Swiffy's Rue

By

Kevin Firth

Cover designed by
Ronnie Firth Photography Services. Email: ronniefirth@outlook.com

This book is a work of fiction. Names, characters, places, and incidents either are
products of the author's imagination or are used fictitiously. Any resemblance to
actual persons, living or dead, events, or locales is entirely coincidental.

Printed in Canada

First Printing: March 4, 2023

ISBN: 979-8-388994-417

Numbers in parenthesis (1) appearing in the book direct the reader to the
bibliography at the end of the book and to the WWW: link.
If you loved this book, please submit a review at Amazon.com or
kevin@kevinfirth.ca

Visit my website at www. http://kevinfirth.ca/

Other books by Kevin Firth:
Below the Surface - ISBN:978-1-98060-169-2
Rengat Ericksen - Chronicles of Humanity ISBN: 978-1-98054-4173
Thor Lindstrom – Chronicles of Humanity ISBN: 979-8-671691-993
The Miner – ISBN: 979-8-420936-863

DEDICATION

At any time of the day or night throughout the world there are men, and these days even some gutsy women who go about dangerous professions far away from home. Some are in three to four weekly rotations; others might only make it home a handful of times a year. Most who generally work at sea can attest to this. Oil field workers whether on land or at sea put up with the loneliness and the many health hazards that come with the territory, until they are forced into retirement. These are generally higher paying jobs than would be available closer to home. For most, it's a 'no brainer' especially when youth is on your side. Why would you not? In the beginning the excitement of overcoming the many dangerous occupations and walking away with a fistful of dollars might sustain them. Well at least until family connections become a concern... and they always do!

For anyone who has worked away from home extensively the saying, 'absence makes the heart grow fonder' is a complete fallacy. The honeymoon is short lived! All the fast cars and fancy homes; the baubles and beads, the jam-packed walk-in closets means nothing when loneliness and temptation become an issue... and they always do!

I would like to dedicate this story firstly to the ones left at home dealing with the sheer loneliness and worry of their loved ones far away from home. Secondly to the ones who work away also dealing with loneliness and fear of the unknown.

Contents

ACKNOWLEDGMENTS

I would like to thank my lifetime friend Bernard (Biscuit) McVittie. We have been friends since a very early age; two backstreet muckers creating havoc in the small local town of Haslingden Lancashire, England. We both later joined the Royal Navy and became divers. Fast forward a few years later and he persuaded me to become a deep-sea diver in the North Sea off Aberdeen, Scotland, much to my wife's (at the time) chagrin. This changed my life considerably mostly for the good (and a little bad). As I look back along my path, it is where my life seemingly began. But for him, my adventure that I can now boast to my grandkids and inevitably take to my grave, would not have happened. Many of the characters in this book are/were mutual friends.

Again, kudos to my patient wife Joan, for her perseverance during the long hours I have taken to write this story.

Huge thanks to Michelle Earle for her literary experience and much educated suggestions during the editing portion of this story.

And again, great big hugs to my talented and loving brother, Ronnie Firth for his excellent and artistic version of the book cover. You da best man!

Swiffy's Rue

Chapter 1

Exercise gone wrong.

"Swiffy, talk to me ya prick, what the fuck is going on down there?" The dive supervisor shouted through his headset mike, getting more nervous by the second. He immediately switched over the helium unscrambler radio to the bellman who was busy donning his Kirby Morgan band mask and preparing to leave the diving bell. "Chalky, I hope you've left the bell already; we've lost contact with Dave. Get a fuckin' move on fer Christ's sake."

This was supposed to have been a standard exercise emergency diver recovery and it was starting to go all wrong. In the pit of the supervisor's stomach, he knew from the series of events that had just passed, this wasn't going to end well. The last communication from Dave Swift was that he couldn't breathe. Shortly thereafter he couldn't even hear him breathing over the comms.

Dave had previously locked out of the diving bell which was only at eighty feet of water below the floating oil rig, drilling in the North Sea off Scotland. He had done this a couple of times before, so he knew the drill. As instructed, he would swim out to the full extent of his one-hundred-and-twenty-foot umbilical hose underneath the massive pontoons that the rig floated on, once there he would inform surface. 'Jock' McCracken, the supervisor would then inform the bellman who was also the standby diver to recover the diver. This was 'Chalky' White's first time in the bell, so he was pretty much dressed in with the standby umbilical connected to his harness and feeling a bit nervous. He already had hot water running through his suit and dumping into the sea via the bell trunk where his legs dangled into the water with his fins on. He had the band mask on his knee and was listening intently to the bell speaker for the instruction to, 'recover the diver.' He would have three minutes to recover the diver, which meant finning out to the diver, and returning him to the lower bell stage. He would then connect his harness to a pulley set up inside the bell. He would then climb into the bell and remove his own mask then commence winching the diver into the bell. Once the diver's head and chest were above water, he would remove his mask and commence mouth to mouth resuscitation. They would do this normally by making kissing sounds over the bell speaker, together with other rude profanities. If he hadn't completed the task in three minutes the diver was pronounced dead and the bellman after a few tries at this and not completing the task on time would risk being sent ashore on the next chopper.

Dave had previously held onto a fitting connected to the hull that he had found on the far-underside of the pontoon as he waited. Even though he had dumped one of the weights in his suit pocket the sheer weight of a hundred and twenty feet of umbilical had been pulling him deeper and was becoming tiring work finning to stay at this depth. The umbilical was suitably named because not only did it supply the breathing gas which at this shallow depth was of course only air. It also told the supervisor what depth the diver was at, via a simple open-ended hose at the diver's chest level. It also had communications to and from the dive shack via the bell. The state-of-the-art band mask had a small microphone in the breathing cup and small waterproof speakers beside your ears in the attached neoprene hood. In nineteen-seventy-five the regulation to have an emergency 'bail out bottle' of stand by air/gas in case of an umbilical failure had not yet come into play. There was also another bulkier hot water line in the umbilical that was connected to his suit via a control valve that supplied his neoprene hot water suit. The other end of the umbilical was connected via a series of valves inside the bell then through the main umbilical that was connected to the surface control room (dive shack).

It had been a nice day with calm seas when they had left the surface. At this depth, the sun reflected down, and the visibility was amazing, unlike many of the dives he had done in the Navy.

This was the life he thought, *I'm making good money for doing little. Two weeks on then two off, I can handle this. Line em up 'till ah fuckin' drop... yes siree!*

"OK, Swiffy time to pretend dead, the bellman is coming to get you. No fuckin' around now, let him do his thing," he had heard the supervisor order in between the loud bubbles of air he was expelling.

He had made a pact with Chalky prior to the exercise. He was a good egg; they had shared a few beers together ashore, and he was ex-navy too.

"Listen, as soon as I see you, I'll come out and meet you and we can both fin back to the bell. It's a right royal pain dragging two umbilicals around. Fuck em they'll never know. That's gotta be worth a couple o' beers, eh?"

He had spent the last week showing Chalky all the valves and equipment inside the cramped quarters of the tiny diving bell and repeating the procedure for the exercise that Jock had also already explained more than once.

His mind wondered as he waited, it had been so long since he had made any sort of deep connection with a female, and he was beginning to think if this was the way it was always going to be.

At that moment he heard a strange difference in the sound of the air that was coming into his mask. Then suddenly without warning the air stopped mid breath. He immediately began swimming in earnest in the direction of his umbilical knowing full well that he would never make it back to the bell. He had learned never to panic in any situation, but this was beating him hands down. His chest ached as he laid under the hull looking into the deep beyond.

His first thoughts were, *this is where they are going to find me, stuck to the bottom of the pontoon's hull.*

Everything seemed to slow down as a strange feeling of elation replaced his fear. The beautiful blue water and his immediate surroundings seemed so inviting. This was how his wretched life was going to end and in doing so all he had to do was allow himself to go. For sure nobody would miss him. Just before he passed out a vision of his late father; the only person that had ever loved him came into his vision.

"Cum on now son tha's gonna be alreight, am reight 'ere fer thi." The peaceful and kind face said.

Chalky swam out as hard as he could dragging his heavy umbilical that he had frantically thrown out onto the bell stage. He was also pulling on Dave's umbilical which didn't seem to have an end. He had realized his awful mistake once he had donned his own mask; the air/gas supply valves he had mistakenly closed instead of opened. It had only seemed like seconds before he had realized his mistake. But it was long enough to asphyxiate Dave.

This practice diver recovery had rapidly become very real. A simple mistake had caused Dave to die. In this business, simple mistakes were mostly always followed by disaster.

Chalky immediately went into top gear as he struggled to winch Dave into the bell where he ripped the mask of Dave's head and quickly performed mouth to mouth. Both masks were hissing and bubbling air in the bell trunk where Chalky had dropped them. Water spurted out of his hot water suit supply bypass valve. Spraying the inside of the bell. Waterproof flashlights and the bell check list had also been knocked into the bell trunk. In his haste he had also knocked the spare carbon dioxide scrubber cannister into the trunk. To say it was pandemonium would be an understatement made steadily worse by Jock screaming down the bell speaker wanting updates and if they could bring the bell up yet. All he could concentrate on during this nightmare was bringing Dave back to life. Through his carelessness he had systematically murdered his friend. He tried to push Dave's chest through the harnesses in an attempt to re-start his heart and constantly gave him mouth to mouth. Eventually he felt a faint heartbeat and passed that information to a very exasperated supervisor, who ordered him to immediately ready the bell to be raised. Chalky haphazardly winched Dave further into the bell and pulled in both umbilicals. Anything that had fallen out of the bell was history as the bottom door was hurriedly closed and dogged. The moment he called topside, 'bottom door closed' the bell immediately began to be raised. '"Bell coming through the interface,'... 'Bell out of the water,'" He informed topside as Dave's seemingly lifeless body hung from the pulley only inches from his face. The moment the deck moonpool door was closed and the bell lowered onto the deck, the bottom door was undogged allowing the bottom door to swing open. Umbilical's fell out onto the bell stage with the two band masks still attached as Chalky immediately lowered Dave into the arms of two of the diving deck crew. The rig medic was there to check his vitals and thankfully there was still a weak pulse. The supervisor made the decision to immediately put Dave and Chalky with the medic into one of the decompression chambers. Much to the medic's concern as he had never been in a chamber. Dave was put on pure oxygen through a mask bibb, as the chamber was blown down to thirty feet. This would supply a higher percentage of oxygen into his blood stream. A rescue chopper had been called and two hours later the medic with Dave, who was still unconscious, was on a chopper heading to the hospital in Aberdeen.

Chapter 2

In the beginning, 1959, Lancashire, England.

He tried to stay dry as he sheltered in the pub entrance while he waited for the double-decker bus to take him to the primary school in the small town of Haslingden. It's not that far by bus from Station Steps on the outskirts of Haslingden center. maybe twenty minutes or so but having walked it a couple of times it seemed quite a way. He'd already got a drenching as he ran down the steep cobble stoned hill from the tiny, terraced house that he and his Dad lived in. He was only nine years old, but he had been doing this since he was seven, so it was nothing out of the ordinary.

Dad hadn't been feeling well when he left for work at six thirty this morning. He had been up most of the night puffing away on his strong 'Park Drive' cigarettes that he always seemed to have perched on his lip. His arthritic hands and bronchial chest were playing up with the change in the weather. Not that the rainy weather changed very much from summer to winter, except maybe for the cold. The frosted windows in the bedroom and the added blankets on the bed were clues as to what was ahead. The ceramic hot water, bed warmer that was filled from the gas hot water geyser above the porcelain sink in the kitchen helped until it got cold. He would then push it to the bottom of the bed, as far away as possible from his feet. Dad was a brick layers laborer on a building site working with Arthur Clarkson who was also a family friend. We called him Uncle Arthur.

Since mum left when he was about six, they had kind of been looking after each other. He vaguely remembered her face and missed her affectionate embrace, stroking and kissing his head. But as much as he had dreamed that one day she might return, Dad said that we should get used to the idea, we will never see her again. Dad was fifty-three on his last birthday, Mum always seemed much younger from the photos he had hidden under his bed. Dad had told him a little while back, after he had asked, that she was not even thirty.

The house is called a terraced two up and two down, which he found a little amusing. There was a front room and living kitchen on the ground floor and two bedrooms upstairs, Dave's was in the back. There was nothing much to see out of the small window except the back of the next street and the rabbit hutch next door. Out the back, downstairs in the small yard between two tall walls, was our outside toilet, the door was kind of rickety and sometimes it fell off. It could get awfully cold out there, so we just used a jerry that we put under our beds, Dad sometimes called it a potty. Dad mostly emptied them every day down the tippler toilet outside.

It wasn't that bad really, particularly on the few nice days of summer. Dad sometimes took him across the Accrington Road and down another steep cobbled hill to the playing fields. We then crossed over the railway lines just before the station that our area of town was named after. Sometimes we would watch a game of footie or If Dad was feeling up to it, we even walked up the grassy hill on the opposite side, almost to the top of the valley. There was a pond where we would sometimes strip off and go swimming. We particularly liked that.

Dave had asked his Dad a few times for a school uniform so that he could be the same as the others, but he said we couldn't afford too many clothes. So, he bought me a suit and told me that I should always wear a tie and try to look tidy, like he did when he was young, I must always wash and comb my hair. It made him feel different from everyone else, and they sometimes picked on him because of that. He did have some pals though that also didn't have uniforms and they would sometimes gang up together and protect themselves against the bullies. They would meet up after school and play footie or spy on the bowling green, old codgers in the memorial gardens beside the school. There was no rush to get home 'cos Dad was never home until after six. He would normally bring home fish and chips wrapped in newspaper. Sometimes it might be his favorite; Hollands's steak and kidney pie, which just happened to be made close to where they lived, with chips and mushy peas. Sunday was really the only day that Dad cooked which was normally pork chops or liver with spuds and peas with gravy.

The bus finally arrived, he wanted to get upstairs at the back 'cos that was his favorite spot, well until the teenagers came on, then he would have to move. Dad mostly gave him enough money to pay the bus conductor and sometimes enough to even buy a Jammy dodger biscuit to have with his milk at school break time for his breakfast. The dinner ladies in the canteen would always smile at him and sometimes give him extra servings at dinnertime. Rice pudding was his favorite, and he could go back two or three times if there was enough. He and his pals were usually the last ones to leave.

So, overall things were pretty good, he just wished Dad was healthier and happier.

Chapter 3

Unfortunate life changing incident 1961.

It had been an uncomfortable night, Dave thought. Dad had been coughing until the early hours of the morning then everything seemed to go very quiet. A chill ran through his body as his senses were alerted. He had felt this before, so he tried in vain to overcome and force sleep, but it wasn't happening. It had been a few years since he had wet the bed, he sure didn't want that to happen again. Dad would curse as he washed the sheets in the kitchen sink and hung them over the drying maiden over the fireplace. He was eleven years old now and had recently been moved up to Haslingden secondary modern school which was basically the same school but was divided by a large double door that had previously been out of bounds by the primary school pupils. Even the large play yard had an imaginary line drawn through it that separated the two age groups. He was now a first former and was being continually tested and threatened by the older third and fourth formers. It was like he had to start all over again proving his mettle. And these bullies had reputations that gave him the willy nillies. It was all he could do to just stay out of their way.

The early morning dim light struggled through the heavily cold frosted windows painting strange patterns on the glass. He watched his breath vapors evaporate in the cold bedroom. He had heard his father's alarm clock noisily disturbing the silence for what seemed many long minutes, and strangely he hadn't stopped the alarm as he would normally do. Covered in the mounds of heavy blankets, a dread filled his body; was his worst nightmare now taking place? Eventually, after what seemed an eternity, he forced himself out of bed. The cold immediately seemed to freeze the naked parts of his skin not covered by his tee shirt and underwear. He slowly walked on the cold linoleum floor to open his door then pass over the top of the downstairs step. He had his hand on his father's bedroom doorknob but for long moments he just couldn't motivate himself to open it.

Finally opening the door, the strong odor of camphor oil filled the frosty air. The bed lay still as he called from the door, "Dad, you alright? Dad, please wake up," he now shouted. He shivered like never before as he slowly walked to his father's bedside to see the glazed open eyes staring into nothingness. He dropped to his knees as tears streamed from his eyes. For many unbearable minutes he cried on his knees before standing up to feel the cold of his father's face.

"Dad what am I going to do, I don't know what to do, please, please help me!" he cried. In complete hysteria he clambered onto the bed and pulled the covers over him and his Dad as he tried futilely to warm his Dad back to life. Seemingly hours passed until he could not bear the cold any longer. He returned to his bedroom and dressed.

OK, I must light a fire, he thought. He curled up newspaper into the fireplace grate as he had been taught then placed coal onto the paper. He lit the newspaper and put the back of the small coal shovel against the fire and placed a newspaper over the shovel causing a draft up the chimney slowly igniting the coal. Having something to do to occupy his mind had given him a respite from his thoughts. He put more clothes on and his raincoat and hovered over the fire until he could feel pain in his fingers as they defrosted from the cold. What was he to do? For sure they would put him into a homeless kids shelter. He had heard many awful stories about that. No, that wasn't going to happen.

He hung on for four days until the last of the small amounts of food in the cupboard had been drained. He found some money in his father's wallet in a drawer then went to the corner shop to buy beans and bread for his toast and some chocolate bars. The coal was also running very low, especially as he had been burning all through the night attempting to sleep on the uncomfortable sofa.

He had not returned upstairs since he had found his dead father. A plan was slowly forming. *I'll go and see Uncle Arthur; he might be able to put me up for a few days until I can find some more food and coal. I might even be able to steal some.*

He dressed as he would normally for school and set off on the long walk to Uncle Arthurs.

"Hi Uncle Arthur, my Dad's not feeling very well and has asked me to come and see you. He needs to borrow some money so that I can buy groceries. Or I could come and stay with you for a while until Dad gets better."

Arthur, obviously not being fooled by the young boy's story, knew there was something amiss.

"OK young Davey, then let's go and see your Dad and see if he needs a doctor or something," he replied smiling.

"No, no, Dad said he didn't want visitors."

"Oh well, how about I drop you off in the truck, it's such a long way to walk back," Arthur replied still smiling.

"Oh, I suppose so, but you can't come in 'cos he'll be upset with me if you do."

"Alright young Davey lets go," as he went into his kitchen to explain to his wife the situation.

"Somethings amiss Emily, stay close to the phone, I think we might have to call the hospital."

"OK," his pregnant wife replied holding a baby girl in her arms, "I'll be right here."

Arthur dropped off Dave and pretended to drive off but stopped at the end of the street and walked back to the house up the back laneway. He came in through the back gate and door which he knew Alan never locked. As he opened the door the vile, fetid smell hit him like an express train. Dave was sitting on the floor beside a smoldering fire.

"Oh my god Davey, where is your Dad?"

"Uncle Arthur please don't tell; I don't want to go into a home."

Arthur ran up the stairs as the smell became unbearable, he put his handkerchief over his nose as he entered the bedroom where his friend Alan lay dead.

Chapter 4

News about his father.

After the funeral that Arthur had kindly arranged and paid for, Dave refused to allow himself to cry, which he found disappointed the many strangers that came to shake his hand. After much pleading, Arthur and his wife Emily allowed him to sleep on their sofa but only until other solutions could be made. Their home was a converted farmhouse at the 'top of the town' just off Haslingden old road. There were three bedrooms, one of which was Arthur's busy office. He, his wife, and baby Mary had the main bedroom overlooking the scenic town of Haslingden which was at the bottom of the hill on the other side of the road. Roy, their six-year-old son, had the other small bedroom. Arthur had built an extension which housed a bathroom that included a bathtub, sink and a separate walled off toilet with a door. There was a large eat in farmhouse kitchen with fitted cabinets, laundry facilities and laminate countertops. In a separate living room, there was a fireplace and a TV. Behind the fireplace was a gas boiler which supplied the house with hot water for the sinks and bath. Over the fireplace was a large, framed picture of a snowcapped mountain. The concrete floor was covered with carpet in the living room and linoleum was fitted on the kitchen floor. The house was bright and cheery with a lot of light coming in through the large windows. Mrs. Clarkson always kept a comforting coal fire burning which kept the house warm. She had instructed Dave to always have the covers on his makeshift bed neatly put away before anyone came downstairs in the morning. His clothes were also to be neatly put away in the closet by the front door. He could feel the tension that he was causing just by being there but tried to keep out of everyone's way, the alternative wasn't worth thinking about.

He had reluctantly returned to school, mainly to stay out of everyone's way. At assembly in the main hall on the morning of his first day back he was shocked and embarrassed; at prayers, the headmaster as usual asked everyone to bow and pray. After the Lord's prayer he then asked for love and encouragement for Dave Swift after the loss of his father. When all the heads were finally raised, he felt many eyes directed toward him, not only from the teachers on the stage but seemingly every student present in the hall. He could feel his face turning bright red and just wanted to disappear into the floor. Even for the next week or so the other students would stop and stare, some in groups pointing in his direction. He hated people looking at him at any time, but this was especially embarrassing. He had always been tall and spindly. His thin muddy blonde hair flopped over his eyes, in an attempt to hide his protruding nose. His father had called it his prestigious Roman nose. It didn't help that he was constantly jibed by the bullies and called beaky, sniffy or hawk face.

But he still had his pals who knew better to never mention his loss. Bobby, Mac, Keith, and Birdie all had single parent families, so they had all witnessed hardships just by looking at the clothes they wore.

We were at the bottom of the pile, he thought. *In the 'D' form we are the lowest educated and had our lives mapped out to be the laborer's, cotton factory worker or worse still, to work in the dreaded coal mines. In most of our classes, we were handed writing paper and pencils so that we could while away our days simply drawing pictures, which became exceedingly boring. At the Monday morning role call to pay for the week's school dinners, the teacher ensured that everyone in the class knew we couldn't pay because our parents, 'if you had one' was on some form of social assistance.*

Just after a month of living at Uncle Arthur and his wife's home in spring, Arthur had asked him to stick around as he had something important to tell him. Dave's stomach churned thinking that this might be the day he was going to be put into a home. Uncle Arthur had driven into town to drop Roy at school and Mrs. Clarkson to do some shopping with the three-year-old Mary in a pram.

As he returned it was plain to see that this was going to be bad news from the look on Arthur's face. He asked Dave to share the sofa with him.

"Davey boy, I've been toiling with this over the last few weeks and for a while there, I was going to keep it to myself as I know you've been going through hell losing your Dad, but you really need to know this."

Dave could feel his stomach churning.

"When we cleaned out your father's house, we found a locked box. I found the key in your father's key fob which opened the box. As you probably know, your house was rented. There was an eviction notice over two months old because of unpaid rent. Your Dad hadn't been making any wages because of his health for months. So, I don't know how he lasted out so long. I feel bad and just expected as always, he would come bouncing back because he was a tough old bugger. At his age he could still handle a hod of bricks. That's a wooden holder for a bunch of bricks that the laborer climbs a ladder with to supply the brick layer."

Dave began to relax somewhat. If this was what this important talk was about then he allowed himself to loosen.

"However, that is not all we found. As you know your full name is Dave Swift Taylor."

"Yes, I know that, but Dad told me years ago not to worry about the Taylor bit as it just confuses my name," Dave added seeing the questioning look on Arthur's face.

"I think that I should probably cut to the chase here. Your Dad was not your biological father," seeing the confusing look on Dave's face, it was time to explain.

"I met your Dad when he was still with your mother. We both went to the same church together; your mother rarely came with him though. I've done a little bit of research since I read the papers in your Dad's safety box. I talked to some of my acquaintances from the old church before the last vicar died. The new vicar let the church go to the point where it had to be demolished. Before your Dad came to work with me, he worked at the cotton factory at the bottom of the hill. It's there that he met your mother, she was pregnant with you."

Dave immediately felt a flush come over his face. "Hold on a minute are you telling me that my Dad was not really my Dad?" he exclaimed.

"Well certainly not biologically but he was the one that has loved and taken care of you all these years. In those days to be an unmarried woman with child was considered a mortal sin. Your father took your mother, Ethel Swift, into his home and apparently looked after her during her worst moments."

"Something horrible happened to your Dad over in France during the war that he never spoke of. When he returned, he was considered 'shell shocked' and apparently, he was later considered an alcoholic. One of his old acquaintances that I spoke to mentioned that he would turn up for work and he could hardly stand, 'pissed as a cart,' were his actual words. It was the past vicar of our church who spent much time with him that saved him... and coincidentally me too. That is how I met your Dad, you see, I was also going through a rough time in my youth. He became a kind of guiding light to me when he quit cold turkey and vowed never to drink again. We are both recovered alcoholics and have looked out for each other over the years. But he never divulged to me that your mother wasn't his actual wife."

"From what I am led to believe, and this is not from one source, so I don't think there is any malice or gossip involved. Your mother later met a man who was more her age. He did not want to bring up another man's child and as you had become accustomed at six years old to your Dad, she reluctantly made the hard decision to leave with her man to another town. She could have even gone to another country, nobody knows. She was twenty-five at the time so that would make her only nineteen when she had you."

Arthur waited in silence as Dave stared at an imaginary object on the carpet.

"It's a lot to take in Davey but one thing for sure and there is no doubt in my mind whatsoever; your Dad loved you more than life itself and, in a way, I like to think you were both good for each other under the circumstances. It would have been so easy for him to step off the wagon and return to oblivion, and with his health condition, it is nothing short of a miracle. And you, young Davey have yourself to credit for that."

"So, my surname isn't Swift Taylor then?" Dave asked.

"No, I'm afraid not, there were no records or papers that showed Alan officially adopting you," Arthur answered.

"Uncle Arthur, please tell me that you won't give up on me?" forcing himself not to cry.

"Davey I can't promise that you'll be able to stay here indefinitely. Emily has her hands full these days. She is OK with this being a temporary situation. She feels for you too, but I must put her health and condition before anything, especially while she is pregnant. The moment she tells me it's too much is when we are going to have to find you other living accommodation. I hope you understand, either way I feel an obligation to your Dad to ensure your safety and wellbeing. Anyway, let's not worry about that right now, you obviously have a lot to take in."

Chapter 5

Life with Arthur.

The weeks and months passed living in the Clarkson's busy home. Arthur had given him an old push bike that he then used to ride to school and visit his pals around the valley. He started delivering papers for a local news agent around Haslingden before and after school. This gave him some spending money, that he did not want to ask Arthur for. On Saturday afternoons he could join his pals to watch the matinees at the local cinema. If he was careful with his cash, he could even have a chocolate bar or an ice cream at intermission. One of his favorite characters was a tough cowboy who finished most of his sentences with, *'yes siree, aham a comin fer you'* or *'you'd better get off that horse before I blow ya full o' holes, yes siree'.* After the cinema they would all go to the local fish and chip shop. "Yes siree... I'd like pie an peas, an be quick about it or a'll blow ya full of holes." The kindly fish and chip shop owner would give them an extra spoonful of peas smiling as he pretended to shoot them with his fingers.

On some Saturdays when the warmer days of Summer came, Arthur would take him with the family on beautiful scenic drives to the Lake district or even Wales. It was a bit uncomfortable squeezed in the back of the truck but being out in the country made it all seem worthwhile. It also gave him a feeling of inclusion in a family that he had never felt before. Sometimes Mrs. Clarkson would come with the baby Mary until she became quite large with her pregnancy then it was just Arthur, Roy, and himself. Arthur was a keen rock climber, which seemed to be the main reason for these excursions. Sometimes they would camp out overnight, but Arthur would always have to be back for church on Sunday. A few years back the family had converted to Latter Day Saints after they had been impressed by the two black suited, fit looking young Americans that had come to their door. Arthur, being a bit of a fitness guru, was also impressed by the weekend sport events, mainly playing baseball that the church hosted. He had been instrumental in helping to build their church in Rawtenstall that gave him much status within the Mormon worshipers.

Although Dave liked the outdoors, the climbing sometimes scared him. He went along with whatever they were doing at Arthurs request, only to impress and attempt to be part of the family. Roy, at six, was completely natural like his Dad and had no fear whatsoever of heights, unlike himself.

On a few occasions he was allowed to bring one of his pals along. Dave and his pal Keith would stay at the bottom of the climb helping with ropes and such. While Arthur and son ascended like a pair of monkeys up the shear rock faces. He would even go to a couple of the Mormon baseball games which was a lot of fun. But he soon felt like he was being quietly indoctrinated into the faith, which apart from the fun and meeting new people he really wasn't interested in. Because of that he often felt Arthur's anger. A few intense arguments had begun to increase, especially after Arthur found out about his truancy from school. He and his pals would stay until the morning role call then conveniently sneak away. They had met up with a bunch of older lads in the Flax Moss council estate on the way to Helmshore that had shown them how to steal sweets from the local shops. They would all crowd into the small shop and while one of the larger boys directed the shopkeeper to items, where his back was to them, they would fill their pockets with chocolate bars or whatever they could grab.

Arthur would increasingly mention how disappointed he was and how Dave was abusing their trust. At one point Dave quietly packed a bag of his meagre belongings and left what he thought of, for good. He just felt that he was a complete hinderance to everyone concerned. He had a very uncomfortable night on a park bench where he tried to sleep overnight. Arthur waited for him after school and apologized for letting his anger get the better of him and pleaded with him to come home.

Mrs. Clarkson was huge and nearing her time to give birth to their third child when he was informed of the bad news. It was another one of those sit-down chats that he dreaded, with just the two of them in an empty house.

God, what now he thought, *I've been trying to behave, even though trouble just seems to follow me around these days.*

"Davey boy, Emily is almost due, so we need to talk about your future. You know we both care for you very much. We only want to do what is best for you. We'll always be here for you no matter what. But the time has come for us to change our own living arrangements. Our Mormon church is still in its infancy, we plan in the future to have accommodations not only for children like yourself but also the homeless adults. They would of course have to convert to our religion and views. In the interim, I have spoken to a catholic boys' home, and they would be willing to take you in for a suitable donation of which we are more than willing to pay."

"No, no Uncle Arthur please, haven't you heard the stories. That's a crazy place, please don't send me there."

"That's a load of old rubbish Davey boy, I have spoken to the bishop in charge and the many nuns there and they all agree. It is just hearsay flaunted by the evil that exists in our society. And anyway, this could just be a temporary thing until Emily has got our household back to normal after the birth. I will come to visit you when I can and if it's as bad as you say, well then, you'll just come home until we can find other suitable accommodation. You know if you hadn't run away, this might not have been necessary, it just proves that what we are trying to do here is just not working. Everyone I speak to agrees that you need discipline at this point in your life. I for sure do not want to be responsible for allowing a delinquent into our society. This is your time to prove to us that you can handle discipline enough to become a credit to our society. Why don't I take you down there tomorrow and you can see for yourself?"

Dave realized that it was pointless to argue his position, the atmosphere had become a little volatile of late and he had witnessed Arthur's anger more than once. But he was still the only person in this whole world that he felt he could rely on. He felt so sad that he wanted to cry, *but that wasn't going to happen... no siree!*

"OK, but you promise to take me out of there if things get tough," he said uneasily.

"Yes, of course but you'll also have to promise me that you will try to make it work, and no more of your shenanigans. How you act from now on will reflect on me and your late father, do you understand that?"

The following day Arthur drove him to the catholic home that had tall walls surrounding the old mansion that had been converted into the home. The large metal gate was closed behind as they entered the grounds. Boys of all ages were playing footie in the green field beside the home. Nuns and some priests were directing the games. Arthur looked at Dave with a smile on his face.

"Looks pretty good to me so far Davey boy," he said.

Inside the large front door, the Mother Superior met them and escorted them up a large, carpeted winding staircase onto a wide also carpeted hallway passing several closed doors. On the walls were many religious paintings, he noticed that most of the portraits of people had halos above their heads. Eventually they reached the Bishop's office. They both sat on creaking wooden chairs. The walls of the plush office were dark oak with several oak shelves filled with books. The elderly Bishop was talking on his phone as he directed them to sit. He leaned back on his creaking wooden swivel office chair. Behind his head was a large photo of the Pope with several other photos of Archbishops and Bishops below. Eventually he put the phone down and stood to shake Arthur's hand.

"Welcome Mister Clarkson to Saint Peters home for boys and this must be young Master Swift we have been hearing so much about," he reached over and shook Arthur's hand as his smile turned to concern. "We are so sorry to hear about your deceased father it must have been such a shock for someone so young. Just so you know he is in a much better place beside our Father in heaven," he solemnly bowed his head, crossed himself as he kissed a cross that hung around his neck. He then quickly turned to face Arthur. "On behalf of our church we would like to thank you for your generous donation. I expect you have many questions of which I am going to pass you over to the Mother Superior to answer any of your concerns."

The Mother Superior, who had been quietly waiting at the door said, "come this way Mister Clarkson," as she directed them out of his office. Dave looked back to see the Bishop, already back on his shiny black desk phone.

"Bishop O'Reilly is a very busy man, there is talk of him becoming an archbishop soon, we are all very proud to say."

The Mother Superior's office was not quite as grand, she asked them to sit, then closed the door to her office.

Arthur had a few questions, mainly about when he could visit, she eventually stopped him short.

"Mister Clarkson, we understand that young Master Swift here has had an extremely shocking experience," as she looked in his direction showing concern. "We have professional help and of course our religious beliefs that will help him on his road to recovery from such a traumatic experience. It is no surprise to us that he has rebelled against society. We have spoken to the head of his school, so we know what we are up against. A lot of our boys have come from broken homes and horrendous situations that they are not equipped at their tender age to handle. You have made the correct decision to bring him to us. Now if Master Swift could wait outside the door so that we may speak privately," as she made her way to open the door escorting him out.

"Master Swift, why don't you go and sit over there on that chair while Mister Clarkson and I finish our discussion."

He sat on the padded bench across from her door noticing that the door next to her office was open with a younger nun smiling at him behind her desk. She came out and sat beside him.

"Now what is a handsome young man like you doing here?" she asked. She had a soothing voice with an obvious Irish accent that seemed to unravel the tension he had been feeling. She reached into her pocket bringing out a bag of sweets to offer him.

"Don't tell anyone," she said smiling.

He smiled and took a sweet and popped it into his mouth.

"Well, it looks like I'm going to be living here for a while," he answered dolefully.

"I'll tell you what then, when the Mother Superior has finished with your father, I'll show you around, OK? By the way, I'm Sister Josephine." As she offered her warm hand to be shaken.

"Oh, he's not my Dad but he's the closest thing right now," he replied.

"Well, you'll have to tell me all about that later, eh? Mister Swift," as she returned to her office smiling back at him.

That was strange, he thought afterward. *She didn't know what I was doing here but still knew my name.*

Meanwhile behind closed doors a different conversation was being had; "Mister Clarkson, you may call me Gwendoline. May I call you Arthur?" asked the Mother Superior.

"Yes of course," Arthur answered.

"Dave is going through an extremely difficult period in his life from all accounts. We see these episodes all the time in our refuge. We are experienced in dealing with this so your question about visiting, you might find it strange that our answer would always be, 'very limited'," she waited for him to realize what she was attempting to explain.

"Are you saying that I can't visit?"

"No, of course, we are not saying that. It's just that it would be best for Dave that you didn't. The most important thing we can give him at this tenure in his life is discipline. You have obviously done an admirable job of giving him a home and love. But you have also noticed his rebelling attitude. You will inevitably be doing him and yourself an injustice by showing any form of weakness."

Arthur seemed to let that sink in before answering. "I knew his father very well, so I feel a responsibility toward young Davey, Gwendoline. How will I know how he is doing if I am not to visit him from time to time?"

"You can of course telephone me anytime you wish for updates on his wellbeing and how he is being treated. If we feel at any time that he needs assistance, rest assured you will be the first person we will call," adding a comforting smile. "Now if there are no other questions, Sister Josephine will now take you both on a tour of our facilities and young Master Swift can place his belongings in his locker beside his bed. I will say my goodbyes now and will pray to our Father in heaven to give us his loving guidance."

As he sat on his small bed looking through the window where he had watched Uncle Arthur's truck disappear then the gate closing at the end of the long driveway, he felt so alone. Seemingly only moments ago Uncle Arthur had held his shoulder with his large, calloused hands and had showed an unusual amount of concern in his eyes. He had known his uncle to be a hard man who didn't show affection easily.

"Davey boy, this is for your own good, you know that I hope. It's not going to be forever. Emily and I care for you. This year has had its difficulties since you came to stay, but you have grown on us somewhat, and have felt like our own. Hard work is a great healer, you need to get your head down with your studies and make us proud." As he softly pushed him on the shoulder with his large fist with somewhat of a hard smile. He then walked down the steps to his truck waving from the window as he drove away.

The high ceiling room seemed cold. A large ornate light fixture hung from the plaster patterned ceiling. He noticed that there were also several sconce light fittings on the walls. The wallpaper was a dark and dismal designed color. The floors throughout the building were wood which constantly creaked when walked upon. He counted ten small beds on each side of the room, between each bed were small wooden cabinets. At the end of the room beside the doorway was a tall curtained off cabinet that he presumed was for hanging clothes. Every bed was neatly made, and nothing was left out on the tops of the cabinets. He had put away his few clothes and belongings into the cabinet and the single drawer as he had been instructed by Sister Josephine. His belongings really didn't add up to much; the wrinkled brown suit and slightly stained white shirt with his tie loosely tied. Even his black shoes that hadn't seen polish in many months. The socks he wore he knew to have holes in the toes. So, he was always embarrassed to take off his shoes during P.E. at school.

As he looked around the room the horrible thoughts returned, they came with no explanation only that he felt terribly low. He had vowed never to return to that feeling when he found his Dad almost a year ago. Those tears were unbearable and painful. He had recently found some respite in inflicting pain on himself. He would dig his nails hard into his stomach below his belt until they drew blood. The pain took him away from the brooding thoughts until the next time. The P.E teacher at school had once noticed scratch marks on his arms and legs when he had undressed in the changing room and had asked him where they had come from. He had made some feeble excuse that he had gotten into a fight in the play yard. Since that time, he always ensured to leave the wounds below his waistline. He had never showered at school with the excuse that he preferred to bathe at home.

His thoughts were immediately interrupted by Sister Josephine entering the room with a white towel folded over her arms.

"OK Master Swift we need to get you cleaned up," she said with a jolly attitude. "I'm going to show you where the bathroom is. But first I'm going to wait outside the door while you remove all your clothes and put this towel around you, OK?" as she placed the towel on his bed and closed the door behind her.

Dave immediately undressed and placed the towel around himself ensuring that the newly inflicted wounds were covered. He followed her down the hallway as she directed him into the large communal bathroom shower area.

"OK, you have a shower and don't forget to dry yourself off good. You are fortunate, because you have the whole bathroom to yourself as the other students are still in class. I'll put clean clothes on your bed and if you quickly get dressed, you'll be in time for lunch. I'll come and get you and take you to the dining room," she said in her reassuring and melodic Irish accent.

He returned to the room to find his wrinkled clothes gone and when he investigated his cabinet so were the rest of his clothes. He felt a little annoyed. On the bed were neatly folded clothes. The pants, socks and underwear looked to be new but the shirt, tie, and jacket, although clean, they certainly weren't new clothes. He immediately heard a loud knocking on the door.

"Come along now Dave Swift don't dilly dally, get a move on, I won't wait here all day you know," Sister Josephine called from behind the door.

He dressed quickly and noted the black shoes were also not new and were a little large. Following her down the stairs to the expansive dining hall at the end of the corridor he began to feel nervous. The large double doors were open as they entered. Many of the long tables were full of seemingly every age group of boys. The reverberating noise of the many voices sent chills through his being.

Sister Josephine clapped her hands and loudly called, "Boys, quiet... quiet please, we have a new guest."

An immediate silence filled the room as many eyes glanced in his direction. He could feel his cheeks turning bright red.

"Please welcome to our home, Dave Swift. I hope you will all show him the courtesy we expect at Saint Peters. OK, now continue... with a little less noise please," she sternly ordered.

She escorted him to a space at the end of one of the tables beside the middle passage. His face he knew was still bright red as he sat with many eyes still straining to look his way. At the front of the hall was a raised stage area with a long table facing into the hall.

The Mother Superior appeared on the stage and the noise of chattering again began to quiet.

She clapped her hands and said loudly, "Silence for our Holy Bishop."

The hall again was immediately silenced as the Bishop, four priest and six nuns were seated. Mother Superior raised her hand to signal a line of kitchen staff wearing crispy clean aprons to enter the room with trays holding plates of food. Some of them wore smaller habits like the Nuns. When everyone was served the Bishop sitting in the center of the table on the stage crossed himself, held hands with the others and bowed his head as did everyone on the table. He felt a strong nudge on his elbow as the boy to his right reached for his hand. The Bishop said a prayer and the boys repeated some of the lines finishing off with an amen. By now the food he noticed had gone cold, but he didn't feel very hungry anyway as he still felt countless eyes on him.

During and after the meal the boys at his end of the table wanted to talk but he made it abundantly clear that he wasn't into talking so they eventually left him alone. As the meal ended, the bishop stood as did everyone else in the room. Once the main table on the stage had emptied. Each table in an orderly fashion was allowed to leave directed by various sisters. Sister Josephine met him at the doorway.

"I know all this must seem very strange for you, but you will get used to it, just give it some time," she said with a concerned smile. "I'm going to take you to where your next class will be, which is with Father Benedict. You don't have to start just yet, as afternoon classes begin at one fifteen, you will hear a church bell ring at one o' clock. Just make sure that you are on time for the class. You may go outside now and get acquainted with the other boys. Oh, and don't go into any of the areas of the grounds that are signposted, 'no students allowed.' You know where my office is, so if you have any concerns whatsoever, just come a knockin', OK?"

She made him feel cared for and protected with her soothing Irish accent, *she might make this whole thing bearable,* he thought. It was futile at this point to fight; he also didn't want to let Uncle Arthur down. He could stick this out for a little while and if things got out of hand, his only friend in the world right now, Uncle Arthur would save the day.

Chapter 6

Life at Saint Peters.

He was past his thirteenth birthday and still felt the disappointment that in the two plus years he had been at Saint Peters, Uncle Arthur had only visited twice. Each time Dave had pleaded with him to return to his home. He missed his friends and the freedom of riding his bike around the town. He had escaped once only to be caught by the police and returned to a painful caning by one of the priests. It wasn't his first caning that he usually had to receive having to bend over and take it on his bum. He had also received numerous canings on the palms of his hands. Each time the priest or nun applying the punishment seemed to have a goal to make him cry. He wasn't going to give them that pleasure... *no siree, bring it on bitch!*

For a while he had tried so hard to be what they wanted him to be. Sister Josephine had always been there to help him through when the brooding thoughts became too much. He remembered one such occasion.

"You know young Davey you're not the only one to have those sad thoughts. Revolting against everything isn't going to help you. I'll tell you a little secret shall I, but you must promise never to repeat this. I also lost my Father; it was during the troubles in Belfast. It was an out and out murder, but the culprit got off simply because my Father was in the wrong place at the wrong time. My Mother was heartbroken and a year later she also passed on, to join our Father in heaven. I was an only child, but I was fortunate to be taken in by the Catholic Sisters. Since I have given my life to God those thoughts rarely come. And when they do, all I must do is simply pray."

He fondly remembered her lilting and soothing accent. Seemingly his only friend in life, but several months ago she had been replaced.

For a time, he buckled down and studied his lessons. He could now speak the Lord's Prayer in Latin. In Mass and various other ceremonies, he knew all the appropriate responses. It seemed the more he learned about the various scriptures the better he was treated.

The Bishop, now an Archbishop had moved on. The new Bishop had replaced a few of the nuns and priests, in a major shake down at the home. He had spoken during his Sunday sermons about discipline and how one should conduct themselves in this life. Dave, among many other students noticed the caning and the severity had increased for seemingly minor infractions.

Dave had filled out somewhat from his past skinny frame because of the regular food and routine exercise and becoming quite proficient at football. There was a small gym where he could also bring on a sweat pushing weights. The few fights that he still seemed to inadvertently get into, mainly because of his desire to be a loner, had started to wane. Even though a few of the older students two years his senior were stronger, they tended to leave him alone. He had learned to fight dirty, remembering the movies he had watched where Bruce Lee used his feet. As they came at him with fist flaying, he would kick them in the shin or knee. Once they were down, he would conveniently knee them in the face, ending the fight very quickly and unscathed. He had gained a small following of fellow students who were always close by for protection from the older bullies.

"Hey, hook nose, think you're so tough?"

It was Judd, one of the older boys who had seemed to have it in for him from the first moment he had arrived at the school. Judd or 'stud' as he was more commonly nicknamed was beside a large tree obviously out of sight from the school. Dave wasn't in the mood as he tried to ignore him.

"I heard your mum was a prostitute and you're nothing but a fuckin' bastard."

Dave just saw red as he ran toward the boy. Two of the other seniors surprised him from behind the tree and struggled to hold his arms behind his back. He tried to kick out but was held tightly as Judd hit him square in the face with a clenched fist. He saw stars as his legs gave way underneath him. Everything seemed to swirl around then went blank. He woke in the sick bay of the school with Sister Genevieve hovering above his face.

"Dave Swift what have you been up to now? Why is it that if there is any trouble in the school you are always a part of it? You're going to have to tell us who did this or you're going to feel the wrath of my cane, my boy."

It took him a few seconds to remember what had just happened as he began to feel pain in his face and nose.

"Well come on boy, you had better speak up before you feel the wrath of God himself?" The angry face of Sister Genevieve, who was the one mostly giving out punishments lately exclaimed.

As his senses returned, he knew that should he tell the nun who was responsible, he would never hear the last of it and the bullying would just increase.

Why couldn't they just leave me be, he thought.

"I accidentally ran into the tree, I just wasn't looking where I was going," he lied non-committedly.

"A likely story, well we'll see about this and if you are lying you are going to regret it," she replied threateningly.

Another nun helped him to his feet as he saw himself in a mirror. His nose was broken and was horribly pushed to one side. A doctor came the following morning to painfully attempt to put his nose back into position and place bandages around his head. Both his eyes were bruised black. For the rest of his life the 'prestigious Roman' nose his father had named would now have a slight twist.

Dave was now required to have special school detention from one of the new priests, 'Brother John' at his discretion. Mostly it was after the last class of the day when the students were in the yard until mealtime. In quiet moments, Brother John would come and sit by Dave pointing out passages in the bible he was reading. Sometimes he would feel his arm around his shoulders which felt mildly uncomfortable. As the weeks passed, he was progressively called for his detention hour, at later times in the evening, during TV hours and sometimes later just before bed. The classroom was noticeably quiet, being at the far end of the corridor. Sometimes he noticed that the priest locked the door to the room which he felt strange. Again, he would sit close and ask questions about Dave's feelings and life in general. In the beginning Dave had taken it as a concern and Brother John's intention to help. He had even shown him Dave's own file in a brown folder. And where he thought he might be able to help him, so his guard was completely down when Brother John began placing his hand on his knee. This developed into stroking.

"You know Dave, I can help you considerably during your stay here. When Sister Josephine left, she spoke to me about your situation and that you need care and love. You need to learn to trust me implicitly Dave," he said in a reassuring voice.

On one evening Brother John had called just before bedtime to do his detention hour which he felt odd. The excuse had been that he had been remarkably busy all day. On arriving, Brother John said he was sorry, but Sister Genevieve had instructed him to administer punishment. Dave asked why and was told that it was because of an infraction that had occurred during the day that Dave as usual had been accused of.

"Let's get this over with before we start the lesson, I will try to be gentle," he said softly. "Now bend over the desk." He ordered.

Dave felt confused, he had begun to trust Brother John and his concern over his wellbeing even though the touching felt weird. And now he was administering punishment? He bent over the desk and clenched his fist waiting for the usual sharp pain as he tried to blank out thoughts. The cane just glanced off his buttocks.

He obviously doesn't know how to do this, was his immediate thoughts, *this is going to be easy peasy.* Then he felt a stroke on his buttocks.

"Sorry Dave that must have hurt," he said quietly.

Then another glancing whip from the cane and another sincere sounding apology. The normal punishment was six canes. After four canes It became even more disconcerting when he was asked to remove his pants and the stroking became longer. This was altogether weird but at least he didn't have to deal with the pain, so he just waited until it was all over. When he stood to pull his pants up, he was shocked to see that Brother John had opened his fly and was pulling on his dick. Dave rushed toward the door to find that it had been locked.

"Let me out of here right now," he screamed.

Brother John had zipped up his fly and came toward him red faced.

"Swift, sit down now!" he shouted. "I can get you into a whole lot of trouble if you don't listen to what I have to say."

"I don't care just open the door, right now," Dave screamed.

"Do you honestly think anyone would believe you if you reported this? I can make life easy for you here or exceedingly difficult. Do you know what a Borstal home for boys is? Probably not but I can guarantee it's worse than you'll ever find here. Or I could try and find ways of returning you to, hmm... who was it, Uncle Arthur? Yes, I'm well informed of your file young man. You'll never feel a cane or any corporal punishment while you're under my supervision. Now I'm going to open the door, so go directly to your room and we'll talk more about this at your next lesson."

Dave was released and he went directly to the washroom to be violently sick. In his wildest dreams he had never thought that things could get worse and now this. Over the next few months, he had to allow Brother John to feel his body while he masturbated himself. Whenever he thought about the abuse he was receiving, it made him feel ashamed and sometimes physically sick to the stomach. It was only two months back that one of the students had jumped to his death from an upper window onto the hard concrete surface surrounding the school. Dave had contemplated doing the same to halt the nightmares and pain that he endured in silence. He pleaded so many times to no avail to see his Uncle Arthur.

Finally, Arthur arrived, he had never felt so relieved to see him. He immediately told him what had transpired, Arthur was furious and told the Bishop he was going to sue the church for what they had done. Dave felt so happy as they left the grounds of the boy's home. The following day, two lawyers appeared at Arthurs door where he was asked to join them in their plush shiny black car for over an hour. Arthur never divulged what transpired but every time the conversation came up, Arthur told him that he was sorry, but it would be best all-around that they kept what had occurred to themselves.

Chapter 7

At 14, Arthur and son on the Matterhorn.

Arthur had converted the second-floor hay loft in the barn, where he kept his building tools and supplies, into an office. He had also decorated his old office into a child's bedroom where little Mary had her cot. Dave had also helped Arthur to install a temporary single bed into the small room for his use. Baby Joan now used the small cot in their main bedroom. Seeing how well Dave had helped, he was now making a small wage working and cleaning around the yard, sometimes even helping on various building sites.

He felt like his life had taken a turn for the better. School was basically still the same and just as boring, but he knew it was a necessity that he had to adhere to. Freely riding around the Rossendale valley on his bike sometimes with his pals felt very special. The relationship between Arthur and the family had developed into what made him feel loved and cared for.

The shame he sometimes felt when his thoughts of what had happened to him in the home, made his stomach churn. It was all he could do to exhaust himself riding his bike or finding work to do. The horrible nightly nightmares he had to keep under control so as not to wake little Mary.

It was in this period of his life that he began to smoke. It all started with hanging around the doorway to the outside school toilets. It looked tough and grown up to be nonchalantly puffing on a cigarette as most adults did at the time. Lookouts were usually posted in case the prefects came to check.

The climbing weekends on nice days had become serious for Arthur and Roy. The photo of the Matterhorn above the hearth in the living room; once a daydream of Arthurs had over the last few years become a serious goal. They had already received much fame and front-page news when Arthur and Roy, now ten years old, had scaled one of the tall factory's smokestacks. (1)

Dave was just over fourteen years old when all thoughts that his life had changed for good were obliterated; Arthur and his son had been lost on the ascent of the Matterhorn. The reports they had received were that the weather had changed, and they had been caught in a snowstorm. Days turned into weeks and their bodies were never recovered.

Emily Clarkson was a quiet lady and would normally go about her household chores without fanfare. She had become understandably distraught and now spent her days in her bedroom. Dave did all he could to help with family chores; cleaning and feeding the children. When she eventually reappeared and was able to return to looking after her children and the home, there seemed to be something sadly missing. A normally healthy-looking lady had lost a lot of weight and was now looking skinny and gaunt. When she did speak it mostly didn't make sense and sometimes was followed with a wild smile. He would regularly return from school in the late afternoon to find her in the same position that he had left her in that very morning, blankly staring out of a window. The baby was crying and had not been changed. The few times the home care or the school truancy officer came to the house she seemed to pick up and attempt to be normal. He had missed a considerable amount of school because of his inability to leave her alone.

Eventually she was placed in care. Her family and Dave were going to be placed into care homes.

That wasn't going to happen... no siree!

He packed his few belongings and headed out to the big city of Manchester where he was homeless, he was almost fifteen when he was caught stealing food from a grocery store. He was then taken to a junior offender's court and given the choice of going into a Borstal home for boys or joining the Royal Navy, which was quite normal in, nineteen sixties England.

To him at that time of life, it wasn't a difficult choice. At the age of fifteen he was given a one-way railway ticket and directions to make his way to Shotley gate in Ipswich. He would report to HMS Ganges boys training facility of the Royal Navy (7).

Dave had not liked his prior life being homeless, so in the beginning he forced himself to get used to the regimental life of the Royal Navy. He received his three-square meals a day, clothes, and a warm bed. All he had to do was keep his, 'nose clean' as it were. He vowed to do his utmost to, 'fit in.' *Yes, sir... no sir... when to get up... when to eat... learn classroom shit and when to march and smartly salute the officers. Try, try, try, to stay out of fuckin' trouble because that parade ground is awful big to be constantly running around. And lastly, when to go to bed and, 'lights out'. Yes, siree bub... aham just a regular sailor boy.*

It wasn't all bad; he enjoyed shooting guns and swimming. He had also volunteered for an unarmed combat training course. The PTI* that ran the course was a particularly revered black belt karate expert. During the one year of basic training in Ganges Dave had won many inter camp contests and made a good friend with the petty officer PTI.

PTI* Physical Training Instructor.

Many of the lads had similar backgrounds to himself; broken homes, no home! petty crimes and abuse from so called trusted adults. In the future he might even see a little of the world. It was a far stretch from working in a cotton factory or coal mine. His future was mapped out for him here and he didn't have to make any decisions; that was up to the authorities. He didn't like climbing the Ganges mast, his fear of heights made his knees shake but like everything else, if he just did as he was told then everything would be OK. The old M.O.D* buildings seemed ancient and had even weathered a couple of world wars.

M.O.D* Ministry Of Defence

It gave him an eerie feeling of what was expected of him and of what boys and men had given for their country. There was so much history which made him feel small and insignificant.

There were times when he felt so alone; he had no one. Emily had been placed into a home for the mentally handicapped and her children had been fostered out. He occasionally had sweet memories of his Dad and even more distant of his Mother. He felt desperate to keep them alive in his mind because at some point, he needed to know that he had once been loved.

As he allowed himself to be led and not to care what tomorrow might bring, the self-harm episodes had almost ceased to occur. It was easy to get cigarettes, as all the Petty Officers and Chiefs smoked so they turned a blind eye too, if boys were caught smoking. His party piece was to dock out his fag on the back of his hand or in his palm if he didn't want the blister to be shown.

At sixteen he and a few others were drafted to the base camp, HMS Excellent in Portsmouth to finalize their seamanship training. After that came the sea training on HMS Ulster, which was an old tub but gained him more seamanship experience. He must have been doing something right because after the training he became Ships Company and his first rating as an Ordinary seaman. Sleeping in a canvas hammock wasn't the most comfortable as it moved back and forth with the motion of the ship.

Work mostly consisted of cleaning decks, painting and polishing the many brass bells and fittings. Helping the Able seaman in the Bosuns store in the forward lower deck of the boat did much to get him over his initial seasickness.

As much as he had tried, he still seemed to get in trouble over minor infractions; not wearing the official clothes in the correct manner or not saluting the right person correctly and was punished accordingly. Number nine punishment seemed to be the hot favorite. It consisted of no shore leaves and having to get up at ungodly hours of the morning to dress into his number one suit with all the corrects creases ironed to within millimeters. The punishment increased if the silk, lanyard, and collar wasn't tied in the correct manner. Inspection was either by the Officer of the day or the Master at Arms who were basically the police onboard the ship. Every dirty job onboard was completed by the boys or men under punishment. Peeling spuds in the galley seemed to be quite popular. He wondered if somebody had to be under punishment or the dirty jobs wouldn't get done.

Prior to the training at HMS Excellent he had signed on for a minimum of twelve years. It was later explained that it would be nine years and three years in the reserve. If war broke out, men would be forced back into service. Even later it was also explained that even though he had signed on at barely sixteen he would not be classed as a man. At eighteen your time began, so in fact you would have completed two years of your reserve already. Meaning of course that you would be twenty-seven years old and still must serve the one year in reserve. He was already having regrets knowing how long that he would have to serve.

Chapter 8

At 18, drafted to a tribal class frigate.

After his time on the Ulster, he was promoted to Able Seaman and drafted to a tribal class frigate just out of refit. He joined the ship during its sea trials off Portland. Weeks later when it had completed the sea trials successfully, it was stationed out of Pompey* and spent the next six months on fishery protection in the English Channel.

Pompey* Portsmouth

Every time the ship returned to home port, wives and girlfriends always seemed to be waiting on the jetty, which made him feel envious. Many of the ships company would generally get a weekend leave pass, leaving just the duty watch onboard. If Dave wasn't on duty, he would join some of the other men on a 'run ashore.' The more senior men who had made the navy their home seemed to know which bars to go to for alcohol and loose women. Many evenings and into the early mornings generally ended in skirmishes. Dave had become quite popular as a run ashore buddy because of his skill at fighting.

He had been taught by senior black belts never to use his skill unless in dire situations as it could be classed as a weapon, if he were to seriously harm or even kill someone.

But alcohol would sometimes let loose his feelings of resentment. Street fighting had become popular, and money was changing hands to fight the local combatants. He would generally finish the fights quickly with two to three strategic moves. PTI's from various shore based naval establishments contacted him on a regular basis wherever he was serving to have him train and fight at official karate competitions. He was now a black belt and had never been beaten. Onboard ship wherever he was in the navy in future years he would train rigorously. Sometimes if he was allowed, he would rig up a punch bag on the quarter deck four-point five-gun turret. An arduous work out would clear his mind, keeping his many distraught thoughts at bay. In the latter part of his late teens, he was no longer the skinny kid and had even grown a couple of inches. Apart from the occasional cigarette he always kept himself in excellent physical shape.

"Swiffy, see that big brute of a guy over there at the end of the bar?" the father of the seaman's mess called over; (the father of the mess was usually the oldest man in the seaman's quarter). "Well, he thinks you're a pussy and he's got a whole bunch of ugly fuckers that don't like us sailors taking their women."

"Hey Dusty, I don't want any trouble, I got my eye on that cute blonde over there and I've had a bit too much to drink to be battling it out with those ugly fuckers. The last time we did this I got my clothes all ripped to shit," Dave said slurring his voice purposely.

The conversation was rudely interrupted as a pint glass came hurtling across the bar loudly smashing into their pints, covering them both in beer.

"Fuck... that's it, they are going to pay for that," screamed 'Dusty' Miller charging over into the fray that ensued.

In minutes, the whole bar was in disarray with chairs, bottles, and glasses flying everywhere. The cute blonde quickly came over to sit with him for protection.

"Please don't let them hurt us, as she pointed to her friends now kneeling below the bar in fear," she pleaded.

He looked across to see the big brute had already dispatched Dusty into neverland, who was now laying over a table knocked out. His other sailor friends weren't doing so well either and were one at a time being thrown out of the door of the pub.

Oh, jeez why me? all I wanted was a quiet drink and a possible fuck and here I am again, gonna be up to my elbows in blood and snot... yes siree... blood and snot.

Two of the gang members from the other side of the bar had come over and now looked down menacingly at him as he sat. He pushed the blonde partially behind him on the small bench seat.

"Listen lads back off, I don't want any trouble. I'll just pick up my buddy over there and we'll leave, OK?" Dave explained.

One of them immediately lunged at him to grab his shirt. He saw it coming and immediately hit him in the throat and jaw with the palm of his hand. He fell backwards having bitten part of his tongue off and had crushed most of his front teeth as he fell to the floor in oblivion. The second man pushed forward to also grab him. Stealthily from under the table, he kicked the man's shin hard. When he looked down to see where the sharp pain had come from Dave used a twisted punch to his stomach below his ribs. The man joined his buddy on the floor as he gasped for air.

"Stay there," he ordered the blonde.

OK, I guess it's time for the ugly brute... yes siree!

The big ugly brute was coming toward him with a broken bottle in his hand.

"Hey sailor boy pussy, I'm going to mess up your face good. These ladies won't have anything to do with you then," as the brute slowly and menacingly walked toward him.

Dave stood up to face him at the bar. The brute lunged at his face with the sharp edges of the bottle reflecting from a light above the bar. Dave quickly moved to one side allowing the brutes' momentum to fall forward. He kicked him in the knee which made a loud cracking noise and as he fell to the floor Dave was able to hit him once in the sternum and with his other fist a lighting fast punch to his throat. The brute was now lying on the floor also gasping for air.

He looked back to the blonde who was now with her two other friends, "I think it's time for you ladies to leave." He then turned to look at the rest of the brute's gang who were staring in disbelief.

"I'm going to help my friend here and the others outside, I suggest you not follow us. I'm going to leave now before the police arrive."

On the Monday after the weekend, he was called to the Master at Arms office. From behind Dave and to his right, a Patrol man; part of the ships policing barked at him, "Able Seaman Swift stand to attention."

"What's going on I haven't done anything wrong," he said resolutely.

"Do not speak unless you are asked to in front of the Master at Arms," screamed the Patrol man. "Stand at... ease and remove your hat."

Dave did as he was told, looking at a framed photo of the ship on the wall above the Master at Arms who was sitting behind his desk looking at a report.

"Able seaman Swift you are in big trouble. We understand from a police report given to me this morning that you were in an altercation at a drinking establishment ashore last Friday night. And before you answer this, should you decide to lie, any forthcoming sentencing will be increased," said the Master at Arms vehemently.

Dave pondered how he should answer when the Patrol man came up to within inches of his right ear and once again screamed, "answer the Master at Arms immediately Swift... no time for thinking."

Dave immediately blurted out, "it was self-defense sir."

"First off, you do not refer to me as sir, which is reserved only for officers. You will address me as Master. Secondly, this is not what the police report describes. Three men are now in hospital; one who is fighting for his life as we speak. Should this man die, you will be tried in a civilian court for murder. Whatever the local civilian boneheads publicize in their tabloids inevitably becomes serious issues for this navy. We are here to serve and protect not to fight with the local riff raff. I need to know who else from this ship was involved because the Admiralty wants heads."

"It was only me, Master, they attacked for no reason, so I defended myself. I was ashore on my own," Dave responded.

"That is not what the report says so unless you confess, there can only be an increase in the grave circumstances that you now find yourself in. The Patrol man will take you to the ships holding cell until you will be tried by the Captain. Swift, think wisely on this... dismissed."

"Able seaman Swift, return your hat to your head... ten-shun, about turn... left right... left right." The Patrol man ordered marching him out of the Master at Arms office.

He was placed into a small, locked room on the lower deck of the ship. It had a small light fitting which was switched on from outside the room. There was a single wooden bed. He was fed at mealtimes from a small sliding hatchway at the bottom of the door. His food was on a metal tray with a plastic spoon. There was a metal bucket for his toilet. Two days later he was marched before the Captain with the Master at Arms shouting various orders behind his right ear.

The big brute in the bar fight had thankfully recovered but Dave was severely reprimanded and sentenced to thirty days at the Royal Navy detention quarters infamously named DQs (2) He had heard stories of the cruelty used to 'crack the hard nuts.'

Two Patrol men handcuffed him, and he was escorted to a waiting covered truck parked by the gangway to the ship. He knew better not to struggle. He was in enough shit!

As they approached the old foreboding, prewar building, he noticed the high surrounding walls were covered in cemented broken glass bottles. Inside there were marching platoons of men in their working number eight clothes with ankle gaiters and polished boots. A Royal Marine Sergeant was at one end of the parade ground shouting orders and a Gunnery Chief at the opposite end of the parade ground doing much the same. Some were marching and others were on double time*.

Double time* jogging in step.

A Gunnery Petty Officer marched him into the building and up a set of metal stairs to his cell. The heavy metal door was opened, and he marched into his cell. They removed his handcuffs, and the metal door was closed and locked behind him. The small inspection door opened, and the Petty Officer shouted through the opening, "Able Seaman Swift you have five minutes to put on your marching boots and gaiters. You will button the top button on your number eights and present yourself for inspection."

He quickly went about this, he didn't own a watch, but he was sure they had opened the door prior to five minutes.

"Able seaman Swift... 'ten shun'," the Petty Officer shouted from the doorway. As he quickly put his hat on and came to attention.

Petty Officer Jones stepped aside to allow Chief Petty Officer Blight to noisily march into the cell. He was a gnarly looking man with a pockmarked face and dark piercing eyes. His voice had a low gravelly tone, Dave guessed from shouting parade ground orders every day.

"Swift, you're a disgrace to this fine navy. You will polish those boots until you can see your face in them. Follow the rules here and your time will go quickly. DO NOT get on my wrong side or you'll wish you weren't born. You will speak to no one. I see you are unshaven, should you not be ready for inspection at any time or adhere to any of the rules, it will earn you a trip to solitary. The Petty Officer will show you how to march out of your cell and be marched to the parade ground to join this floor level platoon. DO YOU UNDERSTAND?"

"Yes Chief," he nervously replied.

He marched out of the cell, down the stairs, given an SLR unloaded rifle and joined his platoon. During the march he quietly asked the rating next to him how long this was going to go on for. The Chief immediately brought the platoon to a halt then ordered a 'right face' then 'order arms'.

"Able seaman Swift take one step forward... 'MARCH'. The rest of the platoon... 'left turn'. Petty Officer Jones, take over the platoon."

The Petty Officer had the rest of the platoon continue marching leaving Dave alone presenting arms. The Chief came almost nose to nose with him, he could smell his breath.

"Swift what is it that you do not understand. You were given the order to remain silent, speak to no one. 'If' you want to make your time here difficult this is going to be a very painful thirty days.

"Petty Officer Jones, take Swift over to the assault course where he will repeat the course for the rest of the day with no rests for meals. This is your first and only warning because I can't wait to get you in solitary, there's nothing I like better than cracking the so-called tough nuts."

Petty Officer Jones was relieved at lunch time for one hour as Dave was continually screamed at, to run faster. By five o'clock every muscle in his body ached, his normal threshold for pain was being seriously challenged. The Petty Officer eventually called a halt and attention.

"Swift, at all times on the parade ground or in the building you will double march unless told otherwise. Able Seaman Swift stand at ... ease. 'DIS... MISSED'."

He later quietly queued up to the galley for the miserable excuse of a meal in silence then was double marched back to his cell to eat.

His cell was about eight feet by ten with a small pull-down single bed and a thin mattress. The only kit he was allowed was strewn across the bed which was the bare necessities. There was a galvanized metal bucket and a spitkid*

Spitkid* a circular shallow aluminum pan normally used for mess deck garbage; cigarettes etcetera.

One of the lads explained that only in the first week were you not allowed to speak but never on the parade ground. It hadn't taken him long to get into the routine because punishment for even the most minor offence was strict and usually painful. There was no toilet in the room and the thought of going in the bucket would only make for more work, so he held on until the wake-up bang on the door. With mug in hand, he doubled down to the bathroom to line up for the toilet. Afterward he quickly filled up his shaving mug with hot water to immediately return to the cell to quickly shave then wash from the water in the bucket. It was imperative to dress quickly then be marched down to receive breakfast. After breakfasting, his cell had to be scrubbed and cleaned with a brush and mop and when finished the metal bucket and spitkid had to be polished to a mirror finish. Any kit had to be neatly placed on the bed then you dressed and made ready for the morning inspection. After that, each man was assigned to cleaning parties to clean the toilets, washroom, and corridors.

The rest of the days were taken up with mainly parade ground drills punctuated by assault courses and seamanship courses.

Should he step out of line, even slightly, or catch any of the Chiefs and Petty Officers on a bad day, the result would usually be agonizing.

Dave wasn't sure that he was going to manage the full thirty days. He had witnessed one inmate being returned to his cell from four days of solitary, he was frothing at the mouth and looked partially insane. They just threw him in his cell and locked the door.

The average age of the inmates he noticed was between the ages of seventeen and twenty-three. Many simply wanted out of the navy and had tried to go AWOL*.

AWOL* Absent With Out Leave or 'On The Trot' as it was more commonly known.

They would eventually be caught and brought back to be punished and returned to duties. This was a military offence of the greatest order and civilian police were even called upon to find absconders anywhere in the UK and sometimes even in Europe.

By the end of the second week, he had already had enough and was set to blow.

"Able Seaman Swift this is the second time this week that your bucket has not been up to standard," said the Petty Officer removing the mattress from the bed with all his belongings and throwing it onto the damp floor.

"Why don't you just fuck off you stupid wanker." Dave screamed completely out of control.

The Petty Officer, knowing of Dave's abilities, quickly stepped back out of the cell and locked the door.

"That was a mistake Swift that you are going to regret." He said through the door.

Moments later the door burst open, and a high-pressure fire hose was trained on him pushing him onto the floor and to the back of his cell. The water was not only very painful but freezing cold.

"Stop, stop please... for fucks sake stop," he screamed.

Three men came into the cell, one stood on his neck while the other two handcuffed him. He was immediately taken to solitary and thrown into an isolation cell. He shivered with cold as he looked at the completely bare windowless room. He curled up into a ball and tried to find some warmth. He had no track of time as he sat wondering just what he had done to deserve this. Eventually after what seemed forever the door opened, and a wooden board was thrown in with a blanket. He immediately crawled over and wrapped himself in the blanket. More time passed and the door opened again, and a cup of water and four slices of bread were passed onto the floor.

His stomach had been churning at the thought of food as he greedily ate the four slices and drank the water. The blanket helped but he still shivered with the cold. Eventually the light was turned off. Which at least gave him an idea of time.

He didn't feel like he had slept because of the constant shivering. It was January and there had been flakes of snow during the parade ground training. There was no heating whatsoever in the room, unlike his previous cell that had a single hot water metal pipe running through it. The lights had been turned on, his legs and arms ached where he had tried to sleep on the hard board. He stood up with the blanket over his shoulders and began walking around the tiny cell. There were many scratched messages and names on the painted concrete wall.

Much time seemed to pass as he walked around and around the room attempting to keep his sanity. Eventually the cell door opened, and a Leading Hand Medic entered. He asked what he thought were silly questions and asked if he was warm enough. Obviously, he was cold by the wrapped blanket around him. The Medic left and later the door opened again with the bread and water plus another blanket. The dull meaningless routine repeated itself, at least giving him a sense of time that just seemed to drag on abysmally. He counted four days and was expecting to be released. He had asked the Medic on his daily rounds how long he would be in solitary, but he apologized that he wasn't allowed to divulge that information.

On day five as he wrapped himself in the blankets, he had begun to talk to himself. He could not remember day six or seven, only the shear relief of waking up in his normal cell on the morning of day eight. It was not morning yet from the lack of light through the small window. He quickly dressed and set his kit on the bed in regulation style. The thought of food again gave him pains in his now shrunken stomach. After his morning shave and wash he waited eagerly at the door to be marched down to collect his breakfast. As soon as he returned to the cell with his food tray, he immediately gobbled everything. As meagre and tasteless as the food was, this morning it tasted soo good.

He had been in DQs for three weeks of his thirty-day punishment and began to realize that *they* had won. All he had to do was prove to them that he was reformed to get through the next week. Even though 'Blighty' had it in for him he concentrated on doing everything he had learned 'by the book'. On his last day of punishment Blighty had again pulled him out of the platoon for another afternoon of agonizing assault course. All through the day he repeated to himself, *Davey boy you're out of here tomorrow... yes siree... go fuck yourself Blighty.*

The following morning, he was marched to a covered wagon. Chief Petty Officer Blight met him prior to boarding.

"Swift... 'ten-shun'. Thought yourself a tough motherfucker, eh? I eat little boys like you for breakfast. It's such a shame that you didn't get the full forty-five, I was just beginning to have fun. Able Seaman Swift... 'stand at... ease ... 'dismissed'."

Climbing aboard the wagon he noticed that he had brought blood to the palms of his hands as he had made a fist wanting dearly to punch Blighty right between the eyes.

Don't do it ... just get on the fuckin' wagon and get the hell out of this hell hole... no siree... just get the fuck out of here.

Chapter 9

At 19, tour of the med.

He had returned to the frigate as it was readying itself for a tour of the Mediterranean. It would go to various ports then keep a presence off the Suez Canal. He was still not allowed leave but was just content to be as far away from the DQs as possible.

The ship visited interesting ports in the Mediterranean keeping a presence with much scrutiny from the Russian fleet. Eventually he was allowed leave again, but the Master at Arms kept an awfully close eye on him, especially during pay week. Everyone onboard would have to line up outside his office with their pay book to collect pay. He had been picked up for long hair and shabby appearance but really, he knew that he was still being punished.

During their stay off the Suez, there was a crew of Navy Clearance divers onboard at various times where they had worked in the canal removing mines. This interested him as the daily seamanship tasks had become very mundane.

His shore leaves in Malta and Gibraltar were very tame not wanting to attract any attention from the authorities. He kept himself to himself and watched his intake of alcohol.

Months later the ship had a minor collision with a freighter that had an unmanned bridge. The ship had to return to Portsmouth to go into dry dock and have the damage fixed.

He had previously applied for a ship's divers' course in Portsmouth and was pleased to find he had been accepted. During the mini refit he was allowed to attend the course. As this was the beginning of the winter months getting used to the freezing water was a challenge. Many of his fellow recruits failed mainly because of the cold. The Clearance diver crew that taught the course seemed to delight at causing the utmost pain to prove how tough *they* were.

Dave was used to pain and willing himself to show his determination even though after most dives in the dirty dockyard waters he couldn't even feel his extremities. It was a satisfying feeling six weeks later as he returned to his ship with the new diver's badge on his sleeve. He was also making six shillings extra a day danger money but only if he maintained the minimum two hours diving per month shown in his divers' logbook. This sometimes meant sitting on the seabed of a filthy dockyard willing the hour to be quickly over with. It was much more interesting once the ship returned to the Suez Canal and he found himself working with the Clearance diving crew. He was basically a bring me fetch me kind of help in the team, but he was soon a respected addition when the going got tough.

During the exercises onboard, he had also proved himself. The team had to attack the ship underwater and place magnetic tin lids on various parts of the hull. These were meant to be limpet mines.

If they were captured, and they always were because it was either that or have your ear drums blown apart by the thunderflash fireworks thrown into the water. The marines onboard were ruthless in torturing the handcuffed divers for information as to where the mines had been placed. Another set of divers would then go and retrieve the tin lids. Dave was impossible to crack and had the bruises to prove it.

The ship again returned to home base in Pompey and apart from the duty watch the ship's company had been moved into barracks at the HMS Victory base during another mini refit. He met up with a friend that he had previously made in Ganges who was also waiting to join his next ship which was going to be an aircraft carrier. They had spent shore leaves together, but Dave was still a little hesitant on hitting the bars, in fear of a repeat occurrence. They had spent much of late Spring visiting Southsea, which was a holiday resort area not too far from Portsmouth.

Bryn 'Taffy' Williams seemed noticeably confident around females and had helped with Dave's shyness around the opposite sex. Although he had experienced sex with one night stands here and there and had even paid for sex occasionally when the desperate need arose. It had all felt too clinical, and one sided, which always left him feeling unsatisfied. He desperately needed to feel a connection of sorts. He had never experienced climax with a woman and was beginning to think that maybe there was something wrong. Unknown to the female he would later look after his climax in a quiet room or washroom later. He had also never experienced a steady girlfriend. The thought of being abandoned, should he allow himself to care for someone, was always in the back of his mind.

Chapter 10

Annie.

"Hey Swiffy check out the two cute ones at the bar, we should go and try our luck. Now don't go all quiet on me ya prick, just take my lead, OK?" Taffy demanded.

It was a Saturday night; they had heard impressive stories from others in the large mess at the barracks that this weekly dance was a good place to pick up women. The joke in the mess was that it was a 'grab a grannie night'. They had as usual come ashore in their civvies as most local women didn't want to be seen with matelots giving them a bad name.

"OK seeing as this was my idea, I take the blonde and you get the brunette... got it? Now don't fuck it up ya wanker," Taffy said smiling.

"O.K, mister fuckin' prince charming but I'm tellin' you they are not gonna be interested in us. Dream on! These are a bit above our standard," Dave replied.

"See... there you go ya fuckup... ease up with the fuckin' negativity. If you want to sit this out sippin' on yer fuckin' beer shandy, be my fuckin' guest but I'm going for it," Taffy explained.

"OK, keep yer fuckin' hat on, I'm comin'," Dave replied already feeling the butterflies in his stomach. As they walked across the huge expanse of the dance floor that Dave thought would never end, his hands began to shake. He was dreading the denial and the impending long walk back to his seat.

He wasn't sure what Taffy had said to the blonde with the noise of the band blaring out, but it must have been funny because the two girls were laughing. Dave stood to one side of the brunette like a stuffed dummy waiting for the denial so that he could quietly return to his seat. He knew his face to be beetroot red when she looked around.

"Hey sailor, what ship are ya on?" she said smiling.

He opened his mouth to talk but started to stutter embarrassingly. He just wanted to get this over as a bead of sweat ran down his cheek.

"H-h-how d-do y-you k-know we're sailors?"

Oh God, let the floor just open and swallow me up, is that the best you can come up with... numb nuts.

"My sister and I have lived here all our lives; we can figure a sailor at ten paces. The hair cut kinda gives you away and there are other clues that I'm going to keep to myself as us girls have got to stick together," she said emphatically but slightly smiling.

God she is beautiful... yes siree... way above my standard. I'll just slink away back to my seat... you're just a fuckup Dave Swift ... yes siree... number one fuckup.

"Oh sorry, then... I'll just... just head off back to my seat." He pointed in the direction he had come in and started to walk away.

"Hey sailor boy you gonna give up that quick, I haven't finished with you yet," she said smiling.

And God, what a beautiful smile... if only...

"We're in V-Vicky barracks waiting for our ships. W-what's your name? Mines Dave... D-Dave Swift. He again stuttered out.

What the fuck is wrong with me...

"Well, I'm Annie Brown and this here is my sister Rhonda," as she held out her hand.

He held her small warm hand just a little too long and realized the slightly uncomfortable look appearing on her face. He quickly let go, snatching his hand back.

You are such a fuckin' idiot... yes siree... a fuckin' idiot of the ninth degree.

In the moment of pregnant silence and not knowing what else to say, she kindly broke the silence.

"Hey Rhonda meet Dave," she elbowed her sister who by now was in heavy conversation with the talkative Taffy. She briefly turned around to hold out her hand which he ensured was shook the correct number of moments before letting go. But he was unable to think of anything to say as he was still dumbfounded that he hadn't been dismissed for his obvious foolishness.

Taffy and Rhonda disappeared onto the busy dance floor and not thinking of anything interesting to say he nervously asked if she would like to dance, which he was surprised she accepted. He was even more self-conscious wondering if his dancing was acceptable. Then the music changed to a slow song. He thought that she would obviously want to sit it out as they had only just met. As he began to walk back to the bar, she stopped him.

"Hey, I love this song," as she put her arms around his waist and shoulder.

This is too good to be true. Don't fuck it up... no siree... not now.

It became more unbelievable when she put her head on his chest. He breathed in her perfume. Her soft hair brushed his chin. It seemed that he had never felt so close to a female as he held her tightly not wanting the moment to end. The music changed to another slow song that drifted him into a wonderful and heady place. He could feel her holding him tighter. He was horrified when he felt that he was getting aroused and was trying to bend away so that she wouldn't feel his erection. At the third dance he was sure that she was holding herself onto him. They had not spoken but she had looked up into his eyes more than once. Eventually, the music changed to a fast dance, so they had to dance apart again. He was thankful that the music was loud, which gave him an excuse to not have to talk. She suddenly stopped and pointed toward a table. She held his hand as they walked toward the table. He resolved that no matter what happened now he was just so happy that she had given him these wonderful moments. He was dizzy with elation as they sat.

"Annie, thank you for dancing with me. You are a v-very beautiful woman; I'm waiting for someone to prick me awake, ladies like you don't normally come my way. I'm having difficulty believing you're still here. I don't think I've felt like this before... you must think this is a line... or that I'm weird," he said quietly across the table.

She moved her chair closer to his. "No, I don't think you're weird. Thank you, Dave, you're sweet. Well first off, you're a hunk of a guy... and I'm not really into the big talkers. You seem a little different from what I'm used to," as she reached up to kiss his cheek.

They danced the night away in the busy dance hall and later lined up in front of the stage to sway to the groovy band. Occasionally they would catch sight of Taffy and Rhonda to share a wave. Dave wondered if Taffy was getting on as famously as he was. He didn't want the evening to end and tried to remove the dejected thoughts that this would sooner than later end, and he would go on his lonely way again.

Eventually the band played their last encore, and the bright lights of the hall came on. He held her hand tightly as they exited the hall and waited for a taxi. The late evening was cool as he put his arm around her holding her close. He had to make the best of these last few minutes before she would disappear into the night.

"Dave, we could all share a cab... if you're OK dropping us off at home, it's on the way to the dockyard. I'm afraid we couldn't ask you in as our Dad probably wouldn't approve," Annie said.

Dave looked across at Taffy who had heard the conversation. "Yes, sure we would love to," Taffy said.

In the cab Annie told them that she was the older sister at twenty-three and Rhonda was still nineteen. They gave Dave and Taffy their home phone number and agreed that they would both like to meet up again. Dave immediately felt a surge of glee.

The taxi came to a halt at their terraced house. Taffy who was in the front passenger seat got out and escorted Rhonda to the door of their home. Now alone in the backseat Annie turned to look into Dave's eyes and reached up to give him a long sexy kiss. He again felt arousal as his erection strained against his pants. She reached down under his jacket to feel his erection as she kissed him again.

"Hey... you two love birds in the back I gotta another fare waiting," the taxi driver said smiling through his mirror.

Annie gave Dave a loving glance as she exited the cab and waved as she opened the door to their home.

Not wanting to seem too anxious he waited until Wednesday of the following week to call their telephone number. She had been in his thoughts constantly. As the phone rang, he could feel his heart pounding.

Hey fuckup... don't get your hopes up. She probably had too many drinks that night and might not even remember your name... No siree!

A male voice answered which he took to be her father.

"Hello, my name is Dave... Dave Swift, could I speak with Annie please," he asked nervously.

"Hold the line," came the non-committal voice.

He waited for what seemed a long time as numerous dismal thoughts came to mind.

"Dave, hi, I've been waiting for your call, thought you'd done a runner," she answered cheerfully.

"I would like to see you again Annie?" he said pathetically as the many prepared conversations he had practiced suddenly disappeared from his head.

"Yes, sure, how do you feel about a walk on Southsea beach on Saturday morning. Rhonda just asked if Taffy could come too? Oh, and bring your swimwear, we could go for a swim it's going to be a hot day."

He could feel the excitement building inside but he desperately wanted not to come across as a blathering idiot. He decided to keep his reply short so as not to wreck a good thing.

"Oh, I don't need to ask, I'm sure Taffy would be more than happy to see Rhonda."

They decided to meet at Southsea, south parade pier at ten on Saturday morning. He placed the phone back on its cradle to allow the next rating inline in the barracks passageway to use the phone.

"YEAH," he shouted jumping in glee to the many queued ratings looking at him strangely.

Saturday morning hadn't come soon enough as he and Taffy excitedly set off walking, thinking that they would have enough time to reach Southsea pier by ten. As they came closer to the pier a few minutes late, Dave felt nervous but excited at the same time and was trying to hide those feelings from Taffy who was walking beside him.

"Swiffy if you walk any faster, you're gonna be setting off into a full-blown run. You're gonna be popping off a load in your trousers if you're not careful. Fer fucks sake take it easy. I don't want you blowing my deal with the beautiful Rhonda," Taffy exclaimed.

Eventually the ladies came into view sitting on the front sea wall. They both stood to greet them as they came closer.

Annie looked positively stunning in her miniskirt and tight top; she also wore a fashionable brimmed hat. Her red lipstick complemented her long shiny black hair. A broad smile lit her face as she came toward him. He could not believe his luck as she reached up and kissed him on the cheek.

"Well, hi there, mister hunky guy, you sure know how to keep a girl waiting," she said smiling very sexily.

He was dumbfounded for words but managed to say, "hello Annie... y-you look amazing."

Rhonda and Taffy had decided to walk down the pier, but Annie suggested that she would like to walk the beach a little. They decided to all meet later for an ice cream at the far end of the pier.

Dave had brought his swim trunks in a rolled-up towel under his arm. "I thought you wanted to go for a swim Annie. I brought this," pointing to his towel.

"Well, yes, I do, I have my swimming costume on under these clothes. You're obviously new to this, I should have explained but no problem. She led him to a washroom on the pier where he changed into his swim shorts and rolled up his clothes into the towel.

When he returned from changing, he saw that she had already removed her skirt and top. She now wore a small very sexy bikini and held her clothes also rolled up in her handbag. She had a body to kill for, but he did notice a small scar on her stomach.

Placing their clothes under the pier they waded out into the cool sea. The hot sun aroused their bodies as they splashed in the surf. Occasionally she would come close, and her perfume would waft his way sending tingles of desire down his spine. They held and kissed more than once, which played havoc with all his senses. He wanted her badly. Eventually she seemed to cool, and her smile disappeared.

Oh, jeez what did I do, was I coming on too strong?

"Can we walk Dave I have something to tell you."

"Was it something I have said or done, if so, I am sorry. I'm having difficulty keeping my hands off you," he explained.

He had an ominous feeling that she wanted to tell him something intense, which started to bring on his usual feeling of dejection.

This was too good to be true, what would this lady want with the likes of me... no siree!

They picked up their clothes and comfortably walked the pebbly beach, she held her tiny, strapped shoes and handbag while he rolled everything in his towel and carried it under his arm. They occasionally waded in the surf to cool off from the sweltering sun. Pleasantries and snippets of information about each of their lives seemed easy to talk about. She then guided him to a secluded part of the beach beside the wall, which was shaded, and they sat.

OK, here it comes, whatever it is on her mind, it's gonna be a whammer.

"Dave, I haven't been very honest with you, and I need to get this off my chest. You seem like a nice man that I wish I had met sooner. I am married but separated from my husband. He just happens to also be a sailor, he is a Petty Officer and he's somewhere in the Far East as we speak. We have a child together, Susie, who is being looked after by my Dad and little sister at home today."

Dave's heart sank as she divulged this information. He had all along felt that this was too good to be true. He just wanted to head back to the base and spend the rest of the day with the punch bag in the gym.

"So why am I here? Why did you allow me to build up my hopes? You are a gorgeous woman, way above my benchmark Annie... I guess I should just go." As he moved to raise himself from the beach.

"No, please stay Dave and allow me to explain. My husband is much older than me. I married at seventeen mainly because I was pregnant. He is due to leave the navy in two years. His hometown is in Sheffield where we had a home close to his family. I spent five very lonely and miserable years there trying to make it work. He was rarely ever home and when he was, he quickly became very abusive, his alcohol consumption had a lot to do with it. He became a much different person to the one I had married.

We split months before he left on his ship, and I returned to live with my Dad and two sisters. It's been almost a year now since I made that move. I have asked for a divorce, but we must wait until he returns to finalize the papers.

I like you Dave, even though it's early days, you come across as a very sincere and caring person. When you held me the other night dancing, I felt a strong connection. I've been with other men, but you seem different. You have placed a spark back into my life that I thought had disappeared forever," she put her hand on his shoulder and looked deep into his eyes.

He leaned over and kissed her as they both fell back to lie on the beach. A raging passion seemed to suddenly envelope him. He didn't care what the next moment might bring, he just wanted to hold her and fantasize that she was his. He placed his hand on her breast and she didn't resist. Her breathing then became heavy. She then reached up and placed Dave's large towel over them. She grasped his hand and pushed it under her bikini top. He felt her firm nipple brushing the palm of his hand. He was blind with lust as she reached down and slipped her hand under his shorts to feel his erection. Slowly he reached down to feel her too, but she stopped him and held his hand firmly.

"Not here Dave, I won't be able to stop if you touch me there. But I do want you very badly right now," she whispered into his ear.

A family had moved into the shade close by and was sitting on their towels. The two young children were staring at them. The mother saw what they were looking at and reprimanded them as a look of disgust came their way.

Annie giggled, "I think we should move on, what do you think?"

Dave smiled, "you're going to have to wait a minute," as they both looked down under the towel to see his protruding erection under his shorts.

They both laughed out loud seeing the funny side of the situation.

"Dave, I do want to make love with you too, we must find the time and place. But right now, let's just go and meet up with Taffy and Rhonda," Annie asked smiling demurely.

They sat and talked as their red faces and passion faded enough to walk the beach again. He felt so at ease with her now as they both divulged information about their challenging lives. Eventually they were at the pier where they both used the washrooms to change back into their street clothes.

"Hey where ya been, love birds we've been waiting ages," Rhonda called as she sat on a bench with Taffy who was smiling like a Cheshire cat. They were both comfortably sitting arm in arm eating ice cream cones.

"Rhonda would like to go on the rides at the fairgrounds up the road. You up to it?" Taffy asked.

Annie smiled at Dave and said, "yeah that sounds great, what do you think?"

"Sounds great to me, let's go," Dave agreed.

They all had a fun and a relaxing afternoon on the rides eating junk food. Dave had tried his luck shooting the tin cans and had won a teddy bear. Annie seemed ecstatic when he gave it to her.

"I know someone who is going to love this," she said, then suddenly stopped short, realizing her out of place comment. "Sorry Dave, I didn't mean..."

"Hey, it is what it is... no problem here," Dave answered attempting to make her feel at ease.

Both ladies mentioned that they were supposed to be home at teatime at five thirty, so they headed off on the long walk back. The two couples were quickly separated because every time Annie found a quiet shop doorway, she would drag Dave in for passionate kisses.

He didn't know where this was going or even if it was going anywhere. He had simply resolved to just enjoy every moment with this gorgeous woman. He even felt that she appreciated his presence and touch.

Eventually they arrived at her address where Taffy and Rhonda waited. Annie and Rhonda asked them both to wait as they entered the house. Minutes later they returned smiling.

"Dad says it OK for you both to come for a visit this Wednesday night. What do you think guys?" Annie asked.

They both seemed to answer at once. "Yes, sure we would love to."

Dave was biding his days going about the brainless tasks of cleaning and the daily mess inspections by the duty Officer. He couldn't seem to take his mind off Annie for a second. Amorous notions crossed his mind during the day but especially at night when the lights went out. He gazed at the moving shapes on the ceiling from the headlights of passing cars. Occasionally his dysfunctional and self-defeating thoughts would return.

What could she possibly see in me? there had to be an ulterior reason for this, sooner than later would come the crash... as it always did.

At times, during the night, his thoughts, good and bad, were interrupted by drunks returning to base crashing around the large mess hall giggling.

Taffy and Dave sat together in the barracks cafeteria for their evening meal prior to their date and talked about what promise the evening might bring. They set off on the walk early which they guessed would take them forty minutes or so to the terraced house on the outskirts of the busy port.

Annie answered the door to invite them into their home. In the small hallway there was a closed door to the left which was the front room. Further down the hallway on the left there were stairs heading up to the second-floor bedrooms. At the end of the hallway was an open doorway into the living room, at the far end was a larger opening into a small kitchen. They passed a dining room table that had a plate of sandwiches and a freshly made pot of tea. On the left side of the room, were two armchairs and a sofa which faced an electric fire and to one side was a TV. A teenage girl who Dave guessed was around fifteen sat on one of the armchairs together with a toddler watching the TV.

Their father sat on one of the dining room chairs beside the table close to the kitchen, he was also watching the TV from the back of the room.

"This is our Dad," Annie introduced them to the rather non-committal man who glanced around and held up his hand as his attention returned to the TV. Annie and Rhonda looked at them both and shrugged their shoulders in mock disbelief.

"Alyssa, bring over Susie and meet our guests." Rhonda called. The teenager held the toddler's hand and made their way around the sofa to meet them.

"This is Dave and that is Bryn you can also call him Taffy," Annie introduced smiling.

Alyssa confidently shook hands with them both. "Oh, you're the two new dancing fools, eh?" she cheekily replied.

"Now, don't be cheeky Liss, that's not nice," Annie scolded embarrassingly.

"And this little sweetie is Susie smoochie." Annie bent down to pick up the giggling toddler into her arms.

"Well nice to meet you all," Taffy confidentially said waving his hand.

"Yes, likewise," Dave said with a wave but obviously having difficulty concealing his slightly blushing face.

Alyssa and the toddler returned to their TV program as Annie invited Dave to sit with her on the sofa. Taffy and Rhonda sat on the dining table chairs. Moments later the father disappeared into the kitchen where he could be seen smoking in the dark.

Annie observing the uneasy atmosphere, said quietly, "hey don't take any notice of Dad he's always like that. It's not because you are here. Would you like a cup of tea? we've also made sandwiches for you."

"We have already eaten in the barracks thanks but that probably won't stop the ol' gutso Taffy back there," Dave quipped to diffuse the tense moment.

"Hey, take no notice of him, he can put it away like the best of us, he's just being coy." Taffy replied grinning.

Rhonda came over to the sofa and whispered to Annie. "We're going into the front room, OK?" She asked.

With her father in the kitchen and the two girls watching the TV they now had a little privacy to talk. As she snuggled up to him, he put his arm around her, which she seemed to approve of.

"Please don't feel uncomfortable Dave, I know this is a lot to take in but if you want to be with me?" She looked at him questioningly.

"No problem, you've probably noticed by now that I'm a bit of a dorf especially around the opposite sex. I should be asking you the same question," he replied as they both laughed loudly causing the girls to turn around shushing them.

She asked him about his past and where his parents were. He tried to answer as honestly as possible without getting into the horrifying memories that still haunted him. She quietly listened and seemed to be touched by the details and squeezed his hand in comfort.

"And here I am thinking that my life has dealt me a bad hand. Both of my parents are still alive. Well, you've met my Dad," she said, raising her eyebrows questioningly. "He cares for us all even though he rarely shows it. Mum left us and it kind of destroyed him for a while but through all the turmoil he still looked after us. He has never had a day off work. The grocery store at the top of the street is where he has worked for thirty or so years. I can't imagine a more insanely boring job mostly stacking shelves. I like to think he has quietly persevered in this for us. I can never replace mum, I tried for a little while... well until I got pregnant that is. It was heart breaking leaving him and my sisters when I had to leave for

Sheffield. Mum lives close by, about an hour away, she married the man she left us for. They have their own family; he has two sons from a previous marriage. When I left, she promised to take more of an interest in her other daughters. I still get on reasonably well with her but Rhonda and Lyss have trouble forgiving her. When we visit it is always fraught with arguments. Happy families, eh?"

Just over an hour had passed when Taffy and Rhonda appeared red-faced from the front room. Minutes later Annie whispered, "come with me?"

Dave followed her into the front room. She closed the door behind him.

"We can have a bit of privacy here."

There was a sofa in the center of the small room facing an electric fire, only one of the bars was glowing red. There was a single armchair to one side and at the back of the room behind the sofa was a teak cabinet with fancy glassware showing through the glass. Annie lit the shaded lamp that was on the cabinet and turned off the main light.

"There that's better, eh?" she asked sitting close beside him. Her eyes glistened as she looked into his eyes and reached up to kiss him. He felt her tongue gently brushing his lips. Her hand touched his thigh which immediately sent shudders of ecstasy through his body. After much kissing and caressing she began lightly biting and licking his ear. All of this was so new and extremely sensual. He had been slightly concerned that he might come across as a bungling amateur, it was painfully obvious that she was far more experienced. He moved off the sofa to her surprise but then pulled her to one side, so she was now laying down. He lay beside her and lifted her blouse up to reveal her bra. He then reached behind to unsnap her bra it took a few attempts, but he had to show that he wasn't completely green in these matters. Even though it was partially dark on this side of the sofa he could see her glistening dark eyes sensuously looking into his. When he revealed her beautiful breast, he just felt the need to bury his face to kiss and caress. He could hear her quietly moaning, which became louder after he reached under her skirt to rub between her legs.

"Dave, I want to make love with you now," she then stood up to remove her underwear and laid on the carpet in front of the warm fire. She pulled him toward her and unbuckled his belt and unzipped his fly. She then reached in to pull his manhood over his underwear. He was now on his knees facing her as she caressed him in both hands. He looked down to see he was dripping wet onto her hands. She laid back and pulled him toward her as she opened her legs and directed him into her. She moaned much louder and he was concerned that they might be heard. He pushed into her while gently kissing her mouth. She immediately wrapped her legs around him and pulled him closer. This was the most erotic sex he had ever experienced; he could feel her squeezing him inside. Her nails dug into his back. She seemed delirious as she kissed and gently bit his neck between her moaning. He couldn't believe that he could have this effect on a woman. Eventually she wanted him to move faster as her breathing quickened.

"Oh god Dave you feel sooo good... I'm going to come," she whispered into his ear. She began to shake and move faster it was all he could do to just hold her tight. She started to moan louder, he tried to kiss again to hold in her scream. It started as a violent rapid movement as she seemed to be enraptured. This happened three times consecutively. During the wondrous lovemaking he felt like he was going to climax but each time he came close, the feeling disappeared, he almost felt fear. Eventually, after the sensuous and loving moments he rose to gaze into her face again; she was flushed but held a wonderful contentment.

"Dave, thank you, I needed that so bad... it's been a while. *YOU*... are a very sexy man, but I knew that the first time I set eyes on you. Why didn't you come? I am on the pill, no need to be concerned."

"Oh, I wanted to, but it's never happened, no slight on you, that was *THE* most erotic moment in my entire life," Dave confessed. He was beginning to feel that he could tell her his intimate secrets.

"Well now, you've set me a goal." She replied grinning. "We had better get cleaned up before anyone comes looking."

They replaced their disheveled clothes and tried to look innocent and presentable. Sitting back on the settee they continued kissing.

"Oh god we had better stop Dave I am already wanting a repeat performance. You have made me so horny. I wish we had someplace we could stay together."

A knock came on the door startling them both. It was Rhonda. "Hey sis you've been in there a while and Dad is looking a bit uncomfortable."

They both squared away as best they could and returned to the living room. Nothing had changed except Susie had been put to bed. Dave glanced into the kitchen to see their Dad in the same position they had last left him. He was quietly sitting smoking a cigarette in the dark looking aimlessly out of a window.

Over the next few weeks this episode was to repeat itself at least twice per week. A couple of times when one of them was on duty watch they would go alone to spend most of the evening in the front room. On the weekends Annie would put little Susie in a stroller pram and they would go for walks together. She had taken Dave to meet her mother on one such occasion. On the way he couldn't help but notice the many men, young and old who gazed at Annie desirously. She as always wore her short miniskirts and tight tops. The slip on strapped mini heeled shoes accentuated her long, gorgeous legs. An elderly lady had stopped on the sidewalk as they passed staring in disgust, tut tutting as they passed her. Annie just gave her a cheeky smile, then turned to grin at Dave.

"Hey, I'm used to that, I'm a sixties flower child... screw them!"

"Are you sure your mother is going to be OK with me coming with you," Dave asked nervously as they came closer to her home. It was a beautiful semi-detached home with a front garden full of roses. There was a modern car in the driveway. Annie removed

Susie from the stroller and let herself into the vestibule where she then folded the stroller. She had a key to the front door that she opened and invited Dave in.

"Mum will be in the kitchen, she loves to cook," Annie explained as she led him down a plush carpeted hallway to the large kitchen. Her mum was on the opposite side of a countertop island slicing vegetables. She had an apron on which was tightly wrapped around her slim waist. It was obvious where Annie had got her good looks from when she removed the apron revealing a tight shapely body.

"Oh, this must be the hunky Dave you've been telling me about," she said embarrassing him. She came around the island to lightly shake his hand. Looking him up and down approvingly. "Hmm you'd better not leave me alone with this one Annie."

"Mum that's enough of that. Why do you have to embarrass me like this," Annie protested.

He estimated her to be in her early forties and had kept herself looking quite young. Her make up might have been a little on the heavy side but she made up for it in her cheerful manner.

He knew his face to be beetroot red as she now held his hand longer than expected.

"Nice to meet you Mrs. Goldman, you have a beautiful house," *Oh god, is that all you can come up with... ya jerk.*

"Ah yes, my husband is a very successful lawyer and has been able to provide more than my last, sad excuse of a husband ever did."

"Mum, if you don't stop, we are going to leave, right now!" Annie said sharply.

"Ah... take it easy Annie, don't have a bird. Did your Father tell you that I dropped in last week to give him a bottle of his favorite brandy for his birthday?" She said, still unnervingly staring into Dave's face then thankfully let his hand go after way too much time.

"Yes, he told us and thank you for that, it was very thoughtful. He's been working quite hard of late. Keeping us all housed and fed must be trying." Annie said with sarcasm.

"I've offered more than once to help him with that, but he is such a proud man and always refuses. You know that I have wanted you and Susie to come and live with us, but you've been so mean to my husband, Levi, that it is now out of the question.

"Dave, you must think we're a crazy bunch. You've just walked in the door and here we are putting out all our dirty laundry. Please sit down in the parlor. Can I get you a drink? We have a healthy choice of drinks in our liquor cabinet," she offered genuinely.

Annie looked at Dave and nodded her head in approval. He needed something to calm his nerves.

"Yes please, do you have a gin and tonic?" he asked quietly.

"Mum I'll have a Coca Cola please," As she escorted Dave into the comfortable parlor. The room was expensively decorated with an elaborate teak chessboard for a coffee table. They both settled into a plush comfortable sofa. Susie had been given a toy and was quietly playing in front of the large ornate fireplace.

"Sorry Dave, Mum can be a pain in the butt sometimes, her heart is in the right place though. I have long since forgiven her for leaving us all those years ago, probably because I have firsthand knowledge of how a marriage can go hopelessly wrong. But Rhonda and Alyssa have not and refuse to come to this house. Thank you for coming Dave, she obviously approves of you. But remind me never to leave you in a room with her alone ha!" she said grinning.

Dave felt a slight flush coming on but was able to keep it under control.

The conversation was light and friendly which put Dave very much at ease and the couple of gin and tonics helped him to relax. Annie's Mum had drunk a full bottle of white wine and was already into her second. Susie was starting to get bored as Annie and her Mum were deep in conversation. He leaned over to pick up Susie and wondered why he had not held her even once since they had met. Annie immediately halted her conversation and quickly stepped in front of him to pick her up.

"OK Dave I'll manage this, it's time we left anyway. Levi will be home shortly, and I'd rather not be here when he does."

On their way back they stopped off at a small café and had a meal before heading home. Annie had informed him early in the day that she had got permission from her Dad to have Dave stay overnight on the sofa in the front room.

"With any luck I might be able to sneak out of my bedroom for some midnight nookie," she grinned.

The evening had gone on as normal, everyone watching the TV leaving them to quietly head into the front room. He wondered what treat that he would be introduced to tonight, there was always a new experience to be had. She was quite deft in the art of making love and it was *always* different. Annie relished teaching him something new. He lost count of all the interesting and highly erotic positions.

Tonight, she had kissed and nibbled his ear, she had learned earlier where his erogenous locations were and had as usual brought him almost to boiling point. She had undone his fly and was stroking him gently and it felt so good. Her head was on his chest actively looking down at what she was doing. She was obviously getting aroused as she watched then suddenly without warning she put him into her mouth. He had heard about this sex act but had never experienced it. It was extremely enjoyable, but he couldn't get it out of his mind at how unhygienic this was. She stopped for a moment to reach up and kiss him and for a moment he pulled back.

"Oh really?" she said. "Don't you want to know what you taste like."

He allowed her to kiss him, although there was a mildly pungent taste. The indecency of it seemed to bring him to a whole new and different level of excitement. As always, her experience was leading him the way. This was an incredible experience as a worrisome thought came to him that he might climax.

"Stop," he asked anxiously.

She stopped and looked up; he could see that she was equally as excited.

"I want to be inside you," he said breathlessly.

She quickly stood up to take off her panties and immediately straddled him. It was an amazing feeling as she slowly moved up and down. He felt completely relaxed yet extremely aroused. He then pulled up her bra and kissed and nibbled her nipples and she was going wild. Then it happened... he pulled her buttocks toward him as he climaxed for the first time inside a woman. She pushed her chest into him to quiet the moan. When he finally returned from this wonderous place he looked up to see her sensuously smiling.

"See what perseverance gets you, I knew I'd get you in the end," she whispered in his ear.

Shockingly, minutes later, they were interrupted as the door opened, and Alyssa leaned over the sofa to witness the disarray.

"I'm going to tell Dad... you're disgusting and shouldn't be doing this," she said angrily.

"Lyss, come back," shouted Annie covering herself up but still straddled mid-coitus.

Alyssa had stepped back into the doorway. And stood with her arms folded in juvenile contempt.

"If you tell Dad he is going to be terribly upset and none of us will ever be allowed to have friends over again. Now if you don't mind just close the door so that we can have some privacy... and stay there, I need to speak to you," Annie ordered.

The thought of the quiet tame man, who seemingly always sat in the tiny kitchen smoking, being angry enough to throw him out onto the street, played heavily on his nerves.

As she was dressing and Dave was zipping up his fly, Annie whispered.

"I knew something like this was going to happen today. Lyss was angry because I'd gone to see Mum. Anyway, don't worry I'll sort this out."

In the hallway he could hear quiet but heated voices, then Annie returned, "little bitch... that just cost me a necklace that she has been after for ages."

She was gone again for about ten minutes which gave him time to think about what had just happened; it was a wonderful feeling to climax like that, he had never felt as close to anyone in his life. What was it that had affected him in the past? He had only known her for a month... was he falling in love?

Annie returned a little exasperated with a blanket and pillow. "We're all heading off to bed now, Lyss is acting up so we should cool things for now. No promises, but when everyone is asleep, I'll try and sneak down."

He laid back on the sofa and covered up as the bar on the electric fire had stopped glowing. He couldn't sleep as he thought about how Annie had changed his whole outlook on life. She extolled the idea and had mentioned it more than once that you only live once so make the best of it. She was indeed a free spirit.

A few hours had passed, and he was beginning to doze off when the door quietly opened. In the dim light he could see that she wore a flimsy black nightgown as she slipped under the blanket. He put his arm around her as she nestled into his chest.

"I hope you're not tired because I still feel very horny from what happened earlier. I just can't get enough of you. Do you think I'm a nymphomaniac?" Annie added quietly giggling.

"Well, I for sure am not complaining but from what I've learned in my vast experience as a 'lover of many women.' That a nympho has issues with climax. Hmm... maybe I'm a nympho? Dave also added giggling.

"So, what is it Mister Casanova, 'lover of many women' that holds you back?"

"Well, I have put a lot of thought into that, especially since I've met you, 'missus lover of many men.' I have told you about my mother and what I learned later when she was pregnant with me; It ruined her life and had she not met who I thought was my Father, she may have perished. I also knew girls at my school who were barely fifteen and had been pregnant. They seemed to disappear from society never to be seen again. I vowed to myself never to be the one to cause that. Could *that* be the reason? I wonder."

She slid her hand down under his pants to feel his erection. "Well, I'm not having babies anytime soon being on the pill so let's try this out again, 'mister lover of many women.'"

She placed the pillow on the carpet and sat on it then pulled him on top of her. He felt her and she was already moist as he entered her. She quietly moaned in ecstasy then asked him to raise his legs one at a time. He did so and she placed her legs inside of his. Her hips were pushed higher because of the pillow, and he immediately began to feel himself being squeezed inside her.

"This is my favorite position, Dave, I need to be a little selfish," she whispered in his ear with a slightly embarrassing giggle.

Within minutes she was breathing heavily then shortly thereafter she climaxed. He was being tightly squeezed and the pulsing of her climax inside seemingly pumping him also into a massive orgasm.

"Oh Dave, I love you," she said breathlessly.

Every time he moved, she quivered. "Oh god Dave don't stop, please don't stop." He climaxed a second time which brought her into another climax.

Afterward they both laid there in silence side by side in awe at what had just occurred. She had moved the pillow up under their heads and Dave pulled the blanket from the sofa to cover them both.

"Dave, I think I'm falling in love with you. I'm not saying that just because of the amazing sex. I know we've only known each other briefly but I can't get enough of you. I want to spend all my days with you. This might shock you, but I've even been thinking about what it would be like having a baby with you."

"Annie I'm not sure what love is as I've never experienced it, apart from the dream like thoughts I have about my Mother. You're the best thing that has ever happened to me. Spending the rest of my life with you would be my ultimate dream. But you will have to be patient with me. I wish I could live like you; like there is 'no tomorrow'. I so envy your outlook on life. You are good for me in so many ways. Let's hold on to this, I think my trust issues will eventually evaporate. Until that time, bringing a child into this world with even the slightest possibility of experiencing what I have, would be my worst nightmare."

"OK mister 'lover of many women,' it was just a daydream at what the future might hold," she said with a little sadness in her voice.

Shortly thereafter they both fell into a deep sleep. He was awakened by footsteps coming down the stairs, then walking down the hallway. It was early morning when he noticed the dim light coming through the curtains over the front window. Annie was fast asleep when he covertly attempted to push her under the sofa. She awoke in a stir as she also heard the footsteps of her father.

The door opened and her father bent down to open a small cupboard in the lower corner of the room that held a coin operated electric meter. He placed two-shilling coins into the slot and turned the latch and the single electric bar element and the small table lamp came on. Dave could see Annie's fearful eyes from under the wooden legs of the sofa. Dave attempted to cover Annie's bare legs with the blanket. The father reached over and turned off the lamp. He closed the door, and they could hear him going back upstairs. Dave looked over to see Annie grinning.

"That was close, eh? He's kind of old school, I'm sure he knows but if we don't make it obvious, he'll just ignore it. He normally goes off to work at this time during the week, but Sunday is his day off."

He pulled her out from under the sofa and they giggled. Her hair was tussled, but she looked so sexy now that he could see the black see through laced nightdress. She immediately noticed the gleam in his eye and straddled him. He lazily watched her beautiful body as she raised and lowered bringing him to climax which seemed to excite her so after a few moments she continued until she had her orgasm. She fell on top of him, and they both laid there saying nothing. With the warmth of their love making and the heat from the fire they both dozed for only minutes.

Annie whispered in his ear, "I'm sorry Dave but I should go to bed now," she kissed him then very quietly disappeared up the steps to bed.

He was exhausted and immediately fell asleep. He woke to a strong smell of burning, as the room was full of smoke. Part of the blanket had fallen onto the electric fire bar and was smoldering. He removed the blanket from the fire and immediately got up to dress then turned off the electric fire. He opened the door and went into the living room. The father sat in his usual position drinking a cup of tea and smoking.

"Excuse me b-but I t-t-think I've burnt your blanket," he stuttered embarrassingly.

What a fuckin' dick I am... yes siree, first class fuckin' dick

The father, seeing the smoke now entering the living room rushed into the front room. Immediately noticing the smoldering blanket picked it up and threw it out through the front door. He left the front door open and also opened the front room window to help expel the smoke. Hearing all the kerfuffle downstairs Annie and her sisters appeared wearing thick nightgowns.

"Are you OK Dave?" Annie asked worriedly.

"Yes, I'm fine but I'm very sorry for burning the blanket. Can I buy you a new one?" he asked the father.

He had never heard the father speak in all these weeks when he said non-committedly, "Its OK son," and looking Dave in the eye knowingly, he said, "accidents happen!" then returned to the kitchen to light up another cigarette.

A few weeks later Dave brought it up in conversation why Annie was keeping little Susie from getting acquainted with him.

"Please don't read too much into this; I just don't want her to be hurt if this doesn't work out... with us. I love you Dave and I think you care for me but there doesn't seem to be much commitment on your part."

He had to admit to himself that there was some niggly feeling that still gave him reservations about their relationship. He would have to go back to sea soon, would their relationship withstand being apart for longer periods of time?

"Annie, I don't know what love is. I feel like I have been lost in a dark void forever, you're the beacon of light that I am heading toward. I have never felt this way about anyone, and it certainly feels like love. You need to give me more time."

After moments of thought, Annie replied. "This began as a fun sexual adventure, but it has grown into much more. Part of me wants to just continue and not complicate a good thing but my heart wants more. I too want more time especially for my daughter. So, let's just leave it at that. All this talk has made me feel horny again." Annie said looking up with her sexy eyes that Dave could not resist.

Chapter 11

At 20, Convoy exercise off Scotland.

Taffy had joined his aircraft carrier and would be gone for six weeks. The carrier would be heading out for a NATO exercise in the North Sea off Scotland. Dave had also joined his ship again and would be on the same exercise but there was no news as to when it would be returning to port. The rumor was that it would be joining yet another exercise and then spending time in Europe.

He had given her a silver necklace that had an engravement on it that said, 'je t'aime.' The jeweler had said that it meant I love you in French.

Annie had walked with him to the dockyard gates in the early morning even though it was a cold and rainy day. He held her tight and kissed her then gave her the necklace. She was taken completely by surprise as she held the necklace. She looked a little confused when she noticed the inscription on the medallion.

"I love you, in French is what it means," he said quietly. She had told him several times over, in the last few months how much she loved him especially during sex. This would be the first time he had conveyed his love. Tiny tears appeared in her eyes then she hugged him tightly.

"Oh, Dave *you* are so romantic, I love you so much. I wish I knew when you would be returning. You must write often. I am going to write you every day until you come home."

"I must go now. I can't be late; they are watching me like hawks and looking for any excuse for more punishment," he kissed her again then waved as he pulled out his Navy ID card to be checked by the dockyard police.

Two hours later the ship left the wall and headed out into the channel. The weather picked up and got steadily worse as they headed North. As usual much of the personnel were on a four-watch system*

*First and second of port and first and second of starboard. The port watches split up into four-hour shifts; first of port would take the 'afternoon' (12:00 to 16:00), 'first' (20:00 to 23:59), and 'morning' (04:00 to 08:00). The second of port would be the first and second 'dogs' (16:00 to 20:00) they would split up the 'dog' watches to allow personnel to eat at (18:00). 'Middle' (midnight to 04:00) and forenoon (08:00 to 12:00 mid-day). They would then get twenty-four hours off (excepting everyone had to work forenoons) while the first and second of starboard repeated the watch system.

Being an Able seaman Dave's watches were mainly wheelhouse duties. This was a small compartment just off 'Burma way*.'

*Burma way - The main passageway's that run fore and aft generally through the center of the ship

He would take instructions via a telegraph system from the officer of the day on the bridge. He watched the magnetic compass and made whatever adjustments necessary on the helm to keep the ship on course. The main engine control room was on the port Burma way where the steam boiler room, engine room and gear room were remotely controlled from. We called them stokers which was an old name given when boilers were heated with coal. They in turn nicknamed anyone in the seamen branch, deck swabbers.

By the time they had joined the convoy exercise the weather had turned into an uncomfortable full-blown gale as they headed west into the North Atlantic. During the day, many ships of the NATO* fleet could be seen far into the horizon.

*NATO - North Atlantic Treaty Organization.

Dave and a few others from the seamen's branch were given the task of setting up strategic safety guide ropes on the upper deck. Only essential personnel were allowed on deck during the storm at the risk of being washed overboard. Dave and a few others took one-hour watches on the quarter deck* beside the hatchway where the elevator for the cordite casings and shells came up from the ship's magazine.

*Quarter deck - Aft 4.5-gun turret deck or the blunt end of the ship.

They were sensibly clipped onto one of the ropes with a carabiner clip. At night during the exercise all ships were ordered to 'darken ship.' During the moonless nights nothing could be seen of the many ships. The Chief Bosun would do his rounds at various times to ensure everyone was adhering to the orders. It was important to extinguish lights when opening hatchways onto the upper deck. A hot cup of kai* was welcomed when returning from the freezing cold.

* Kai - Dark unsweetened chocolate in a large block that was grated into a mug and hot water applied.

They had heard that on one of the ships nearby, a rating had been washed overboard. A life ring was thrown overboard in hopes that a following ship might rescue him. Not only was It too dangerous to turn the ship to have the weather on its beam but a possible collision with other ships in the convoy.

The big brass takes these games so darned seriously. Some poor fucker is on his way to Davey Jones locker... yes siree suck in that water oppo... better than a slow death freezing yer bollocks off.*

Oppo - Short for opposite number - for the person doing the same job as oneself in another watch or ship. In the former case, since you relieved each other, it behooved you to become friends; thus, the word oppo came to mean chum.

It was just over a week before the weather calmed enough to run various exercises. Dave showed his experience when setting up the lines for a refuel at sea, commonly termed a RAS. The ship came up alongside the supply vessel which was doing twelve knots at approximately one hundred feet apart. Dave fired the pneumatic shot line thrower which landed perfectly on the supply vessel to a cheer from the personnel on the bridge. A messenger line was pulled back to the frigate through a series of blocks to eventually allow the large oil hose to be pulled across and fixed to the deck fueling connection. One of the men onboard had come down with a bad case of appendicitis. Through the jackstay it was then possible to transfer him across to the supply vessel that had a naval surgeon and hospital set up.

Later that day he was instructed to report to the Jimmy*. He asked for what reason and, try as he may, could not think of anything he had done to expect punishment.

*Jimmy – First lieutenant, second in charge under the Captain (Skipper). In this case he was a Lieutenant Commander denoted by two and a half gold rings around his coat sleeve.

"Just be outside the Jimmy's office at fifteen hundred sharp in yer number eights* and hat and don't ask questions," The Joss man** said noncommittedly.

*Number eights – everyday working clothes – light blue shirt and dark blue pants, general working clothes.

**Joss man – Master at Arms (ships equivalent of police)

Dave was ceremoniously marched into the Jimmy's office, who stood behind his desk with the Seaman's Divisional Officer.

"At ease Able seaman Swift and remove your hat," the Joss ordered.

Oh, I know this fuckin' routine... yes siree... bend over Swift and take it like a man... bastards!

The **Jimmy** was the next to speak, "Able seaman Swift after this morning's impressive show of your knowledge of seamanship we think you have earned your hook*.

Hook* – A badge worn of a fouled anchor on the right arm above any four-year good service stripes signifying a leading rate, equivalent to a corporal in the army.

From this day forward you will be **Leading** seaman Swift. We are also going to overlook your previous tarnished record and time served in her **Majesties detention** quarters. **You** will also receive your first four-year good conduct stripe. Congratulations Leading seaman Swift," he said holding out his hand to be shook.

"Thank you, **Sir**," Dave said feeling slightly bewildered while shaking his hand.

"Leading seaman Swift, hat on... ten shun... about turn... quick march," the Joss ordered marching him out of the office.

"**Swift**, I've got my eye on you, you might have fooled them upstairs, one bad move and I'll have that hook and stripe off your arm quicker than you can sew it on... Got it?" The red-faced Joss said once they were out of earshot of the wardroom.

Dave walked into the Seamen's mess feeling quite jolly and explaining to his two onboard buddies' 'Buster' Brown and 'Spud' Murphy. "Guess what? I just got me hook. You'd better watch out you scoundrels it just might go right to my head. I might get you to polish my boots fer starters," he joked.

"Hey... shitinit I just did a fuckin' middle, keep it quiet," one of the men called down from the top bunks. At sea most of the mess decks onboard were in partial darkness because of the busy and tiresome watch system.

He laid back in his bunk thinking how this might change his life onboard. Being a Leading hand or Killick as it was more commonly termed was the first advancement up the ladder. There were a few badge men in the mess who had all three four-year stripes yet had never reached Leading hand. They were known as lifers. He had passed certain exams two years prior for Leading rate, but it was up to the Divisional Officer for any advancement. What interested him the most was the marginal increase in pay. With his divers pay he might even be able to save up for a car. He had been taking some driving lessons while in Pompey. He dreamed of picking up Annie in a car and taking her places. It would have to be a cheap secondhand car which he had seen on the bulletin board in Vicky barracks. Cars would continually change hands as men were transferred overseas for up to a year at a time.

Things are looking up... must be doing something right... for a change... Yes siree! He quickly fell asleep dreaming of being with Annie in a future home with a car in the driveway.

The convoy turned around to head back to Scotland somewhere in the mid-Atlantic. They had been at sea for almost six weeks when they arrived at Scapa Flow, which is a series of islands off northern Scotland. The men were allowed to go ashore to, 'stretch their legs' as the Skipper had put it over the **Tannoy** speakers earlier in the day. A couple of the ships at anchor had set up a football game ashore. Dave quickly put his name down on the list that had been posted on the ship's bulletin board. He was off duty and desperately wanted to get off the ship. A tugboat came alongside to take them to the MOD base. It gave everyone an eerie feeling walking around the old prewar rusting buildings. This was where the convoys during the Second World War had begun and ended their dangerous journeys across the Atlantic in a bid to protect the many supply freighters. Horrific stories had drifted down through the ages in the mess decks of the thousands of sailors that had met their premature deaths at sea.

The men wanted to put the creepy base behind and find a field where the games could begin. In the late afternoon, the grey skies opened, and it rained heavily. **Arriving back onboard** it was a fight to get into the showers to get cleaned off. Climbing down through the hatchway and ladders into the mess, after his hot shower he was pleasantly surprised to find a pile of letters on his bunk. At sea letters from home were like gold. The fortunate respondents would sometimes even share their letters with the less privileged.

"You might have a couple of juicy ones there looking at what's on the back of them. So don't be a tight arse, pass them around when you're done." 'Knobby' Clark the father of the mess asked, crudely rubbing himself between his legs and grinning,

"Hey, how about you suck my dick and maybe I'll think about it," Dave answered.

He checked the dates and put them in order, noticing the curious acronyms written on the seal. All of them had an imprint of a lipstick kiss. Some of them had SWALK which he knew of course was, Sealed With A loving Kiss, but NORWICH, BURMA, and SIAM?

He asked one of the long-time older married men who then laughed and said: Nickers Off Ready When I Come Home and Be Undressed Ready My Angel and Sexual Intercourse At Midnight. The evening flew by as he read each letter more than once. He missed her so much and wondered when he might see her again. Everyone was asking the same question when the good news came over the Tannoy, they recognized the Jimmies voice.

"Men, we will weigh anchor in the morning and make our way to Rosyth dockyard where weekend leave will be allowed for everyone not on duty watch. And just a reminder for those taking trains out of the local area; being late is considered ADRIFT which is a punishable offense.

Dave checked his roster and was delighted to know he would be off watch. He immediately applied for weekend leave and a free railway ticket to Pompey. The Navy allowed three free railway tickets per year, anywhere in the UK.

In one of her letters, she had mentioned that she had apologized to her mother's husband, Levi. She would be allowed to have Dave stay with her in their house but only for short periods. He immediately wrote another section to the long letter he had been writing over the weeks since they had been at sea; he explained his intentions of travelling down on the following Friday.

The 'airy fairy' chopper pilot would be taking mail in the morning to the mainland of Scotland and picking up some important parts for one of the ships' main engines.

The overnight train from Edinburgh to London was packed, mostly with sailors from different ships. He tried to sleep in the passageway with his head on his navy issue holdall bag with his white hat on the side. He was told that by showing his hat it would be much easier to hitch a lift, should he need it. He had telephoned from the dock and had told an excited Annie of his intentions and his arrival the following day at the train station in Pompey.

His heart skipped a beat when he first saw her waiting at the turnstile. She looked stunning in her short black dress and heeled shoes. Her shiny black hair glistened augmenting her red lipstick. She also proudly wore the silver pendant he had bought her.

"Annie you are a sight for sore eyes," he said as he hugged her tightly.

"Dave, I have missed you so much. It seems like you have been gone forever," she said as they kissed.

Thrills ran down his spine as he held her tightly and looked into her glowing dark eyes. "Annie, you have been constantly on my mind, I have thought of nothing else since I left. I want to be with you always."

"Dave the same goes for me, I have never felt this way about anyone."

He flagged down a cab outside the train station, he felt a little tired and didn't want to walk the distance to her mother's house. They were very pleasantly surprised that the house was empty when they arrived. Annie explained that her mother had probably taken Susie to her father's house as she would do on occasion to share a cup of tea and a fag* with him.

fag* cigarette

They both ran up the stairs to her room and were taking off their clothes before they even hit the bed. The lovemaking seemed frantic and quick, but both felt satisfied as they lay back afterward. She had her head on his chest stroking his lower stomach. Even though he felt tired he was beginning to feel aroused again.

"Hmm look at that are you ready for round two," she said sexily, now lightly stroking his erection. She slowly kissed his chest and made her way down to put him into her mouth. He groaned as she made a humming sound of pleasure. He was in another world when suddenly they heard the front door open. He had left his holdall bag beside the front door.

"Annie are you home, Levi is going to be here soon, so you'd better put lover boy down and be presentable. Let's at least start off on the right foot," her mother said calling up the stairs.

"Yes, mum we'll be right there, I'm just showing Dave the rooms upstairs." Annie replied quietly giggling.

They dressed quickly and Dave used the washroom to splash water on his glowing, red face.

"Hello Dave and how are you? it's been a while," her mother asked. "Look, we need to get this out of the way before Levi arrives. He can be quite broad minded as he has had two boys who have now left home... thankfully. It's no secret that they drove me crazy. I might have been looking for husband number three otherwise, anyway, I digress. Annie has recently apologized for being rather ignorant with him in the past. And I have been successful in persuading him to allow Annie to stay with us. It was a little harder to convince him that it would be OK to have you also stay. Annie says that it will only be for tonight as you must leave on Sunday evening, is that right?

"Yes Mrs. Goldman. I must go to London by train, change stations then the overnight to Edinburgh, change trains again to Dunfermline. Then it's a cab drive to the dockyard and be there by eight o' clock sharp on Monday morning."

"Wow, this must be love or... lust," she said grinning.

"Mum, we've also talked about this too," Annie interrupted glaring at her mother in contempt.

"OK... OK I'm sorry. You two are going to have to be discreet while my husband is around. I've convinced him to take me out to dinner tonight to give you some privacy. Even though Levi has forgiven you, you're still on thin ice with him Annie," her mother said emphatically.

"OK, Mum... point taken now can we change the subject," Annie asked derisively.

"You know, I like you, Dave. Annie's husband is a drunk and a bully. When he hit you causing that black eye," as she looked at Annie with sad eyes, "well, that was the last straw for me. I wanted to personally strangle him. Nobody harms my girls and gets away with it. It was only because he got you pregnant that you were married in the first place. I disliked him from the get-go. Apart from the fact that he is also too old for you."

"Alright **Mum** enough of the lectures, can we move on now. We will be respectful and always watch our p's and q's*, OK?" Annie answered assertively.

*Mind your p's and q's" is to say, 'mind your manners!' or 'be careful about the details!'

Shortly thereafter a shiny black Mercedes car pulled up in the driveway. A short and overweight man entered the **house,** he wore round rim glasses and a rather obvious toupee.

"Oh, hello young man, you must be the infamous Dave we've been hearing so much about," **Mister** Goldman said holding out his hand to be shook.

Dave immediately stood up to shake his hand respectfully, "thank you Mister Goldman, and nice to meet you too." *Hmm... that didn't sound too convincing.*

They all sat making idle and proper conversation. Dave was on his fourth cup of tea. He needed the washroom, and he was struggling embarrassingly to stay awake. He excused himself to use their washroom and splashed more cold water on his face. On his return, he sat next to Annie then inappropriately fell asleep. When he awoke, seemingly only moments later the clock on the fireplace showed that he had been asleep for over two hours. He found himself alone in the parlor and noticed that someone had put a cover over him where he sat. He could hear voices coming from the kitchen. He embarrassingly walked into the kitchen to see surprised faces looking at him.

"I'm so sorry, I didn't mean to..."

"Hey, don't worry Dave, you must be exhausted after your journey. Come and sit next to Annie here and let me make you a snack, you must be starved." Mrs. Goldman interrupted.

Mister Goldman excused himself and disappeared into an office just off the entrance to the house.

He devoured the snack that Mrs. Goldman made. He wasn't sure what half of the finger food varieties were, but they tasted amazing. She pointed out to Annie in the fridge what she could make later for their meal because of course *they* were going out for dinner. They would probably stop by for a few drinks with friends at the Jewish country club, Mrs. Goldman informed them.

Annie and Dave went for a walk pushing Susie in the stroller. There was a park nearby that had a pond and swans. She had brought bread rinds and they spent a few peaceful hours showing

Susie how to feed the swans. When they **returned**, Mrs. Goldman had dressed a little too elaborately for his taste; she wore a sparkly mauve dress, and her face flaunted an overly amount of makeup. They were almost ready to leave for dinner.

Mrs. Goldman came into the parlor where he and Annie sat, "OK, we're ready to go. Have a nice meal together. And try to be good and if you can't be good... be careful," she glared with a slight grin at Annie.

"Mum, you can leave now... please," Annie accentuated.

Later Annie made a meal, and they sat on stools beside the kitchen island having lots to talk about, while they ate. Afterwards he helped her wash the dishes and they returned to the parlor where they continued the conversation.

"Dave we shouldn't waste this time we have," as she smiled then led him to the stairs with a sexy smile. She lit some candles and they both bathed together in the plush bathroom. He wanted her so bad, and he could see in her eyes that the feeling was mutual. They dried and she led him to her bedroom.

The **foreplay** was as usual very arousing and as he was about to mount her, she gently pushed his shoulders down. It was plainly obvious what she wanted him to do. It took him a few minutes to will himself to do it but when he kissed her there and lightly licked, she seemed to go wild. It gave him an amazing feeling of control. Annie always had complete control over their love making. This felt so different and gratifying. He could take her wherever he wanted her to go. Eventually she pulled him to her lips as he entered her. Sending her into a complete frenzy.

"Dave hit me," he wasn't sure he had heard her correctly.

"Hit you? What do you mean? he whispered in her ear."

"I want you to slap me across the face. Do it now."

"He very lightly slapped her face."

"No harder... please."

She held his wrist and pushed it toward her face.

"Yes, like that," she said breathlessly.

He did it a little harder and she immediately climaxed. He wasn't sure that he liked this; inflicting pain on her was the opposite of what he wanted to do. They had explored many kinky sex acts before, but this felt very wrong. He pulled away and lay beside her.

"What's wrong Dave? You weren't hurting me. It's called sado masochism; in this case I was the masochist, and you were the sadist. If both partners mutually accept, then there is nothing wrong."

"Sweetheart you've taken me to places I never knew existed and I've enjoyed every moment. But this doesn't turn me on, I'm sorry. It probably stems from experiences I had as a child."

"No problem, Dave, and by the way you seem to know your way around a woman's body that was amazing."

He knew what she was talking about, he could still taste her which brought on another erection.

They made love most of the evening until they heard the door open downstairs. "Oh, oh we'd better be good," she said. He saw her cheeky smile in the twilight coming through the curtains.

She curled up in his arms and they both fell asleep. He was woken in the early morning by her stroking him. Laying on their sides he took her from behind and they quietly made love again.

Mrs. Goldman put on a huge breakfast for the three of them. Mr. Goldman had taken a coffee and disappeared into his office. Later in the morning she dressed Susie and they returned to the pond. It was a beautiful morning as they talked about their future. Her divorce would eventually transpire, and she would be free.

She went quiet for long minutes. "Annie, is everything OK? is it something I have said?" Dave asked.

"No love, but you do know I have responsibilities with Susie. I am still receiving a navy allotment from my husband. He could have made things difficult for me if he had stopped paying. I could have taken him to court but thankfully he didn't take that route. We agreed to separate on good terms, and, on his return, we would commence divorce proceedings. He still thinks that there is a possibility that we could reunite. He loves Susie very much and I have no intention of ever changing that, but she will always live with me. I could never chance having her taken from me. So, you see we come as a package. Are you sure you want to take that on?"

"I would be lying if I said that it *didn't* bother me. It's important that we are always truthful with each other. My life before you was a complete disaster. With you I can only see good things happening. If you were single right now and ready to give yourself to me, I would have no reservations; I want to spend the rest of my life with you."

Annie leaned over and kissed him sweetly. "Then that's all I could ever hope for Dave."

Chapter 12

Return Pompey.

The trip back to Rosyth was extremely tiring, the only thing keeping him coherent enough to ensure he caught the correct train on time, was the thought of Annie. If she was there, then everything else would be tolerable. He anxiously made it back to the ship with only fifteen minutes to spare.

The ship was sailing at noon, his duty watch had the dogs, middle and forenoon. It was three days later before he had a full night of welcoming sleep. The scuttlebutt going around was that they were returning to join the remaining of the NATO ships from the past convoy and visiting various ports heading toward Norway. Basically, a show and tell.

Yes siree... we got bigger guns than you hoo!

The only good thing that came out of it was the various runs ashore and seeing some of Europe. But as usual the lads only saw the inside of the first pub.

Annie was true to her word and wrote almost every day, much to the extreme jealousy of his mess mates.

Six weeks seemed to go by before the good news came from the Jimmy over the Tannoy; a big cheer could be heard in every mess of their return to Pompey. And it didn't stop there, Dave was granted two weeks' leave. Although he had been granted leave before it was usually spent in a barracks somewhere, with other sailors who simply didn't have a home to go to. There were other rare occasions in various ports to stay cheaply at a Seaman's mission or at an Aggie Weston's. (8)

Many letters had passed between them, and the other good news was that Annie was now living in her own flat. Levi, not liking the situation of having her around, somewhat disrupting their life, had found her the flat. He had used his business connections to keep the cost low enough for her to afford.

He couldn't believe how his life had turned around since meeting Annie. He wanted to be with her always and was beginning to dream what it would be like to *not* have to leave. She had also given him the courage, not to put up with the norm. All his life so far, he had followed the path that others had forced upon him. Why couldn't he decide to be happy for a change and take his own course? He was coming to the realization that he wasn't cut out to mindlessly take orders. Memories of DQs and how they had humiliated and tortured him were still fresh on his mind. He wasn't the only one who wanted out, there were many frustrated individuals that had simply had enough. Still boys in their mid-teens had signed a document to spend the best years of their lives basically in a prison. The punishment for attempting to escape was extremely painful and demeaning to say the least. One of the lads in the stoker's mess, that he had spoken to had signed papers to buy himself out.

How crazy is that; as a boy you basically get conned into signing your life away, then when you are a man and old enough to realize your mistake, you must save for the best part of a year to buy yourself out. Oh, and one more hit... before you are even allowed to buy yourself out, you must have served two thirds of your man's time... hmm quick calculation... I would have to be twenty-three... Yep siree... that's fucked.

The ship returned to home base at Pompey docks. There was excitement in the crew of the ensuing leave. Dave had his holdall packed and ready the night before not wanting to miss a minute of his upcoming leave. He had helped to secure all the lines for the ship and prepare the gangway to the shore. Eventually when all was complete the **Chief** Bosun gave the order to secure. At twelve hundred hours all who were not on duty watch would be allowed liberty to go ashore.

There was a queue at the dock telephone box but eventually he made it to the front and called Annie, who would be at her father's house, as they had previously arranged in their last correspondence.

He ran the last half of a mile as he couldn't wait to see her. When she opened the door, he almost felt overwhelmed, she looked beautiful. They hugged and kissed. Her familiar perfume seemed to waft through his brain. She was his **home** that he had waited for so long. They wasted no time preparing little Susie in the stroller.

The flat was about a thirty-minute walk away. The second story of the old building had been converted into three separate flats. Annie's flat had a small kitchen facility with a modest basic sink and a tiny fridge. It had a table with two chairs. In the same room was a sofa and chair in front of a three bar electric fire. In a separate room was a double bed and a walled off bathroom with a tub, porcelain sink and toilet. At the bottom of the bed was a cot that Annie had brought from her mother's home.

"It isn't much but it's mine, I have the freedom to come and go as I please. I just feel that for once, I am in control of my own destiny, and if I have my husband's navy allotment and my government family allowance then this is all I need," Annie said assertively.

"This won't be forever my love. Once you have your divorce, we will eventually have our own place. I have a little sad news that I should get out of the way. After this leave, the ship is returning to the Med. The rumor has it that we'll be gone for about four months. We have something to look forward to because by the time I return you will have your divorce and we will be together forever."

Annie hugged him tightly. "Oh, Dave I can't wait for that day. I feel like I belong to you completely," she said then kissed him. "Do you want to try out the bed? You will have to give me a hand to move the cot into the other room. Susie is ready for a nap."

The two weeks had gone by quickly. They had lived like husband and wife; grocery shopping together; watching the small TV that Dave had bought her; visiting her Mother and Father, on occasion. Sometimes her parents or her sisters would babysit while they went to the weekly dance in Southsea where they had met. It had all felt very normal, yet dreamlike. He couldn't believe how his life had changed. She had asked him again to have his child and wanted to stop taking the pill. The painful memories were all from the past and he was slowly learning to be more positive and look to a brighter future. Annie was always positive and refused to even hear anything negative on the occasion if he were to bring it up. Her past life with her husband was always an area to avoid, she would remind him of that whenever he broached the subject. It made him feel a little uneasy, but he just put it down to his inherent pessimism.

With Annie, there was always something new to explore. They had set up the stroller and were going to spend a leisurely few hours walking around the local mall. At the doorway before they left the flat Annie held him tight and whispered in his ear.

"Sweetheart I have a little surprise for you."

"Oh, and what would that be," he replied.

"Well, it wouldn't be a surprise if I told you," she said smiling demurely.

As always, she looked amazing in a mini skirt and a spaghetti stringed tank top. She wore her tiny strapped mini heeled shoes which enhanced her shapely legs.

When they arrived, she excused herself to go to the washroom. Dave held the stroller as he waited for her. On her return she took the stroller from him.

"Dave from here on you just follow me, I am going to pretend that I don't know you. This is called, 'role play' as she smiled wickedly... just follow my lead," she said giggling mischievously.

She had waited at the bottom of a stair escalator until it was completely empty, he had no idea what she was going to do and just thought it was because of the stroller in front of her. He did as he was told, to stay a few steps behind her. They were halfway up the escalator before she bent down to fix something with Susie. He noticed very quickly that she wasn't wearing any underwear.

Oh my god what is she doing. As he looked around to ensure no one else was looking. He followed her into a small café. There were people sitting and busy talking as she went to the back wall seat but as she passed a table that was directly in front, she covertly pointed to it. He sat where he was told. Under her table he could see under her short dress as she opened her legs. She was looking at a menu completely disengaged with what was going on underneath the table. The waitress came to take her order, she ordered a coffee and an orange juice for Susie, the same waitress also took his order of a coffee. From where he was sat, he would be the only one to see underneath the table. She opened her legs again and reached down with one hand that wasn't holding the menu. She was stroking herself even though her face showed no emotion whatsoever. This felt so wrong to be doing this in public which just made it even more erotic. He kept nervously looking around to ensure no one was watching but they were all completely oblivious. He could feel his erection uncomfortably straining under his tight jeans. He could also feel his heart pounding, he wanted her so bad.

Eventually as a bead of sweat rolled down Dave's face she stood and turned the stroller around to go to the counter and pay for her order. He waited for her to leave then did the same, covering his bulging pants with his jacket over his arm.

He followed her as she walked around the mall and in the quiet areas where no one was watching she would bend over the stroller to reach down to Susie giving him a full view of everything under her skirt. Again, this felt very wrong but at the same time highly arousing. After about an hour of this extreme teasing, she made her way over to him. There was no one around when she surreptitiously reached down to stroke his erection.

"Well, hi lover boy what's your name she said squeezing him," she had that suggestive and carnal look on her face.

"Annie, we need to go back to your flat right now or I'm going to bend you over that rail and take you right here, that has got to be the most erotic experience that I have ever felt."

He had spoken to Rhonda a few times when they had visited her father and was surprised that the girls had seemed to have developed a minor rift. Dave had put it off as a normal family dispute and expected that it would eventually pass. Taffy had been away for a month, but she had let on that marriage was on the horizon.

Leaving was as always heartbreaking, Annie had even wept the night before which he had felt strange and upsetting.

"Dave, I love you so much, whatever happens in the future you must always remember that. I wish you did not have to go. I hate being lonely, I count the days when you are gone. Every day seems so cold and empty, I'll never get used to that," Annie said weeping.

"Hey Annie, I won't be gone forever. And I won't be in the Navy forever either. I have plans to buy myself out when the opportunity arrives. We must be patient. What we've had these past weeks will then be forever. My dream also is for us to have a baby, I can't think of anything more that I want, in this life." Dave said hugging her tightly.

They had agreed that they would say their goodbyes in the flat. He didn't want her to come to the dockyard. It would be just too sad.

Chapter 13

The Med for four months.

The ship had spent just over a week in Gibraltar. He sent a letter to Annie explaining that the ship wouldn't be returning for four months. The ship then headed to Malta where they spent ten days. There were also short stays in Naples, Izmir, and Athens. Their final stop was anchored off in Port Said where again, Dave and the other two Ships divers onboard helped the Clearance Diving team.

The CDs detonated or neutralized the mines. It was interesting work, sometimes diving in clear, warm water and seeing lots of undersea life. The CDs were serving on a small minesweeper ship and would regularly invite him onboard where they shared many beers. It felt like a different navy to the one he served in. Chief Coxswain Allan Broadhurst was also a CD and would regularly join them. The Jimmy onboard was also a diver and seemed different from any Officer he had ever met. This would be forbidden anywhere else in the navy. It was obviously a dangerous job, and everyone had ultimate respect for each other. If only the ones in control in the rest of the navy had the same respect for their men as they demanded, what a difference it would make. He fully understood that an armed force must have discipline, especially on the frontline. But to treat their men as imbecile cannon fodder was unconscionable.

It was around that time that he received a cheery letter from Taffy with several beautiful photographs of his wedding to Rhonda.

Sorry mate we both really wanted you to be our best man until Annie told us that you wouldn't be back in time. Be sure to look us up when you're next in Pompey. I've applied for married quarters in Gosport*

Gosport* is a short sea ferry from Portsmouth Harbour.

Annie's letters started to dwindle and sometimes when mail arrived there was nothing. He was beginning to be worried that something had gone amiss. It was around the two-month mark that the cheerful letters ceased to arrive. He sent off letters to her to no avail. In frustration and shear panic he sent a letter to Taffy on the aircraft carrier. Two weeks later he received a reply from Taffy.

Dave me best oppo, I have some sad news for you; Annie has gone back to her husband and is now living in Sheffield. From what Rhonda is telling me, it would be just as well that you forget about her altogether. She is bad news all around. I hate to be the bearer of this, and I can imagine you to be pretty pissed off.

Come and visit us when you're next in Pompey, here's our address in Gosport. Keep your chin up buddy. Believe me, it's for the best.

He hastily wrote down the Gosport address in his thin address book.

Sadness came over him like a tidal wave. He had never cried before but he felt that it was the closest he'd ever been to completely lose it. He went on to the upper deck and continuously walked around the quarter deck trying to think where he had gone wrong. What had he done? Should he have agreed for them to have a child together? Desperation engulfed him. He needed it to stop. He couldn't allow the tears and knew that if he broke down not only would he not be able to stop but he was also surrounded by other men; the embarrassment would be insane, and he would be a complete joke and ridiculed forever and a day. His control was being severely tried and nearing a point of no return. Through everything he had gone through in his life it was the first time he considered suicide. His thoughts were becoming very dark. He needed to do something to occupy his mind to overcome these awful, morbid thoughts. He went down below and collected his punch bag. As he was tying up the punch bag to the gun turret, he could feel the beginning of tears coming from his eyes. He had to fight this. He punched the bag until his fists and feet bled.

The following day he was diving to check a leak in a sea cock for the Chief stoker. He listened for the tapping coming from the engine room and attached a fiberglass patch over the through hull fitting. When it was done, he swam down and sat on the seabed while they checked on the inside of the hull if the leak had stopped.

How easy it would be to just pull out the breathing tit from his mouth. His dark thoughts were disturbed by several individual pulls on his lifeline from the standby diver on the surface. The signal asking, 'if the diver is, OK?' He ignored them. He then received several four consecutive pull signals denoting, 'diver return to the surface.' He knew if he didn't reply with a one pull denoting 'I'm OK' or repeat the four pulls denoting, 'diver coming to the surface,' the standby diver would then be committed to follow the lifeline down and attempt a 'diver recovery.' He had his hand on the harness that held his breathing set. He could quickly dump the SABA* breathing set and swim away and no one would find him. With his weight belt on; he surely wouldn't be floating to the surface any time soon. Seconds later he came to his senses and gave the 'four pulls' The standby gave the four pulls to say, 'OK diver is safe to return to the surface pulling up your line.'

*SABA Self-contained Air Breathing Apparatus

It was a week later that he received a letter from Annie. There weren't any lipstick kisses or acronyms, but he recognized her blue envelopes. He quickly opened the envelope.

Dear Dave,

I am so sorry for not replying sooner. Rhonda told me that Taffy had sent you a letter. The last weeks have been a nightmare. My husband stopped the allotment payments a month after you left. I thought it was just a screw up but then he suddenly returned unannounced as he had been awarded compassionate leave. He gave me an ultimatum to return to him and his home in Sheffield or he would divorce me on the grounds of adultery. Apparently, he has had a private detective who has evidence from you and I in the flat. Not only that but he says he has evidence from other men proving that I am a bad mother. He is also going for full custody. Levi investigated it and said that he has a valid case.

I can't chance losing Susie, Dave no matter what. He has basically forced my hand. He says that he is a different man and has curbed his drinking habits and will never lay a hand on me again. He will also be leaving the navy which will lose him a pension, he says that he is more than willing to do that. He has asked me for a trial reconciliation. I'm afraid my dream of having a happy life with you has ended. It is best all-around that you forget about me and get on with your life. You're a good man and someday you will find someone more deserving of your love.

Sincerest

Annie

The sadness remained, leaving him feeling drained and as the weeks moved on it began to change into anger. He had read the letter numerous times and had mistakenly left the open letter on his bunk during a watch change. He was horrified to see his letter had been pinned on the main bulletin board in the galley dining area. Above the section was written 'The Best Dear John award.' There were a few other heart rendering messages of broken hearts explaining why they could not wait for their loved ones to return. Some of them even had photos attached. Alongside each letter was a section where readers could put their comments and marks out of ten.

He immediately felt extreme anger at the intrusion of privacy and wanted to rip it off the board. Then the anger returned, and he walked away to leave it there for all to see. No one would know that he was the Dave in question except of course the messmate who had stolen the letter. The following day it got an average of eight out of ten. Someone had written 'fuckin' whore, best rid of mate' another said, 'Hope she gets the dreaded pox.' He left the letter there for days until he was bored of seeing it, then unobtrusively ripped it up and threw it in the food garbage bin.

Chapter 14

Return from the Med.

In the few ports that they visited before returning to **Pompey**, he had gone ashore with the intent of just getting drunk. He had even received a number nine punishment, a loss of leave for two weeks followed by a two week loss of the privilege of civilian clothes going ashore. He had returned onboard and swore at the young Midshipman who was the officer of the day on the gangway. It was a light sentence considering what he had said.

Fuckin' piglet* ya think am gonna salute you... fuck off!

Piglet* Officers of Her Majesties Royal Navy were nicknamed, 'Pigs' by the lower deck. Midshipmen therefore were... piglets!

Five weeks later they were back in Pompey. He visited Taffy and Rhonda who were now pregnant. "Wow congratulations you two, a little sprog on the way, hope it doesn't inherit that horrible Welsh accent. It'll never get anywhere with that." Dave joked.

"Jeez it could be worse with a dopey Lancashire accent, I suppose," Taffy replied smiling.

They told him their plans; Taffy would be going back to sea soon but would hopefully return before the baby was born.

Eventually Dave steered the conversation toward information about Annie.

"How is she doing with that jerk of a husband?" Dave nonchalantly asked.

Rhonda answered, "Dave, you would be best to leave well alone for your own good. You're a good man, we both think a lot about you and don't want to see you hurt anymore."

"To be honest before I can put this to bed and move on, I need to see her one more time. I know it's over and she has chosen to go this route. If she can tell me face to face that it's over then I'll live with that. Just give me her telephone number or ask her to call me here," Dave asked sincerely.

Taffy looked at Rhonda inquiringly. "OK, come here tomorrow at the same time, we'll have dinner together. I will ask her but don't be surprised or disappointed if she refuses to call.

The following day he was at their place at the appointed time.

"I telephoned her today and she said that she will call here," Rhonda informed.

When the phone rang, he felt a nervous excitement and tried to be calm, not wanting to show sadness. Rhonda answered the phone then handed it to Dave, "we'll leave you to it," she added as they both left the house to go for a walk.

Annie was the first to talk after a brief silence.

"Hi Dave, how are you?" she asked.

As much as he tried, he couldn't help himself, he immediately imagined her from the time she had met him at the train station. Dressed in black with her dark hair and red lips. His chin began to tremble, and he couldn't speak.

"Dave are you there," she asked cautiously.

"Y-yes, I'm f-f-fine how are you?"

Come on get it together ya piece of shit.

"Dave I'm so sorry for how all this has developed but it really is for the best... for us both."

"Annie, I need to see you. I thought I'd got over you until a few seconds ago when you first spoke. I need closure before I can go on to whatever is in my future. I don't think I can get that without seeing you one last time. If I meant anything to you, you must at least, grant me this."

"Dave, we both must be strong; do you think that I don't have the same feelings?"

"Do you love him?" he asked, feeling his voice beginning to tremble.

"Dave, life isn't black and white, nothing in a relationship is ever consistent. There is more happening here that is hard to explain."

"Annie, do you love him?" He repeated a little more forcefully.

"I think I did once, I was young and naïve, becoming pregnant certainly forced the issue. At this moment in time, I'm not sure... it certainly doesn't feel like it. But honestly Dave that isn't the point. Susie needs a Dad and a settled home. I know he loves her and would never let any harm come to her. He is older than me, as you know. He has a home and a car and close family ties with his mother and siblings all living close by. He can be vindictive and would not have any qualms about taking Susie away from me. I can't imagine my life without her."

"So why did you leave him, if that is what you wanted?"

"Dave you already know that; he was an abusive alcoholic. It was sometimes a relief when he *wasn't* home, but I was then left on my own in a town where I only knew his family. I don't like being alone, I have never been able to get used to that. When you left, I found myself alone yet again.

He says that he has reformed and so far, he has lived up to that promise. His discharge papers are expected in the next few months. So, in the not-too-distant future I won't ever have to be alone again."

"Annie, I really need to see you. I promise that if you still don't want to see me again after, I will leave you be."

"That would be very unwise. You know my situation; I could lose everything if he were to find out. But I will give it some thought and let Rhonda know in the next few days. Goodbye Dave, I must go now."

"Bye Annie," he said sadly as she hung up the call.

He had dinner with Taffy and Rhonda. It was a quiet affair neither wanting to bring up the subject of the phone call.

Returning to the ship again, he felt like his heart had been ripped apart. He couldn't understand why he was making matters worse by reading her letters that he had kept stored in his locker. In the days following he went about the mundane tasks on deck and in the Bosuns store which was his new part of ship. He was now in charge of all the ropes, pulleys, and assorted equipment. In the evenings he lay on his bunk and inevitably the letters would reappear. Going ashore with the boys seemed to be the last thing on his mind. He was also afraid of what might occur should he use alcohol or whatever else he could get his hands on. It wouldn't be the first time that he smoked marijuana either. He wondered what the Navy would do if they found out about that, he'd probably be hanged from the yardarm, knowing their reputation of severe punishment.

Five days had passed before he called Taffy and Rhonda. The ship would be leaving the following week for the Persian Gulf and the Far East and not returning for eleven months.

Taffy answered the phone, "Hi Dave, how's tricks? Heard you were leaving for the Middle East. The carrier is heading out there after a trip to the Med, well that's the rumor anyway."

"Yeah, mate, can't say that I'm enthralled about it, I'm about as popular as a pork chop in a synagogue with the pigs upstairs," Dave said gloomily.

"Listen mate, I don't know if I should be telling you this as Rhonda asked me to keep schtum. Annie called a couple of days back and she wants to see you. She has given me a phone number for you to call. Rhonda isn't here right now so you can't tell her I gave you this, she'll be pissed with me if you do. The way I see it, you're both adults and it's none of our business really. Having said that, as a **friend,** you need to make sure she is being honest with you," Taffy implored.

He immediately felt a lifting in his spirit but didn't want to let it get out of hand. He rushed back to the ship to collect as much change as he could, beg steal and borrow for the shoreside telephone box. He returned, and immediately called the number.

"Hello who is this," Annie answered.

"It's me, Dave. I heard that you want to speak to me," he replied with expectation.

"Dave, after our call the other day, I did a lot of thinking and I agree it is only fair that we meet one last time. Although you need to know it will not change my decision. We will have to be careful and discreet. Can you get away this weekend?" she asked.

"Yes, pretty much everyone is granted leave this weekend apart from the duty watch because the ship is leaving next week for the middle East."

"OK, call me tomorrow night, at this same time. I'm due to visit **Mum** and Dad. Mum will go along with this. I will have my husband's sister look after Susie, while I supposedly visit my **Mum.** You and I will meet somewhere. It obviously can't be here or in Portsmouth, we will have to meet somewhere mid-way say... Nottingham would be good. I can't stress how important it is that we be incredibly careful. In two months, my husband leaves the navy for good, and I return to being a dutiful wife again."

"Thank you so much Annie, I really appreciate this. I can't get you off my mind, but I am prepared to go along with whatever you wish." He then ran out of cash for the telephone, and it hung up the call.

Damn it yes siree damn it... fuckin' telephone.

The following night he ensured that he had enough cash for the coin telephone. It was, however, a quick call; she would meet him at the Nottingham railway station. She gave him the name of the station and the time of arrival. There was a café in the station where they could have a few hours together before she would continue her trip to Portsmouth.

On returning to the ship, he immediately requested weekend leave and a free rail ticket.

As the train pulled into the station he felt excitement in his stomach, he had not been able to eat all morning. Part of him was hoping that it would develop into more than a simple meeting and another part was reminding him of the hurt he had felt and what he should expect.

He sat in the café and was sipping his third coffee when she entered. He waived as she looked for him. She looked gorgeous as always. Her shiny black hair had grown and was now tousled over her shoulders, but the red lips and trim body was the same as he remembered it to be. She had a knee length beige gabardine trench coat on with a belt knotted on her slim waist. His heart began pounding in his chest.

As she made her way to his table she smiled. He recognized that almost mischievous smile and the dark glistening eyes that sparkled, it always had the same effect of turning him on. What had he done to ever deserve this amazing woman's attention? What could she possibly see in him? All these thoughts ran through his brain as she took off her coat to sit down. She wore a tight bright red dress which was almost the same color as her lips.

"Hi Dave," she said simply, then sat down with that same enduring smile.

"Annie, you look positively amazing, thank you so much for this."

She stood up and leaned across the table to lightly kiss him on the cheek. "Thank you, Dave, I assure you the feeling is very mutual."

"How long do you have, I want to make every minute count," Dave asked.

"Well, it all depends... have you brought your toothbrush," as she placed her hand on his knee. Looking at him with the sexy smile he remembered only too well. "We shouldn't waste this time."

Yes siree... could this mean nookie... I had better be reading this right.

"Please tell me that I'm reading this right, we can be... together... like...?" he placed his hand on hers and lightly squeezed.

"Well, it's entirely up to you Dave. Mum is going to cover until tomorrow... bless her little cotton socks."

"You mean we should... find a ... hotel."

"Well yes Dave... unless you want me over this table. I'm sure the other patrons would be OK with that," she said mischievously.

Dave immediately stood, leaving money on the table to pay for his unfinished coffee.

"OK... lets go," he said to a grinning Annie.

They hailed a cab in front of the station and asked the cabbie to take them to the nearest hotel.

"There's a B and B I can take you to if you like, I know the owner," the cabbie answered resetting his meter.

"Yes, please that will be fine," Dave answered.

The taxi had barely moved from the station when Annie reached over to kiss him deeply. "Dave, I have missed you so much," she whispered in his ear. "When I left this morning, I knew that I couldn't just walk away if I saw you again."

"Oh Annie... is this for real, I'm having trouble believing this is happening."

"Dave, please don't spoil this brief time we have together. Let's not ask any questions of each other. Or even read too much into this... Tomorrow we will go our separate ways but today I am yours... And you my love are mine again, even if it is just for a brief time," she kissed him again deeply.

The owner of the bed and breakfast asked if they had any baggage and could they sign the register. Dave was stumped for a moment as Annie stepped in, "no, my husband and I will be leaving first thing in the morning for London... no luggage," Annie said covertly nipping him in the leg.

He smiled and repeated, "then the register please? and how will you be paying?"

Dave said, "w...we'll b...be paying cash," Dave stuttered as he hoped there was enough cash in his wallet. He paid then put his wallet away.

The owner looked at Dave questioningly, "Thank you sir... the register?"

He was a little flustered, he had never done this before as he quickly looked at Annie for support, who slightly shrugged her shoulders and smiled.

"Ah, Mister and Mrs. Smith... welcome," he said looking at what Dave had written with a seemingly knowing smile, "follow me, I'll show you to your room."

As soon as the door was closed, they both laughed hysterically.

She removed her coat and again she looked so beautiful. He immediately embraced her tightly. "Somebody prick me, am I dreaming this," he whispered into her ear.

Breathing in her familiar perfume and again feeling the softness of her hair against his face, he felt dizzy with desire. Tingles of electricity seemed to reverberate through his fingertips where they touched the soft bare skin of her arms and neck. They kissed as she gently removed his jacket. He found the zip on the back of her dress and slowly unzipped it down her back. She trembled and he could feel her excitement as her dress dropped to the floor. He stood back to look at her, she wore black silky underwear and bra and looked so sensuous as he laid her on the bed. She reached up to unbuckle his belt as he removed his shirt. He pushed her back on the bed as she groped for his underwear. He pulled her panties to one side and began to gently kiss and lick her. She was already very moist. She held his head pushing him into her. From experience, he knew where and how she wanted to be touched.

"Oh, Dave I'm going to come but I want you inside." He took off his clothes and removed her panties as she removed her bra. She lightly screamed as he entered her. Dave, I have missed you so much, you will never know how much as they both climaxed together.

They slept arm in arm for hours as the light from the window disappeared.

"Are you hungry? I'm starved." Dave asked.

"Yes, I am, I was so nervous and excited at the thought of seeing you again, I forgot to eat," Annie admitted.

"That makes two of us. I had no idea how this was going to go. I certainly didn't expect this. Thank you, Annie."

"No, Dave it should be me thanking you after the way I have treated you, how can you ever forgive me."

"I don't want to think of it, remember what you said in the Taxi. I'm going to take a page out of your book Annie and live only for this moment, now let's go eat before I pass out."

They found a restaurant and ordered sirloin steaks. They both ate heartily and laughed at the way the B and B owner had treated Dave. He was taking on his accent and snotty attitude. Annie was laughing and in tears as he imitated and came up with different situations.

They finished the wonderful meal and decided to walk a little. Nottingham was an interesting place. It was strange how they had decided to meet here. They found a nightclub that was packed and were pleasantly surprised that Rory Gallagher, the famous guitar player, was performing. They danced the night away free of all thoughts of the real world that they would be returning to, only too soon. She was beautiful in every way as the night weaved its mysterious and sensual way, he felt closer than he had with any other living person.

In between dances he reached and pulled her toward his chest. "Annie, I know I'm breaking our rule here, but I just want to tell you. I love you so much, whatever happens in our future I want you to always remember that. She put her head on his chest as he kissed the top of her head. She was very still; he pulled her back to see her face and saw that she was crying.

"Sorry my love I shouldn't have, have I spoilt this? Just ignore me, I'm getting sappy. Let's go, our time is running out. We must make the most of this," he whispered in her ear.

They left the club and began the walk back to B and B. She seemed quiet for a short time before she spoke.

"Dave, I have loved you since the first time we met, you are a wonderful and thoughtful man. When I'm with you, you make me feel like the woman I dream of being. I have dearly loved showing you the way a man can please a woman. In some ways it makes me feel like I own you and you belong only to me. You are a handsome man that now knows all the intimate ways to treat me. But I can never have you, and you deserve so much more. Now I'm getting sappy which I vowed I wouldn't do today, because this is our time to be happy."

They headed back to the B and B and had a heavenly night of erotic sex. The morning came and he was the first to wake. He pulled the covers down to see the shapely back of this wonderful woman that shared his bed. He slid down the bed under the covers and turned her onto her back. He couldn't see her face, but he knew she was enjoying it as she shuddered and gently stroked his head.

Without warning there was a knock on the door. The B and B owner suddenly entered their room placing two cups of tea on a tray on their bedside table. Annie immediately covered her chest with the blankets and Dave attempted to make himself as small as possible under the sheets.

"Good morning... Mister and Mrs. Smith, breakfast will be served in half an hour. Thank you," the owner said then immediately left closing the door behind him.

Annie began laughing.

What must he be thinking?... Yes siree... This is too damn embarrassing.

He rolled up in a ball under the sheets and refused to come out. He knew his face to be red raw.

"Aww come on Dave... this is just too funny," She giggled attempting to pull the covers off him, "I'm sure he's seen worse."

They showered together and found toothbrushes and paste in separate sealed plastic bags.

It took some convincing to have Dave enter the dining room where there were other guests quietly going about their breakfast.

"Can we just go somewhere else for breakfast. I don't think I can face that snotty owner again." Dave asked.

"Come on Dave, you have to see the funny side of it," Annie said again giggling.

Eventually they sat down, and the owner came to the table to give them suggestions as to what the cook was preparing that day.

Dave could not look at the owner and knew his face to be beetroot red. Annie told him how she would like her eggs, bacon, and toast. The owner then said quite loudly and with much conviction so others could hear. "And sir... what would you like for breakfast?"

Dave looked up and was sure the man was about to say. *I think you've had your breakfast today son.*

They walked around the beautiful city again. It was a sunny and warm day. They wouldn't have to be at the railway station until later in the afternoon and wanted to make the best of the little time they had left. Dave spotted a notice board with information about Sherwood Forest.

"Hey, isn't that where Robin Hood used to hang out," Dave asked, "we should go check it out, what do you say?"

"Dave, I don't care what we do as long as we make the best of our remaining time, sure let's go."

The taxi took a bit of time to arrive at the popular tourist destination, but it was worth it once they began the walk. They both kept their conversation upbeat not wanting to spoil what little time they had left. He held her small hand in his and wanted to treasure every single moment. Today she was his treasure; the best thing that had ever happened in his horrid life. It was a bittersweet few hours as they wandered through the trees and meadows. In one moment, he wanted to kneel and cry like a baby and plead with her and in the next, rejoice with happiness to have this wonderful woman by his side.

Time was moving on too quickly. They found a beautiful meadow with long grass and buttercups that were flowing back and forth with the gentle breezes. They both moved off the path and walked through the deep grass touching the tops of the grasses with the tips of their fingers. Annie sat down on the grass and pulled Dave toward her.

"Dave, can we do this one last time before I must leave. I am feeling dreadfully sad and want to remember you and I just like this."

They made love slow and passionately, eventually they both climaxed and as he raised his head to look into her eyes she began to sob.

"Dave part of me wished we had never done this and that it was a huge mistake, but I am also thankful to have shared our love and bodies like this one last time. Our love was never meant to be. Just an unattainable dream for two people asking too much out of this life. You will find someone else Dave; a man like you doesn't stay single for too long. She will be free and able to give you the love that you deserve, disentangled from outside issues out of her control."

"Annie, I can wait for you; we can make this work. Why do you make this sound so impossible? People get divorced and still see their kids."

"Dave, you don't know my husband and what he is capable of, not only with me, but he has even mentioned doing you harm. At this point he has all the chips in his favor, also I could never live without Susie; I would surely lose her, and she doesn't deserve that. Dave, we need to stop this, and I need to go. If you care for me then please let us leave on good terms."

They made it to the railway station and neither had said too much on the journey.

"Dave my train will be here soon, let's just say our goodbyes here. I don't want to embarrass myself here in front of all these people."

"OK Annie I too want to leave on good terms and no matter what you say or what the future brings. I will always be here for you. Eventually, I *will* be out of the navy... believe me. Can I at least kiss you, goodbye?"

They kissed; it was a short kiss as he felt her trembling. When he stepped back, he noticed that tears were rolling down her cheeks.

"Goodbye Annie."

"Goodbye Dave... take care of yourself."

He turned around and did not look back fearing that he might also break down. He stayed in a waiting room for her train to arrive and covertly watched her through a window as she boarded the train. The train gently pulled away, taking part of his heart with it.

Goodbye my sweet love... see you in the next life... yes siree!

He made it back to the ship on time in the early hours of the morning. As usual it was a grey rainy morning as he saluted the side. Later in the day the ship sailed, and he was back in the wheelhouse.

Weeks later he kept feeling the familiar sadness when he glanced at her letters tied with a piece of string in the back of his locker. It was time to remove them and all the reminders simply because he could not stand the pain any longer. One evening he made his way up to the quarter deck and one by one he dropped each letter into the sea. He watched as the wake from the propellers swallowed up the tiny pieces of his heart until there was none.

Wherever you are now Annie, I will always remember what you were to me. I hope you find your happiness.

Workin' Away Blues

Come and get your love here

Come and get your love right here, right here, right here baby

I'm on a sinkin' boat

An' I can't float

I got a years' worth of cryin'

I'm drownin' in my tears

I got the work away blues

I got the work away blues honey

One of these late nights

I'll come home

And keep you warm

Come and get your love here

Come and get your love right here, right here, right here baby

You say you're lonely

And been so sad

I got your letter

Now I'm feelin' bad

Come and get your love here

Come and get your love right here, right here, right here baby

If I can ever

Get outa this can

I could take some leave

Would be my plan

I gotta invest some time

To be your man

Kevin Firth

I got the work away blues
I got the work away blues honey
One of these late nights
I'll come home
And keep you warm
keep you warm honey

Kevin Firth May 2011

Chapter 15

At 21, Persian Gulf.

The ship finally arrived at the entrance to Beira (3) in the Mozambique channel. They would be relieving another RN ship that had been there for three months. An oil embargo had been placed on the Rhodesian government because they had unilaterally declared the former colony's independence. In rebuttal the Royal Navy had been tasked to ensure no tankers entered Beira. It was a maddingly boring patrol where two ships patrolled continuously back and forth. In the three long months they had twice taken short breaks, once visiting Madagascar and then the Seychelles.

When they were finally relieved, they visited Bombay* and Karachi before their next patrol in the Persian Gulf. The Royal Navy base, HMS Jufair on the island of Bahrain would be their base for the next three months. Spending most of that time mainly showing a military presence in the Gulf protecting the supply of oil to the United Kingdom.

Bombay* now known as Mumbai

But they would also patrol the area in an attempt to stop the illegal gunrunners. It was embarrassing as the innocent looking fishing dhows would fire up their gas turbine engines and in a puff of smoke disappear over the horizon. Even the illustrious chopper pilot onboard would lose them in the outcroppings and island that dotted the Gulf.

Dave had been, 'volunteered' by the Chief bosun to be included in the boarding party, should they ever have to board a 'runner'.

"Chief, I haven't volunteered for this; I really do not want to do it. Everyone else has volunteered... not me!" Dave protested.

No siree... like what the fuck.

"Shut it Swift... you volunteered OK... don't get into my bad books," he replied forcefully.

Oh well I guess it's all right then... fuck face. Oh, it's OK when you throw me in DQs for protecting myself but when you want protecting its OK... Yes, siree, this is fucked.

The boarding party had done training at the base with three SBS Marines*. They had obviously heard about his ability, so he was excused from the unarmed combat training part of the instruction.

It was also plainly obvious why he had been chosen.

SBS Marines* Special Boat Section similar to the renown SAS Special Air Service.

One of the marines deviously asked him for a sparring competition. The other two seemed to be encouraging him.

"Hey, listen pal, I really do not like pissing competitions. I don't even want to be here," he realized that everyone had left, he was alone and was beginning to think that they had set this up.

The marine then lunged at him with a fist. Dave immediately dodged the fist and landed three lightning-fast punches into his body. The man went down, and Dave leapt on his back in a scissor lock and had him in a strangle hold facing the other two marines. The two marines didn't look so happy about this and were about to come to his rescue.

"I told you I didn't want to play this game. Now step back or your buddy here is going to go to sleep for an awfully long time," Dave shouted.

The marine who was choking lifted his hand toward them signaling them to stop.

Dave let go and calmly walked away from the three marines, who were looking incredibly angry. Back onboard he found the Chief Bosun and again asked him that he wanted out. He just felt that somehow, he was going to end up back in DQs. The Chief gave him a resounding NO!

Occasionally they would be alerted to board a suspected gun runner. Mostly it was for exercise purposes, but they had boarded a couple of suspicious dhows only to find that they were harmless fishing boats.

Again, he had been woken in the middle of the night on his off-watch time and ordered to muster for boarding patrol.

Hope this isn't another waste of time exercise. Can't they think of anything better to do? Fuckin' wankers... yes siree fuckin' wankers... all of 'em.

The Chief Bosun handed each of the six-boarding party men their sub machine guns. They always knew when it wasn't an exercise because they were asked to load a live nine-millimeter, thirty-two round magazines into the gun. The gun would be cocked with 'one up the spout' but with the safety on. Once the dhow was boarded then the safety was clicked off. At the practice firing range previously, he had found that it was almost impossible to fire less than four rounds once the trigger was pulled. This was the same Chief Bosun who had placed him under punishment for being drunk and disorderly in Karachi after a shore leave.

They had been following this suspicious dhow for three days and now it was cornered in a small bay. The ships bright searchlights were trained on the dhow and the port, forty-millimeter Bofer gun was also aimed at the small vessel.

They had boarded the zodiac dinghy and were slowly making their way over to the dhow. The Chief was repeating what they already knew; "Leading seaman Swift, you will hand your sub machine gun to Marine engineer Price, board the dhow first and tie up the forward painter* of the zodiac.

Painter* A rope attached to the bow of a 'generally' small boat for tying it to a ship, quay, etc.

Price, you will then hand the gun back to Swift once he is aboard. The rest of the boarding party will then join Swift to move all the ragheads onboard up to their forward deck. Able seaman Young will join you to guard them while Price inspects the engine room. The remaining will inspect the rest of the vessel."

Dave had to admit even though they had done this a few times he still felt nervous as he climbed onto the dhow. 'Pricky' Price handed him the forward painter rope and he began to tie up the zodiac. When suddenly Pricky screamed at him, "Swiffy behind you!"

Dave turned around and, in the semi, dark, he could make out an Arab clothed man running toward him with a scimitar sword held above his head ready to cut him in two. In a crouching position he was in a weak defensive position, but he was still able to roll across the deck surprising and tripping him up. The man was about to turn around and he still had the razor-sharp sword in his hand. Dave leapt onto his back and grabbed his head, twisting it in a quick, sharp turn. There was a cracking sound as he broke the man's neck.

'Pricky' Price and 'Brigham' Young had now boarded the dhow and was pointing their guns at the dead man. Dave stood and collected his gun from Pricky. "No need for that, Pricky... he's dead."

The rest of the crew came aboard and went about their task of securing the vessel. Dave stood guard over the nine men corralled in a kneeling position on the front deck of the Dhow. He had left the safety of his gun on because his hands were still shaking, and he was in fear of doing unnecessary harm to the obviously terrified men.

Having found only a small amount of opium, the Chief had departed back to the ship. Minutes later he returned to the dhow bringing the Medic and an Arab translator who had been assisting them.

The Chief noticed Dave's shaking hands and had him relieved of duty.

The translator who was also a Trucial Oman Scout* questioned the men at length then explained to the Chief that they were innocent.

Trucial Oman Scouts* Paramilitary force of the United Arab Emirates UAE raised by the British in 1951

They feared that the navy ship was a pirate, which was quite common in these waters. When asked about the opium they said the Captain of the vessel was a user. It was him that was defending their dhow.

"It's hard to believe, if they are in fact telling the truth but I will be sending off the results of my questioning and the subsequent death of their Captain to my headquarters as soon as we arrive back to the ship," the translator informed the Chief.

The Medic came to the forward deck and informed the Chief and the translator that the dhow captain was indeed dead. The Chief looked over at Dave with a strange pitiful expression as he walked out of hearing range to speak to the **Skipper** on the handheld radio.

He then ordered all the crew to immediately return to the dinghy. On their return trip back to the ship the **Chief** informed them not to breathe a word of this to anyone until the **Skipper** had made his decision.

Back onboard Dave was about to go on the morning watch. When he was relieved of duty and told to go to the bridge. The Chief and 'Pricky'* Price were there talking to the Skipper. The Jimmy met him and asked him to follow. They entered a small room behind the bridge and the Jimmy told him to sit and wait. The room was eerie as it was lit with red night lights.

'Pricky'* Price. Almost everyone had a nickname in the Navy.

What now? They gonna hang, draw, and quarter me... yes siree... splice the fuckin' mainbrace (4)... not!

Shortly thereafter the Jimmy returned with the Skipper and the Chief. It was the Skipper who spoke.

"Swift, *trouble* just follows you around. We could have an international predicament on our hands that could have severe repercussions. We have interviewed Price and have of course the Chief's statement. It does seem that you acted in self-defense, be it a little severe... I might add.

I have spoken to the Trucial Oman Scout Officer onboard and he has agreed to not report this incident until we have dropped him off at the base in HMS Jufair. This does not completely offer a lengthy silence as we must expect the dhows crew story to be much different from the actual truth. The easiest and sensible path would be to hand you over to the authorities and hope for a fair trial. I will be asking the Admiralty tomorrow for leniency and a way out of this mess. If I were to have my own way, it would be to depart and leave this to the relevant political authorities. It is only expected that there would be casualties when we are asked to help in these illegal smuggling affairs on behalf of the UAE. In the meantime, it is imperative that you speak to nobody about this incident. We have already interviewed the remaining boarding party crew. It is crucial for your safety that this is kept quiet.

Later in the day the Trucial Oman Scout was dropped off at the HMS Jufair Base by helicopter and the ship left for Singapore via Ceylon*.

Ceylon*. Known today as Sri Lanka

Weeks later they arrived at the HMS Terror dockyard in Sembawang outside the city of Singapore. The Chief, Dave and Pricky were escorted to an office in the Army barracks. They stood before an enquiry to give their recollection of the events leading to the death of the Persian dhow boat Skipper.

The Skipper of our frigate was also part of the big brass behind the long table together with an Arab looking gentleman. At the end of the long frustrating day Dave was acquitted of any wrongdoing but would still lose his hook and his good conduct stripe. Which of course meant a loss of pay.

Feeling extremely annoyed, he later went ashore and took a taxi drive with a few of his mess mates to the city of Singapore. They ended up on Bugis street which was a strictly off-limits area for all military personnel. They had taken the suggestion from a rickshaw driver to see a live sex show. After many drinks and the show, feeling aroused he and his buddies sat beside a sidewalk table talking to two good looking girls who were obviously whores, but they were sadly disappointed to later find that they were transgender* men.

*In those days they were 'locally' more commonly known as kyties or Catamites.

Holy moly... put my hand up her dress to find a nut and two bolts... no siree... not my cup of tea.

He seemed to want to get well and truly plastered to numb his brains for a few hours. Waking up for work at five thirty on the ship's tropical routine* not only was he extremely hung over, but his right arm and right hand hurt like the blazes.

Tropical routine* because of the shear heat and humidity, work began at five thirty and finished at one in the afternoon.

When he could focus his eyes, he saw a heart tattoo on his arm with Annie written in bright blue across it. Then looking at his hand he was shocked to see, 'I hate the fuckin the navy' tattooed on the side of his palm. Every time he now saluted an Officer, they would read the bright blue message... very clearly.

Oh, Davey boy you are in big shit now... yes siree... humongous, big shit.

It was later in the afternoon when he was saluting the Officer of the day before going ashore that he was not only denied shore leave but also received two weeks number nines... again!

Well, somebody must peel the damn spuds...

For the remainder of the time docked in Singers he was under punishment and the Joss made doubly sure that he had the worst jobs believable. During the three frustratingly long weeks he had come to a decision that had been brewing for a long time; in one month, he would be twenty-two years old. He once thought that he might make the best out his time by reaching for advancement, he had passed every exam for promotion up to Petty Officer. But with his record up to date, he would not have a chance of bettering himself and would constantly be at the bottom rung to take whatever they gave. He desperately wanted out. He felt that he was now a man and no longer a weak pawn to be used by the authorities in any way they chose to see fit.

It would be another year before he could even buy himself out, and that would still be at the Captain's discretion. He had spoken to other men onboard who also wanted out and there were very few ways it could happen.

One method would be to be found in bed with another man. Homosexuality was a big 'no no' in this modern Navy, a discharge would be imminent should the so-called experts prove it. He put some thought into that and knew as much as he wanted out, he just couldn't go through with it. He also knew that constantly being in trouble was one way but the Navy in their glorious and historic preeminence would simply look at that as, not allowing a criminal out into society.

*No siree... just punish the shit out of him until he begs for mercy and obeys the rules. This is my life and I have had enough of this bullshit... yes siree... enough is enough. ROMFT**

ROMFT* Roll On My Fuckin' Time, a naval phrase used by many disgruntled and trapped individuals.

He had been ordered to muster (meet with other crew members) at the Master at arms office and was deliberately a little late which had angered the Master causing his normally red face to almost turn purple.

Dave couldn't resist as he had been practicing it. "I musta missed a muster master," He answered.

Oh well more hard labor... but it was worth it. Master, if I just, 'thought' you were a fuckin' idiot... you really couldn't do much about it right? Hmm... yes Swift that is correct. Well master... I think you're a fuckin' idiot.

The ship then sailed for the navy base HMS Tamar in Hong Kong. Before they came alongside the jetty he was again taken to the Joss's office, which unfortunately had been a familiar pastime.

"Swift your Divisional Officer has granted you shore leave. If it was up to me, you'd never set foot ashore again. However, I'm only going to allow you, 'Cinderella leave'. Yes, you know what that is; you *will* be back onboard... sober by midnight," the Master ordered with a sly grin.

As the gangway was being installed Dave and Leading seaman 'Swampy' Marsh were on gangway duty. This basically meant checking each person going ashore handed in their station watch card and handing out condoms to anyone that asked. When Officers left the ship or returned, they had to be saluted. There was a ship telephone installed to call the Officer of the day or the Petty Officer on duty and the ships Tannoy for any calls (pipes) to be made throughout the ship. The Leading hand would be the Quarter Master and Dave would be his run about.

The Supply Officer had gone ashore as soon as the gangway had been placed. When he returned Dave smartly saluted him. The Officer was obviously reading what was on the side of his hand.

"Able seaman what is that disgusting remark on your hand," he asked in his posh accent.

"Sir, it says, I hate the fuckin' navy," Dave replied curtly.

"I can read what it says you imbecilic. We simply can't have this on the gangway for all to see. Get down below NOW," he ordered. "Quarter Master, call the Duty Petty Officer immediately."

Dave was relieved of gangway duty, given a bucket, and a scrubbing brush and ordered to clean the mid deck.

A portly Chinese lady, followed by a procession of coolies came up the gangway. Dave could hear the conversation from where he was scrubbing.

"Hello saila my name Jenny, Jenny sidee pa'tty. We cum clean boat sum good, no need saila scrub deck," as she pointed toward Dave. The procession of coolies came aboard and two of them snatched the brush and bucket from Dave's hand and commenced busily scrubbing.

The Quarter Master seemed flustered as he tried to stop them coming onboard. "Swiffy go and get the duty PO... quick."

Dave rushed down the ladders and across Burma way to the PO's mess to explain what had just occurred.

"Ah no problem Able seaman, that'll be Jenny side party (5). I'll come up and sort it out." The PO had obviously been to Hong Kong before as he spoke to her.

She greeted the PO like a long-lost friend. "Ah Billy Bunta long time no see, wea you bin. I got velly nice gil for you... likee befo, yes?"

Petty Officer Bunter looked a little embarrassed as he looked over to see Dave grinning.

"Good to see you Jenny, you know you're supposed to ask before coming aboard?"

"Oh, cum on Billy you kno we safe... all peopo safe in ma creu, no cause proble."

"OK, just wait here while I check with the Officer of the day.

Within an hour there were lots of coolies busy cleaning and polishing all the brass. Jenny had disappeared with the Officer of the day with four coolies to clean the wardroom.

Dave had changed from his white top and shorts on official gangway duty to his number eight working clothes. The duty Quarter Master, Leading seaman 'Swampy' Marsh and himself were drinking a cool and refreshing chocolate drink that they had bought from one of the coolies, for only one Hong Kong dollar each.

The following day there were more coolies hanging from roped chairs cleaning and painting the ships side. It had been a hot and sticky morning and he had bought a few of the delicious chocolate drinks.

In the afternoon it was a glorious feeling to be free to go ashore with the lads. He had even been allowed civilian clothes like the rest. They stopped at the first bar in Wanchai. There were many sailors from various ships, including a few Bootnecks*

Bootnecks* Royal Marines.

This was about as far as most of them would get, going ashore. It was mid-afternoon, and it was plain to see that some were already three sheets to the wind. The 'buy me drink ladies' wouldn't be present until later. Some of them would be on the game but most just making a few cents here and there from the barman by drinking cold tea disguised as booze.

Saila you ansome man... you buyee me drink? Yes siree... you come sit on my lap and we'll talk about the first thing that comes up.

He stayed with his messmates for the remainder of the afternoon closely watching his alcohol intake. The noise in the large bar increased in a direct relationship to the amount of alcohol consumed.

There were two entrances to this semicircular bar. One would generally enter from the closest door to the docks and depart from the other if you were heading into town. This was also the era for naked streaking made popular by a gentleman running naked across a highly televised national football game in the UK.

Of course, the Royal Navy matelots not wanting to be outdone had a different version of this nicknamed, 'the dance of the flaming assholes.'

The sun was setting as the evening advanced when suddenly without warning a naked sailor appeared at the incoming doorway. He immediately jumped upon the bar and as he raced along the bar at great speed knocking drinks and jars of peanuts hither and thither, he was seen to have something protruding from his rear end. It was in fact a tightly curled newspaper in a cone shape shoved up his bum. The tight end of the cone was of course held in place tightly with his buttocks. The newspaper had also been set aflame and he desperately needed to reach the outgoing door rapidly not only because the flame was being fanned by said speed and spilled alcohol. He was also being chased with the infuriated Chinese bar staff waving sharp kitchen cleavers. He leapt off the opposite end of the bar expeditiously and rapidly headed out the door. He was seen boarding a waiting taxi with said messmates cheering him on obviously winning some sort of bet, most probably including alcoholic beverages.

After the hilarious exposé, the bar had gotten very rowdy, and it was obvious to him that the evening would not end well. He had enough of punishment onboard, so he exited the bar and headed off into town. Walking up and down the bustling streets of the mercantile area of Hong Kong, he was head and shoulders taller than the traders on the street.

His stomach rumbled as the odor of delicious food wafted toward him. Finding a street chef masterly cooking over a hot wok, he wasn't sure what he ordered but it tasted wonderful. The ship's food was minus any taste. It was a known fact that upon joining up one had to have their taste buds surgically removed. After the interesting walk he made it back onboard prior to the bewitching hour.

The following afternoon he hiked to the top of the famous twin peaks. The views were breathtaking. Although it was a strenuous hike, almost five kilometers to a height of over five hundred meters he needed the exercise. He felt like he was in a rut with no escape in the foreseeing future. It had felt like months since he had trained with his punch bag onboard. Like most places the ship had visited he was fond of going off the beaten track and bypassing the bars. By doing so he had witnessed amazing sights. He also liked to be alone with his thoughts and dream of a different future. The books he had been reading of late also gave him hope of more positive opportunities.

In the next few months, the ship had visited interesting ports in the far east mainly in the Philippines and Malaysia always staying clear of Vietnam and the ongoing war. Although the ship had covertly taken wounded Americans soldiers to hospitals in Hong Kong. As a thank you, everyone onboard received a little blue medal.

He was put back on Cinderella leave until he agreed to have a skin graft to remove the offensive tattoo. He tentatively agreed after pressure from the displeased authorities onboard. An appointment had been arranged at a hospital in the U.K for their return later in the year.

The ship had returned to Singapore and on his first run ashore he had spent an enjoyable afternoon discovering the interesting sights. He liked to imagine himself to be free, like the many tourists he came across. He had borrowed a camera from one of his messmates and had taken lots of photos during the day. He also desperately needed female company. He had been with prostitutes in a few of the places they had visited. But it always left him not only dissatisfied but guilty for using a woman like that. Sure, it was the oldest profession in the world and kept the local economies able to feed and house the poor. Being a young man at sea for many weeks sometimes even months it was the norm. Moving from one port to the next was not conclusive to making lasting relationships.

While touring a large Buddhist temple he made conversation with an Australian lady. She was cute and very talkative which made him feel at ease. She introduced herself as Jodie. When she asked him what he did for a living and where he was from, he was momentarily stumped. He knew if he told her the truth she would move on very quickly. Creating a story that he had hurt his hand which he had earlier bandaged to hide the tattoo made him feel slightly guilty. The rest of the lie seemed to surprisingly fall into place as he explained that he was taking a short sabbatical from a college in UK while his hand healed,

"Oh, that's interesting and what are you taking... in college that is," She asked.

He had to think quickly and knew he was getting in deep with this fabrication.

"I'm taking... photojournalism," and held up his camera and quickly changed the subject. "Jodie, do you want to find a café somewhere, I'm parched for a drink."

They spent an enjoyable afternoon taking in the beautiful sights. The conversation was light and deeply satisfying. It had been so long since he had enjoyed female company, but he didn't want to come on too strong. She seemed to also be enjoying spending their time together.

At dusk she explained that she was with a group of girls, and they were going to have dinner together and go to a show.

"Can I see you tomorrow then?" he asked a little feebly hoping that he might extend this surprisingly fun encounter in his miserable existence these past months.

"Yes, I would like that Dave, lets meet at the door to the temple."

The next couple of days were wonderful, at one point, four cute ladies surrounded him, all seemingly wanting to make his acquaintance. The guilt he had previously been feeling had evaporated. They would be returning to Australia in a few days and his ship would also be departing in two days. Why not make the most of this interlude in his miserable life onboard? Jodie was also smitten by his attentiveness.

"Dave you are such a gentleman, unlike the boys back home."

They had bought sandwiches and bottles of chocolate milk and had found a quiet spot lying on the grass in a beautiful park. She leaned over and kissed him; it was a deep sensuous kiss and he responded with like. After an hour of mild petting, he asked her if she would like to come back to his hotel. Just by the look on her face he knew she was ready. They caught a cab and Dave asked the cabbie to go to a certain hotel that he had seen earlier. Once there he asked her to wait outside as the hotel might not be OK with other guests.

They had an afternoon and evening of sex as he used some of the moves, he had learned from Annie. She seemed to be in heaven but explained late in the evening that she should leave and join her friends at their hotel. They decided to meet the following day and after she left, he returned onboard.

During the hardworking morning, thoughts entered his head. Why was he using this innocent soul like this? The hurt he still felt by Annie's breakup was still front and center. Was this revenge? Sure, he felt some guilt but really, this wasn't hurting anyone. They would share a sad goodbye the following morning and he would return before the ship sailed. It was so overwhelmingly worth it to be free with this alter ego he had conjured up. Everybody happy!

He packed a few things in his holdall bag including his toothbrush in case she might wonder why he had no luggage. He sure did not want to hurt her by admitting to his lie. This would be one of those innocent holiday romances that everyone read about.

The following day he met her, and they had another exceptional day touring the town with four beautiful ladies who had obviously heard of his amorous advances. Whenever there was a quiet moment away from view, she would kiss him and whisper in his ear, "can't wait until tonight."

He had booked the hotel for another night so when they returned, she would be none the wiser now seeing his holdall and toothbrush. They had made love much of the night and in the tender moments in between, it began to feel special and reminded him of his time with Annie. He was surprised that she wanted to stay the whole night.

"The girls know what we are doing, and they are all quite jealous ha! But I've got you all to myself. Why don't I stay with you here until you have to leave? You know I think I'm starting to fall for you. Have you ever thought of coming to Australia?"

He knew this wasn't the love that he had for Annie, but he could see that given time it could progress into something different, and she wasn't married. What started out to be an innocent fling was beginning to become something else... besides shear lust. The morning quickly came and the time he would have to leave to return to the ship before it sailed. She was nuzzled in his arm with her head on his chest. He would have to admit to his lie which he knew would break her and make him feel like the heinous person he felt that he had become. Everything about his life in the Navy he abhorred, why should he have to feel like this. He closed his eyes and remembered the lesson he had learned from Annie about living life for today. With those thoughts he shortly fell into a deep sleep.

Later In the morning they awoke and had a hearty breakfast. They joined the other girls continuing the tour of the city. In the evening they went to a busy nightclub and danced the night away. He felt like a gigolo sitting at a table surrounded by beautiful females wanting his attention. Many men looked in his direction with envy. He just smiled and gave each lady a tour of the dance floor just to rub it in. When he allowed his mind to think about the trouble, he was in, he remembered a passage in a book he had read; *'be in the now, for tomorrow hasn't happened yet and yesterday has been and gone.'*

They made it back to the hotel and another evening of wonderful sex. They were immediately awakened in the middle of the night as three burly Marines with white arm bands showing the initial MP* loudly entered through the door. They held pistols pointing at Dave.

MP* Military police*

"Able seaman Swift you are under arrest for being absent without leave. Get dressed then turn on your front to be handcuffed. We know of your skills so don't try any sudden moves as we have permission to shoot."

As he laid on his front being forcefully handcuffed Jodie who held the covers over her chest looked at him in complete bewilderment.

"I'm so sorry Jodie, please forgive me?" he said regretfully.

As he was being pushed out of the door, he heard her scream. "You are a horrible deceitful person. I hope they put you away forever. You're just lowly scum."

Once they were in the paddy wagon* The Marines joked "Oh you're such a naughty boy, I gonna scratch your eyes out.

Paddy wagon* an enclosed motortruck used by military police to carry prisoners.

You have more than that coming Swift. Me thinks you're going to be taking a long trip to her Majesties DQs hotel. They have the finest cuisine, and the rooms are to die for."

"Hey cement for brains, whose dick did you suck to get those stripes. You had better shitinit and hide behind those pea shooters because I'll take you both on, *with* my hands tied behind my back." Dave said emphatically.

He was placed in the Terror barracks army jail until he was flown back to the UK a week later. It was a long eighteen-hour flight on a royal air force passenger plane where all the military passengers faced backward. He was cuffed on his hands and his feet and had two MPs escorting him.

He shuddered as he entered the fearsome gates of the familiar and evil detention quarters in Portsmouth... Again! This wasn't going to be a paltry thirty days; no, he had been given ninety days.

Chapter 16

D.Qs the second time around.

Chief Petty Officer Blight met him as he exited the covered wagon. He felt another trembling shock run through his spine. Blight was Dave's nemesis, the most hated person he had ever met. Dave had dreamed of beating him into a pulp for how the Chief had brought him to almost beg for mercy.

"Take these chains off him men, *we* can manage this from now on." He said with his barking deep voice.

"Able seaman Swift, what a pleasant surprise, just when things were getting boring around here. I love a challenge, but you already know that don't you? This time I've got you for the full ninety, just enough time for us to get fully acquainted. Now let me see this disgusting tattoo, that your record shows. Why don't you give me a smart naval salute? You will of course remember our assault course for an incorrect salute."

Dave nervously saluted him in the proper naval fashion, remembered by the shortest way up and the shortest way down.

"Well, I'm sorry to share this news with you but we have booked you a spot this morning with the dockyard Medic who will be removing that eyesore. You know he laughed at me when I asked him to make it as painful as possible. We can't have you running around here making a mockery of this fine establishment, now can we. Swift you have ten minutes to sort out your kit for inspection before you will be escorted to the sick bay. Able seaman Swift... 'ten... shun'. Petty officer, march this miserable excuse up to his cell."

As he laid on his front with his right hand laid on a table, he wasn't sure if the Medic was adhering to Blight's order because even though he been had injected numbing fluids into his hand and his right buttock, the pain was excruciating. After the skin graft, he was hastily bandaged and asked to stand. His hand began to throb and every step he took seemed to stretch the skin on his buttock. Given hardly enough time to adapt to the pain he was marched out of the sick bay by the DQs Gunnery Petty officer and into the covered wagon with his legs chained. He stood up in the wagon and winced at every bump in the road. When they returned inside the gates of the DQs, the chain was removed, and he was marched back to his cell. He lay on the bunk on his front as tears of pain ran from his eyes. He felt like he was adjusting somewhat to the pain when his cell door opened, and he was ordered to report for cleaning party duties. It was extremely awkward and painful to be on one knee with his right leg stretched out because of the pain and use his left hand to scrub the floors. Every time he stopped to catch his breath and wipe the involuntary tears of pain from his eyes. The duty PO screamed to get to work or risk an assault course. The thought of attempting to do that wanted to make him vomit.

He was relieved when he heard the pipe for lunch. The PO had them replace the cleaning equipment then doubled marched the men to the galley. He wasn't feeling well enough to eat but he remembered that would be a mistake. Although the food was awful and not very nutritious, it was important to keep up your strength. He had made that mistake before and remembered the hunger pains after all the exercise. He stood in his cell while eating as it was too painful to sit down. He was dreading the afternoon marching instruction.

"Swift, swing those arms and keep in step. Platoon... double march. Every step shot pain through his backside like a knife. He was sure that Blighty was doing this on purpose. He remembered what he had learned on the diving course: *these people are in their position to cause pain; this is just a duel of personalities. He is not going to beat me... no siree!*

He felt an immediate charge of electricity going through his body. *You will, 'not' beat me you miserable fucker.* He repeated it over and over under his breath.

As the long days wore on into weeks, again, he remembered what he had learned the first time; simply not to fight and make it worse. Just toe the line and give them what they want. Complete surrender!

This of course was not enough for Blighty. He would not stop short of having him beg for mercy. Sadly, on his second one-week bout of solitary in the three months he found himself doing exactly that... begging for mercy.

"Please don't put me in there again. I'll do whatever you want." *You want a blow job Blighty... just pull it out... I'm game... yes siree... pull out that tiny dick!*

He couldn't believe the day when he walked free and was billeted in Vicky barracks again. He showered and it felt luxurious but looking in the mirror at the skinny face that looked back he knew there was something missing. He had also lost a lot of hair and he knew that he would not be the same person ever again. They had taken something from him.

He had been silent for so long that when anyone in the mess spoke to him, he would just growl and tell them fuck off. They knew to leave him alone after that. But as the weeks wore on, he began to be able to speak to anyone without the feeling that he wanted to severely choke them.

He had kept his eye on the main notice board and had seen an advertisement for an inexpensive secondhand car. He felt the need to have something, anything to occupy his damaged mind. Within a month he had bought the car and had passed his driving test.

He found enjoyment and a healing from driving out of town and spending time hiking the surrounding fields and forests. Feeling a little more recovered from the traumatic experience of DQs, it was high time to visit his friends, Taffy, and Rhonda. It was fortunate that Taffy was home waiting for a new draft.

"Hey Taffy, how are you doing," Taffy had opened the door looking incredibly surprised.

"What are you doing here Swiffy aren't you supposed to be somewhere on the way back from the middle East." Taffy asked, inviting him into the house. Rhonda was sitting on a chair nursing a tiny baby.

"Ah it's a long story. Well look at you two, when did this happen, pointing to the infant? congratulations."

"Oh, this is little Arwyn, he's only one week old, and a hungry little horse." Rhonda said covering herself as she struggled to get up to hug him sincerely but looking surprised.

"Dave what on earth happened to you. Have you been ill? You're so skinny and what happed to your hair."

"Well, I don't really want to talk about it right now, but I just did another spell in DQs. Three months this time." He really didn't want to go into details as to why, as he was still embarrassed at how he had treated the Australian girl, Jodie.

They invited him to stay for tea as they updated each other with their plans. When the subject came to Annie, they both became strangely silent.

Rhonda spoke first. "Dave, we care for you very much and talk about you often and how we all met. You really need to forget about Annie. Like I warned you before, even though she is my sister, from the way she treated you and the life she leads you would be better off letting her be."

"What do you mean, *the life she leads.* Isn't she still with her husband in Sheffield?"

Taffy then looked at Rhonda with questioning eyes. "Rhonda you might as well tell him, he needs to know, no matter what we think."

"What is it, can one of you please tell me what's going on? Annie and I are history even though I might still have fond memories of her."

Taffy spoke first. "Dave, she has left her husband and is now back in Portsmouth. She has lost the custody of her two kids."

"Wait, two kids you say? How old is the second child?" He asked immediately.

Rhonda spoke next. "Dave, she thought Brendon was yours, as it does work out from the last time you both met. But the last time we spoke, she now says he is not. Dave, if you want the truth, she has been with many men, mostly sailors. I believe her latest was an American."

"But that is since she left her husband, right?" Dave interrupted.

"No, Dave I am so sorry to tell you, she has always been like that. Most of them are younger men much like yourself."

"You mean she was seeing others while we were dating?"

There seemed to be a long silence as Rhonda and Taffy looked at each other questioningly.

"Please tell me this isn't true?" Dave asked quietly.

Taffy spoke next. "Dave, we knew how much this would probably hurt, which is the reason we kept telling you to leave well alone."

Dave leaned back in his chair while he let this latest information sink in.

"Where is she now?" he asked.

Rhonda answered more emphatically. "Dave, please, this is for your own good, forget about her and get on with your life."

"Thank you, Rhonda, I appreciate your concern, but this is all new information, and much like before I need to see her to bring closure... finally! This child, *Brendon*, might very well be mine, surely, I deserved to know... for sure."

Taffy interrupted Rhonda. "Dave, we don't know where she is living but I believe she goes to the dance in Southsea where we all met. You might find her there. Do yourself a favor, if you must find her, just don't get drawn into her web again."

Chapter 17

The final goodbye.

Dave drove around Southsea much of his time off in hopes of bumping into her. He even went to the dance on two consecutive Saturday nights to no avail. He was getting quite concerned as he had received a notice of his next draft to a ship based in Chatham, Kent finalizing a refit in the dockyard.

It would be his last Saturday in Portsmouth when he finally saw her. She was sitting beside a man who by his haircut was obviously a sailor. He viewed her from the end of the bar. She looked a little inebriated as he came closer to hear her voice. His mind immediately cast back to when he first met her. They were warm thoughts that he had nurtured over the last year when he had allowed himself to go to that wonderful place. The thoughts immediately ceased when he saw her stagger to get up and dance with this man. He watched as she laid her head on his chest and he again remembered those touching moments. He was torturing himself and his stomach churned as he made his way toward them on the dance floor.

"Excuse me, may I cut in," he said to the young man. He looked at Dave incredulously and he was about to make a big mistake in picking a fight when a surprised Annie interrupted the heated moment.

"Dave what are you doing here?" she said slurring her words.

"We need to talk Annie, you had better ask your friend here to butt out before I make a mess of him."

The man was readying himself to fight when Annie saved his bacon. "Tony, sorry but I need to speak to Dave. I can see you later if you like," she said sounding a little more sober. Tony made a silly threatening gesture then sensibly disappeared into the crowd.

He directed her to a table far away from the noisy band. And as they sat, she seemed to have a strange distant look like they had never met. She had aged and her face looked gaunt. There were shadows under her eyes and her hair was not the long shiny black like he remembered but was short and a little unkempt. She had always been a little on the thin side which had been a bit of a turn on for him in the past but now she looked unhealthily skinny.

"Dave what happened to you, you look different. Have you been ill?" She said, slightly slurring her words.

"Annie, I hear you have had another child?" he asked, needing to get this out of the way.

"Oh yes, lovely little Brendon. Don't worry he isn't yours if that is what you are thinking. I thought he was at one time, but he is his Dad through and through," She was slurring her words even more. He needed to speak to her sensibly.

"Annie, can we go somewhere quiet, we really need to talk about this. Let's go for a coffee or something... please?"

"OK, let's go," she said standing a little bit wobbly.

He walked her out to his car but watching her stagger a little he put his arm around her.

"Oh, look at you, driving a car now, I'm impressed," she said smiling as he helped her into the passenger seat. "Always a gentleman, eh? Dave," she added hiccupping.

For a brief moment he felt a deep pang in his heart as he remembered that smile.

They found a quiet restaurant and ordered a coffee. By the second coffee she was beginning to make a little more sense as she was sobering up quickly under the situation.

"I just couldn't live with him anymore. He fell short of all the promises he made. In all honesty, I thought I could make it work but I just didn't love him anymore. I stopped taking the pill earlier and immediately became pregnant. At first, I thought it was a good thing and might bring us closer together. He accused me of adultery and his jealousy got completely out of hand. Dave as much as I wanted Brendon to be yours, I know he isn't."

"But you were seeing other men when we were together, isn't that so?" he asked. Surprisingly, she seemed to be completely taken back by this new information.

"Dave, I loved you, don't let anyone, 'ever' tell you any different," she said vehemently.

"So, it's a lie then? you weren't seeing anyone else then?"

She went completely quiet as she looked away from him out of the window of the restaurant. He waited for her response.

"Dave, I need to go. Can you please drop me off at my home? None of this, matters anymore. Why do you want to keep being hurt? I'm not the woman you think I am. I once thought I could be that person, when we were together you made me feel incredibly special. All I ever wanted to do was please you in return.

My life completely changed when I first became pregnant as a teenager. I had no idea how to be a mother and when he proposed it just seemed like the right thing to do. Trying to be a dutiful housewife in a town where I knew no one also seemed like what I was supposed to do. But there comes a time in everyone's life when you eventually come of age and see that there is more to life. Meeting you and feeling wanted brought me into a different world. At least that is what I thought, until you too also left me alone. With you, in the beginning, I had dreams of having it all; a man that I sincerely loved and a family. I'm not blaming you, but you never really gave me a feeling of commitment. Dave, I've said enough, now will you please take me home."

He drove her into a seedy looking neighborhood and stopped in a quiet car park beside the flat were she presumably lived. He wasn't sure what to believe anymore.

"Annie, why can't we start off again on a clean slate. You have been the only love I have ever known. Surely, we could make it work," as he leaned over to the passenger seat to kiss her. She didn't completely respond like he remembered but there seemed to be something there the longer they kissed. She suddenly stopped when he thought she was beginning to respond.

"Dave, stop we can't do this anymore, I really need to go," she asked abruptly.

"Annie, I want you so bad. I have dreamed about making love to you again," he said feeling like he was becoming unglued.

"Dave is that what you really want? Then let's go," she said climbing into the back seat and taking off her underwear. He was hoping that she wanted him too but there was something strangely wrong and somewhat phony with this outcome. He felt blinded as they had sex, and she wasn't responding. He tried harder to make her feel him until she finally asked him to stop.

"Dave, you're hurting me. But if that is your intention, then don't let *me* stop you."

He eventually climaxed but felt extremely guilty at losing control like that. She dressed and sat quietly looking out of the window. He could see tears in her eyes.

Dave was the first one to speak after the embarrassing silence. "Annie, I'm so sorry, I don't know what came over me, please forgive me."

"Dave, I wanted to remember you different to this. We can never be together. It ended in that train station in Nottingham. Our relationship was never meant to be. Let us say our goodbyes forever here and now," she opened the door and began to walk away.

He jumped out of the car and ran to her.

"Dave, please, it needs to end here," she repeated tediously.

He held her tightly and gently kissed her neck.

"Goodbye Annie," he whispered into her ear.

"Goodbye Dave," as she pulled back with tears in her eyes and walked away into the darkness.

Young love (straight out'a the box)

Cold hearted woman she did me wrong
It was a cold-hearted woman who took my heart
They called it puppy love; then I'm just a dog, because
Cold hearted woman she sure took my heart

Because -- Young love, straight out'a the box
Young boy, far from home
He gotta broken heart from runnin' away
She castes her spell and he's blinded by lust, he got
He got no chance
He's drownin' in her

Because -- Young love, straight out'a the box
She was an angel; in fact, that was her name
She had jet black hair and ruby red lips
Let me tell you now she was so fine, she had
She had this young boy all tied up in knots

Because -- Young love, straight out'a the box
Now here's a moral, ain't no mistake
You handle fire, you're gonna get burned
Stay away from divine ruby lips
'Cos, fall in the hole, you might never get out

Because -- Young love straight out'a the box

Kevin Firth Sep 2009

Chapter 18

Chatham.

He would be leaving in the morning to make his way to Chatham Dockyard, feeling a bit nervous about the drive through London. He decided to visit Taffy and Rhonda one last time knowing that his future draft would be based in Chatham, and he might not see Portsmouth again. In as much as he was still feeling the sadness of his goodbye with Annie, she would always be precious in his memories, but it was time to move on. When sadness came over him from time to time, he was now able to place those thoughts where they belonged.

The fond visit went well. He didn't want to get into details about his meeting with Annie. They seemed to know this and not dwell on the subject only that Dave had said his final goodbye. However, when he held their baby boy in his arms and looked at the cute little face smiling up into his eyes, he couldn't help wondering what could have been. Was there a little boy somewhere that could possibly have called him, Daddy? As the emotions encompassed his being, he handed him back to his mother.

He hugged Rhonda and shook Taffy's hand tightly, they almost felt like the family he had never had.

Cheerio my friends, let's hope our paths cross again... yes siree... love you guys.

The drive was indeed complicated but eventually, and with anxiety, he made it to the Chatham Royal Navy base, HMS Pembroke. The ship's company was billeted at the base until the ship finalized her refit. He was told to report to the Mountbatten block where he was given a bunk and a locker to store his kit. It was a large mess deck of many men. The crew seemed quite friendly, and the local town of Gillingham was a decent place to share a run ashore. In the few weeks before the ship was ready for sea, he had met a couple of girls on separate evenings. One seemed smitten by his attentions. He had bedded both at various times until one found out about the other and there was hell to play. He didn't seem to care and searching his feelings it almost felt like he wanted to hurt.

The ship was an old county class, diesel propelled frigate, and so he was told, it should have been scrapped or at least mothballed. Although below decks there didn't seem to be the amenities that he had been used to on his last two ships but the crew and even the Officers were almost friendly. He didn't feel like he was being constantly picked on. The three-ring Commander Jimmy even had a London accent which was very unusual. He must have been one of the rare breeds that had come up from the ranks. The Skipper was a four-ring Captain unlike the two Commander Skippers on his last two ships. He was an older man, he guessed this was probably his last commission before retirement.

Dave hadn't trained in such a long time and decided he didn't want to advertise his skills. It had always seemed to have gotten him into so much trouble in the past. In just less than a year he would be eligible to buy himself out which he wanted badly. It would still be up to the Skipper's discretion. And he knew only too well that this Navy did not want to give up men... easily. He had to toe the line between the threat of returning to DQs which haunted him and ensuring that he was willful enough for them to want to let him go.

The ship sailed and passed its sea trials, it was destined to protect the shores of the UK from illegal fishing. The patrol was cut short by a leak in one of the engine sea water cooling lines through a hull fitting. The ship had to come alongside the South Shields fishing dock just outside of Newcastle, while they decided what to do. The Chief Engineer Artificer had said that unless they could somehow block the through hull fitting that supplied the engine, they would have to return to Chatham for emergency repairs. This would be an embarrassment to the dockyard and to the Naval shoreside inspection team that had given the final go ahead for the ship to sail.

Dave was the only Ship's diver onboard and not only would it go against all the rules of not having an emergency stand-by diver and a qualified supervising tender, but the diving equipment also seemed to have had better days. He was asked to report to the Jimmy's office. As he entered the small office, he was also introduced to the Engineer Officer and the Chief engine room Artificer*.

Artificer* more commonly known as Tiffs. Qualified technicians who are allowed to take apart the engines.

"Swift, we seem to be in a bit of trouble here. Unless we can somehow block off this through hole fitting from the outside, we will have to abort the patrol and return to Chatham. Also, in manning the ship, we failed to check that we had adequate Ship's divers onboard in case of an emergency, such as the one we find ourselves in. I will be having this out with the relevant drafting department very soon. As you are the only Ship's diver onboard and this is an emergency, would you be willing to collaborate with the Chief here to resolve this issue? I understand you have checked the diving equipment stored in the tiller flat. Is that correct?

"Yes sir, it's a bit rough but with a bit of TLC and help from the Chief Tiffy it might be possible to set up a dive. We would need to get the air compressor working to charge up one of the breathing sets. It might be workable." Dave replied.

"OK then off you go, and Chief whatever this young man needs, make it a priority."

The Chief had one of the Petty Officer Artificers work on the air compressor while they went to the Engineer's workshop to figure out how this issue could be resolved.

"Chief have you got a sheet of strong rubber or plastic onboard? He asked.

"Why, what have you got in mind?" He replied.

"Well on my last ship we had a similar issue, and we came up with this idea and it seemed to work. The patch might still be on the underside of that ship, as far as I know."

He had them cut a piece of quarter inch steel plate about one square foot then glue a thick rubber sheet to one side. They drilled a hole in the center and put a quarter inch threaded bar through the middle. He explained that on the inside of the through hole fitting there is usually a grate to stop seaweed and the like from being sucked into the cooling lines in the ship.

"Bend one end of the threaded bar into a hook and I can thread it up and grip the inside of the grate. At the other end place a tight rubber washer over the hole in the steel sheet and give me a large butterfly nut and washer so that I can tighten the plate to the bottom of the ship. The rubber sheet will then be sealed against the ship's hull. Of course, you won't be able to use that sea water supply line as it will be blocked off until the ship is returned to dry dock." Dave explained.

"Hmm you know what Swift that might just work. We can rig up another sea water cooling line to the engine. I'll get the Mechanic on duty to work on that, now why don't you go and get the rest of your diving equipment checked out. It's going to be pitch dark when we do this. Are you going to be OK with that?"

"Yes, no problem, Chief, it's usually shitty black in harbor anyway. Just have someone tap a hammer on the through hole fitting in the engine room. I'll give you two pulls on my safety line to tell you when I have found it. I will also reply with two taps with my diving knife to whoever is on the inside to also let them know. One tap means I'm still looking, OK?"

Three hours later he had carefully rolled into the cold sea from the side of the ship's dinghy which was tied alongside the outboard side of the ship. He had previously found the only rubber dry suit that seemed to have no holes in it stored in a container. He borrowed two pairs of long johns and put on a warm wool sweater as there were no wooly under suits to be found in the locked store. With the air compressor now working they were able to charge up the only SABA set that looked in decent working order. He had cleaned the green mold from the breathing tit and the face mask with a mix of disinfectant and water.

The sea water was freezing cold and as usual trickled down his back through the neck seal. This was the worst part, getting acclimatized before reaching up with both arms allowing the air to escape from the suit and slowly submerge. He could now feel water also trickling in from a hole in one of the legs and it was slowly filling up the leg of the dry suit. He shivered at the extreme cold until he remembered the catchphrase; *safety is always number one, then comes the job at hand, then way down the ladder of importance is diver comfort.*

On entering the water, he immediately heard the tapping as the sound travels much faster in water. He swam toward the sound feeling the hull above his head. He was quite used to working by feeling alone in the darkness. The dive tender was obviously untrained and was holding his safety line too tight. He had to constantly pull on it to move ahead. Eventually he found the through hull fitting. He reached into the fitting, they were in luck; even though feeling was rapidly disappearing from his fingers, he could still feel that there were openings in the grate inside the fitting. Now that he had an idea where it was, he swam back to below the dinghy and pulled on the plate hanging in the water. Not only was the plate not moving, but his lifeline was also being held tight. He came to the surface and pulled the corrugated hose holding the breathing tit out of his mouth.

"For fucks sake stop holding me so damn tight and come on down with the plate until you feel me pull my safety, three bells," He had already schooled them the difference between a pull and a bell. A pull is exactly what it sounds like, a bell is like ringing a bell, one–one-----one, would be three bells.

After several bells and pulls he was able to return to the tapping through hull fitting with the plate and complete the job at hand. He had difficulty untying the knot someone had tied on the threaded bar, as his freezing hands were almost numb, so he used his diving knife to cut it. He gave the tender four pulls and didn't wait for a reply, the tender wouldn't have a clue anyway. He was just hoping that the slack safety line would not snag and hinder his return to the surface. He then held on to the side of the dinghy and removed his breathing tit and mask.

"OK, it's done, ask them to test it before I come out," he ordered.

Minutes later he heard the Chief call down from the deck that it was a success the patch was holding and to get the diver out of the water.

When he climbed up the rope ladder to the ships deck from the dinghy he was pleasantly surprised to be met with applause from the Skipper, the Jimmy, and the Chief.

"Well done Swift, good work," the Skipper said before leaving him with the Chief. When they were both gone the Chief reached behind a deck hatch and gave him a full glass of pure navy rum.

"Now don't you go telling anyone about this, you'll get me trouble." The Chief said smiling.

For once in such a long time, he felt good about himself.

The ship sailed the following morning. The Chief Bosun, who was his direct boss, met him as he was clearing up his diving gear from the night before. He was an older man and quite pleasant. He seemed to know when to be stern but also when to give praise for a job well done.

"Swift, go through all the diving equipment onboard and make a list, also another list of everything we might need for any future such emergencies.

"OK Chief, will do but it won't really make any difference. I broke the rules last night which I don't like doing because it's my life I'm risking. Diver training states that to run a dive one must have a second diver completely dressed-in ready to go as an emergency. And a separate tender who is experienced with diver safety line signals, preferably another qualified ship's diver."

Two weeks later they had come alongside in Peterhead, Scotland. Two qualified ship's divers joined the ship, one was a seaman like himself, and the other was a Leading Marine Engineer Mechanic better known as a Stoker. There was also a container on the dock with everything he had requested to set up three complete divers. There were also spare parts for the air compressor that the Petty Officer Tiffy had ordered.

He was impressed that they had provided everything and more than he had requested. Even though the Leading hand outranked him, Dave was still put in charge of any future dives that they might have. It was put to the test only six weeks later when both the ships' props were entangled in a fishing net. They had been chasing a Belgian trawler who was caught well inside the legal fishing zone of the U.K. The trawler had made a few strange maneuvers, the result being entanglement and a trawler Skipper giving the finger as he disappeared into the night. The three divers were taking turns with hacksaws and sharp divers' knives and were eventually successful in removing the old, entangled nets with no damage to the ship's propellers.

It was cold and demanding work, particularly being in the dark of night and not the ideal weather conditions. But it was good to be accomplishing something at last where he felt appreciated. He had been in the Royal Navy almost eight years and apart from the accolades he had received from his karate competitions, it had been one long miserable existence. They had punished him to the ninth degree, humiliating and severe punishment for what he believed to be unjust. And now, when it was his time to break free from this dreadful experience, they suddenly want to be pleasant?

He was beginning to wonder if his damaging record had been received yet by the brassy authorities upstairs in the wardroom.

It was high time to put in his request to buy himself out and not be boondoggled. At one hundred and twenty pounds it would be a difficult expense knowing that he was barely making twenty-two pounds a week, even with his extra danger pay of four shillings a day.

He made out the correct request and gave it to a surprised Chief Bosun.

"Swift are you sure about this? You've still got a good future here even though I know you have had issues in the past. These events can be forgiven in time. You'll be due to get your hook back soon I expect. Especially with the splendid work you've been doing diving," the Chief said optimistically.

"Thanks Chief, I know you mean well. I assure you my decision has nothing to do with how you or the rest of this ships company have treated me."

The Chief passed it on to the Divisional Officer who then passed it up, where it finally ended on the Skipper's desk.

The following day the Chief met him on the quarter deck where he was splicing the ends of some ropes.

"Swift, secure all that rope back in the locker and get yourself cleaned up. The Skipper wants to talk with you. Come and find me in the Chief's mess and I'll escort you through the wardroom."

Dave felt nervous tension knowing that this would be his bid for freedom. During his shower then dressing into a clean pair of number eights, obscure thoughts entered his head. As a boy sailor all he had to do was obey orders. He had once been keen to please in hopes of advancement. The comforting memories of when he first received his hook and good conduct stripe was still fresh in his mind. But then came the horrible recollections, also still very fresh of what they had done to him in DQs. He had obviously burnt any bridges to any meaningful advancement. But that wasn't 'it' that truly bothered him; he was so tired of being led. He couldn't remember a time when he wasn't being taken down the path of someone else's direction. The experience he had gained with Annie together with what he had learned in the Navy had also made him into a man. What would it feel like to be free to make your own decisions? He could see in his older mess companions; men who had just given up. There had to be something else to this life. This could be the turning point to a new life of his calling. He nervously waited outside of the Skipper's office while the Chief knocked on the door.

"Come in Chief and bring Swift with you. Swift why don't you sit," as he pointed to a seat across the desk facing him. "Thank you, Chief, I think we can manage this from here," he dismissed the Chief who closed the door as he departed.

"Able seaman Swift now what is all this nonsense about requesting to buy yourself out of the Navy?"

"Yes Sir, I'm afraid this isn't just a wild request. I have thought long and hard and would like to buy myself out when two thirds of my man's time is complete as per the regulations. Which would be in the next four months."

"Swift, I won't beat about the bush, you are aware that it is my job to persuade you to change your mind. We have all witnessed your capacity to solve problems. Viewing your record, you have had some serious discipline issues but have been punished accordingly.

I have aways been of the mind to give a man a chance to redeem himself. Youth is a difficult period in a person's life when one is challenged to make better choices that generally only come with experience and age. In less than a year you will become eligible for Leading Rate again. Based on your exemplary work, be it a brief time since you have been serving with me, I can tell you that it will be guaranteed on the assumption that you of course, stay out of trouble. The Navy needs men like yourself. You have shown courage under duress, and I can think of no one better during conflict, should it occur, to be serving with. You have put a lot of time and effort in this Navy to just throw it all away."

"Thank you, sir, I appreciate your comments. The crew onboard this ship are quite different from what I've been used to, because of this I've felt encouraged to do better.

This isn't a careless decision sir. I have put a considerable amount of thought into this over the last few years, which has no detriment to you or the crew. It is time for me to seek a new life, and whatever challenges that might bring."

The Captain thought for moments before answering. "OK Swift I will think this over and give you, my decision."

"Sir, with all due respect. I hope I have made it abundantly clear, inasmuch as I appreciate your comments. I need to know that in four months, when I am eligible, I will be leaving the Navy," Dave replied sternly.

"Swift, I said I would give it some thought now let's leave it at that."

"Sir, if needed I can get into an awful lot more trouble. I hate to make this a threat, but you will leave me no alternative."

The Chief was waiting outside the door. "Chief, come in, our discussion is over. Swift, you are dismissed," the Captain said noncommittedly.

The following day Dave received his request which showed that he was accepted for voluntary discharge on payment of one hundred and twenty pounds. Dave felt relieved when the Chief gave him the request and warned him to stay out of trouble because it could easily backfire.

"Chief, no worries there. I have absolutely no issues with you or the rest of the crew. I just want out... that is all, thank you."

Chapter 19

Goodbye Pompey.

The ship came alongside in Rosyth, Scotland, this would be his last night aboard a Royal Navy ship. The lads had taken him into the Dunfermline Lounge bar to ply him with drinks and much to their disappointment he was limiting his intake of alcohol beverage. He had been warned that punishment could still be given, and his discharge delayed for unruly behavior. He had dreamed of this moment as he said his farewells to his close shipmates.

The following afternoon after the long train journey, he arrived in Chatham to pick up his car, of which he was pleasantly surprised that it started. He then drove to Vicky barracks in Pompey to finalize a week of, 'leaving the navy training.' He had laughed when he was told of the requirement but meeting with the rest of the men in the mess, he could now possibly see the point.

There was such a variety of ages and characters, and he was pleasantly surprised to also meet Taffy.

"Taffy, what the heck are *you* doing here?"

"Ah you know, it was time. We have two kids now and I didn't want them to grow up hardly seeing their Dad. Rhonda was also delighted. We've moved to my hometown in Wales, Rhonda loves it there."

The rest of the mess was a mixed bag of men, some who had served the full twenty-two and even longer. There were also two men who had given themselves up from being AWOL for numerous years, one of which had been AWOL for over ten years. He wanted to marry, and his future wife had made him give up, not wanting the police to one day show up and throw him in jail. The other had come accompanied by military police in handcuffs.

The course was mainly about what to expect in civilian life. Dave suspected that it was also 'scare tactics' and a last-minute bid to have them change their minds. It would also inform the military seasoned men how to find and keep a regular job and how to find suitable living accommodation. There would be no sick bay or even a galley for regular food. On the last day he felt like they had finally given up as the motley crew lined up for a ceremonial handing in of all the kit they had collected in their naval career.

He and Taffy had long conversations and laughs about past exploits. The subject had only once come up about Annie.

"You know Dave we haven't spoken to her in ages. The last we heard she had moved to London. Rhonda saw her once before she disappeared, she was in a bad state and might even be on drugs. Lord only knows what she is doing in London."

On the very last day Dave and Taffy said their sad farewells and promised to stay in touch.

He would never see or hear from him or Rhonda again.

As he drove out of the main gates of Victory barracks and the Royal Navy he felt his heart racing, he had looked forward to this day for so long.

I am free at last; they no longer have a hold on me. I can choose to do whatever I like with my life from this day forward... yes siree... fuckin' free at last. Blighty eat your fuckin' heart out.

He looked in his rear-view mirror one last time at the Victory gate. He would never see Pompey again. In various ways it had been his home; there had been awful periods that would give him nightmares for the rest of his life but there were also fond and tender moments that he would cherish. He decided to drive through Southsea passing the beach and the sea wall then by the dance hall. He had mixed feelings as he departed driving North to his new life.

Goodbye old Pompey, good and bad times... yes siree... good and bad times.

He had absolutely no plans and had decided to just see where life took him from here on. He had heard the phrase, 'life is your oyster.' Would he eventually find his pearls?

OK, let's go where it all began and have a restart.

He had not been to his birth town since he had joined up. After Pompey it was the closest place, he had ever called home.

As he drove into Haslingden after the long drive North he had mixed feelings. Everything seemed smaller, would any of his old school chums still be around. He did a quick pub crawl and asked questions of many of the unknown but familiar looking locals. Most of his old buddies had married and left the area. He finished off in the Commercial pub in the center of town and asked the friendly landlord, John if he had a room for the night.

The room was small, but he had a comfortable night even though his mind was racing. In the morning John made him breakfast as Dave gave him a quick rundown of his exit from the navy and where he had once lived in the town. John told him that he had been in the army. Dave guessed by his age that he had probably been in the war so decided to change the subject.

He later drove around the town passing familiar areas that brought on more mixed memories. He drove past the house where he had lived with his father. It was quite nostalgic but sad that it was now boarded up, as were most of the other houses on the street, waiting to be demolished. He drove down to the playing fields and parked his car. It was a nice day, so he walked up the hill to the pond where he had paddled with his Dad. He folded up his pants and waded into the pond.

Hey Dad, I'm back. I know you've been with me through all my hardships. I wish you were here now to give me some direction. Either way I'm good... and somehow, I'm going to make you proud.

He drove down Grane road on his old paper delivery round remembering the freedom and pleasurable feeling that it had once given him. He even drove by the Clarkson's house which also looked very run down. He wasn't even sure if anyone was living there anymore.

He had a very enjoyable fish and chips and mushy peas meal that brought back many warm memories with his Dad. On returning to the Commercial it was only early Friday evening, and it was almost full. A loud band played in the corner as many couples danced in the smoke-filled room. He finally made it to the bar where many people were waiting to be served. He eventually got John's attention. He had a scantily dressed young female busily helping him serve the noisy crowd.

"Hey Dave, do you want to work off your room costs? If so, get behind here and give us a hand." John shouted above the din.

He quickly got the hand of the busy bar and had been given a few free drinks as tips that were having a pleasant effect.

Hmm this isn't so bad; I could get used to this no prob. Think I've landed on my feet here... yes siree!

Shortly before closing, a fight broke out by the pool table. John was about to call the police when Dave said, "No worries, John, I can handle this," as he made his way to the pool table. He was able to quickly stop the fight with the minimum of moves and not severely hurt anyone then help them out of the pub. When he returned to the bar a few of the patrons were clapping. "Eh yup pal that wus reight gud." One of the elderly men at the bar said.

John patted him on the back, "Well, well, I think you have a job mate. It's almost closing time, give me a hand to get rid of the riff raff and we'll have a quiet drink later, OK?"

Ten forty-five rolled around and John rang the bell for the last orders. There were still a few people drinking that he guessed were regulars. The doors were then locked, and the thick curtains drawn. This was the illegal after-hours drinking crowd, whom Dave was introduced to. John disappeared into the cellar and returned with four bottles of red wine. After placing them on the bar he left for the kitchen returning with a plate full of select cheeses and homemade pickles.

In the early hours of the morning Dave made it to bed feeling quite inebriated but happy to have met this friendly crowd. The following morning, he wasn't so happy, he had a massive headache and didn't stir until after twelve mid-day. John was busy stocking the bar, completely unscathed by the consumption of much alcohol. Dave guessed that this was obviously a regular occurrence and he had simply built-up tolerance.

Saturday evening was almost as busy but not like the Friday crowd. He was able to make conversation with the many friendly locals as he served drinks.

"Eh yup Davey, it's me Bobby... from school. How are yer doin?"

Dave looked at the familiar but quite different face of his old school pal. He was much taller but skinny with a slight stoop to his shoulders. His face was an unhealthy ashen grey color. He held out a boney and heavily nicotine-stained hand to be shook across the bar. When he smiled his teeth were also nicotine stained showing many black cavities.

"Well, well Bobby how the heck are you? It's been a while, eh?" Dave asked cheerfully.

"Oh, yu know, I gets me ups and deowns. Yer lookin reight gud though, 'spect the navies ad a lot tu do wi thad eh?" Bobby answered.

Dave tried to remember if his own Lancashire accent had ever been that pronounced. Not only did Bobby look older than his years but he also sounded like he was.

"Ah don't normally cum in ere, specially on 'tu weekends. Its waay tu busy fer mi. I likes a pint in 'tu Legion its open later an it's cheaper thur an all. Anyways, don't fuck aren'ed. Gi yer ol pal a free pint, ya skingy fucker."

The relatively busy evening wore on as Dave and the young girl pulled pints. John had gone out for dinner with some of his friends and would return before closing time. When he had a free moment, he would carry on his conversation with Bobby who was on his third free pint. Dave had used his two free tipped pints to give to Bobby and had once put money in the till from his own pocket. Toward closing time Bobby had said he was going to 'the club' for a closing hour pint.

John returned and relieved Dave and the young girl as the earlier rush had thinned out.

"The customers have either gone over to the club or the Trades at the top of town as they are allowed by law to stay open longer," John explained.

"OK, I'm going to pop over to this Legion club, as an old mate is there. I've got a key to the back door, so I'll let myself in. If that's all right with you John." Dave asked.

He was met at the door to the club asking if he had membership or if he was ex-military. Dave fished in his wallet to find a watch station card from his last ship, explaining to the man that he had only just left the Navy. The man seemed impressed and escorted Dave to the busy bar area. The doorman explained to the barman what he had just heard from Dave as a group of men in earshot glanced his way.

"Hi everyone," Dave said, feeling a little embarrassed at the looks he was receiving.

The barman reached over the bar to shake Dave's hand. Which made him feel even more embarrassed as more people along the bar looked his way.

"You're most welcome here son, most o' these reprobates 'ave to pay a membership but ex-military will always be free in here. I'm ex-army myself, as he looked across the bar grinning at all the people staring.

"Yer a fuckin' wanker is wot yu are, now gi the lad a pint on me, reight smartish," one of the obviously inebriated men at the bar said coming toward him with an open hand to be shook. "Am

X navy tu, ah did three years to'ord thend o' war. Bloody rough goin al tell thi." He said shaking his hand roughly.

"Leave the poor lad alone yu fuckin' dipshit he's my ol' pal from secondary school oer yon. An yer a lyin git; It wur only last week yu wur tellin uz yu wur fightin wi Montgomery in North Africa." Bobby said making everyone laugh at the bar.

Dave was handed his dark mild beer and they headed over to a seat at a table with many other men and older couples. The bar was thick with cigarette smoke and noise not only from many voices but there was also a piano player banging out old tunes that some were singing to.

It was difficult to have a conversation with all this going on and Bobby looked well sloshed. Dave's beer glass was almost empty as he waited for Bobby to get his round in. Eventually Bobby leaned over and said, "Go on git uz a nuther beer, ol pal, jus fer ol time's sake, eh?"

"Dave made his way back to the bar and ordered two pints and paid for them having various conversation on the way. It was good to see Bobby again, which gave him a link to some of the few good memories he had from his youth. OK, so he was a bit slow in buying a round of drinks, he's probably skint and he felt mildly sorry for him. He wondered what had happened in his life to bring him to this. He remembered that he was an only child living with a single elderly mother, who at times seemed a little overprotective. Bobby had told him earlier that she had died a few years back.

Dave finished his beer and before Bobby could ask for another, which he certainly didn't need, Dave told him that he was leaving and maybe they could meet up tomorrow. Bobby explained that he lived in a trailer caravan to which he gave rough directions. Dave told him he would come out and visit, probably in the afternoon.

The following day he had a quick check on his finances and approximately what he had remaining in his savings bank account. He had only been here two days and it was obvious his finances were not going to keep him for very long. It was a bonus to know that he could work off his board and breakfast working in the bar and was beholden to John for that. But it was imperative that he find temporary work to help pay for his other living expenses. The petrol cost to drive this far north had made a sizeable dent in what was remaining in his wallet and eventually the car would need service, it was already burning oil.

He had showered in the old bathtub down the hall and was now lying on his bed contemplating what should come next. What is it that he wanted to do with his life, as there were so many possibilities? One of the lads that had been on the 'leaving the navy course' told him that the merchant navy were always looking for experienced deckhands. He wasn't exactly enthused by the thought of returning to the long and lonely hours of being at sea. But he did have warm memories of the thrill of visiting foreign countries, how would it feel to have that, without the extreme discipline and forthcoming punishment. And if he didn't like it, well he could just quit no holds barred. But what if he found something of interest, here in his hometown? To lay down some roots, be married and bring up some kids of his own. It was early days, and he should at least give it some more thought, he had certainly felt some sort of connection.

What would Annie do? she was the queen of just living for today, whatever is going to happen will eventually happen, maybe not the way you expect it to. Just enjoy the moment and the rest will fall into wherever it wants.

He was already feeling better. For now, he would make small decisions and see where it took him.

He headed out to the trailer park to see Bobby. He arrived at two thirty in the afternoon and Bobby was still in bed. His sleepy face answered the door still in his ratty looking underwear and soiled vest.

"What the fuck yu doin' 'ere this time o' day. He said sounding very hoarse.

"Bobby, you said to come here this afternoon. You don't remember?

"Oh, yea thats reight, sorry mate, ah need a fuckin' coffee cum in yer lettin all tu fuckin' heat out."

The inside of the trailer smelled of urine and every chair were piled high with dirty clothes. The tiny kitchen sink was also piled high with moldy dishes. He filled an aluminum kettle with water and lit the grungy looking propane gas stove then fished out a tea-stained mug from the dishes. "Du yu wan a mug o' coffee or tea?"

"No thanks mate I just had one, you go ahead," Dave wasn't sure that he might catch leprosy or some vile disease from those filthy mugs.

He poured his coffee while lighting a cigarette which was constantly replaced the whole time Dave was present. The fag hung precariously, from the side of his mouth as the long strands of ash eventually fell to the floor, making Dave wonder why the trailer hadn't gone up in smoke. Bobby sat across from Dave showing his piss-stained underwear and reached down to drag a ratty blanket from the floor to put over his shoulders. "Ee its reight bloody parky in 'ere eh?" he said shivering.

They stayed talking for over two hours until... well simply, Dave couldn't stand the smell of urine any longer.

Bobby had a sad story that made Dave's past sound like a holiday in the park. He had lived with his mother until she passed away two years previous. She had obviously been his rock and had taken care of his every need to the point of smothering him. Dave had remembered her like that. He had worked at various cotton factories as a laborer. Dave could only guess at the miserable conditions. He had been sacked from every one of them for constantly not showing up for work. But mum would always stand by him and take care of his everyday needs. She had been on social assistance for many years, which was their only finance apart from Bobby's miserable wages. After her untimely death he soon lost the only home, he had ever known and moved in with a divorced woman ten years his senior who had three kids. For a period, he had managed to keep a job to bring home a suitable wage to contribute, somewhat illegally because the lady was on social assistance. Because of that he was allowed to stay in her home with some conjugal rights and help pay her rent and feed her kids.

He went on to further explain that the lady had violent tendencies and would sometimes beat him up and throw him out on the street. But he could always wheedle himself back into her charms because, 'she loved him, and he loved her too.' He fully expected to be back in her home in the next few weeks as this was only temporary. She always forgave him in the end.

Wow this sounds like a Walt Disney story, if ever I heard one... yes siree a romantic love affair... sniff sniff!

He asked about Keith, Mac, and Birdie? Bobby wasn't completely sure, but he thought that Keith had moved to Australia and Mac had married a girl from down south, maybe Bristol. And Birdie lived in Helmshore which was a few miles away from Haslingden.

His fond memories of Birdie always seemed to include his sweet and kind mother. His mostly absent father like most men of his era were heavy drinkers and sometimes quite violent. Birdie, he remembered, probably because of his short stature, wasn't one to back down from a fight either. Being his friend meant always being on the ready for a scrap or two. He heard that he had also joined the Navy at fifteen probably for the similar reasons to himself.

The few pubs he visited in the old and decaying cotton weaving village of Helmshore told the same story that he almost expected; his reputation for drunkenness and fighting preceded him. He had been banned from most of the pubs but a familiar face from Dave's school days directed him to Birdie's latest drinking hole.

It was early evening when he found him quite sober sitting alone beside an open coal fire drinking his dark frothy beer. The pub was a small, converted weavers' cottage beside a tea coloured river.

They had greeted each other as old friends would and had a pleasant evening sharing stories and a few of the strong beers. It was no surprise that Birdie had a similar experience to himself in 'Her Majesty's Service'. He had also bought himself out and on returning home his wife had soon left him for another.

He noticed that Birdie had gained a few more scars on his face. The small room was eventually filled, and the music had gotten steadily louder. Some of the younger crowd where even attempting to dance. Birdies drink was knocked over sending him into an uncontrolled rage.

Although the few beers were certainly taking effect, he knew it was time to depart. As he had previously thought, it was obvious how the evening was more than probably going to end.

After a few similar altercations Dave made a feeble excuse to leave, much to Birdies' chagrin, making him feel like he was leaving his old friend to his own devices.

He visited Birdie a couple more times which all had similar outcomes. He felt sorry for how his old school chum's life had progressed leaving him in this loop of alcohol induced anger.

Chapter 20

Haslingden.

In the beginning, he felt that things were looking up and he seemed to be laying down some seeds to his new life. The country was just coming out of a major recession that had caused a lot of unemployment, especially in the industrial north.

Serving the many men and some women at the bar he was surprised that very few of them had regular employment. It seemed unemployment benefits or 'the dole' as it was mostly known in the north was the norm. It was sad to see that most of that benefit after food and rent was being spent at the pub. It was also a known fact that many people were doing side jobs to mostly finance their habit. There was a whole underground tax-free economy happening right under the local government's nose. Driving around the little town it was somewhat sad to see the lineup of men waiting outside the pubs and off license liquor outlets to open. It would inevitably be their first 'fix' of the day. He was determined not to end up in that queue.

Each day he scoured the local newspaper classified section looking for suitable work. Dave had been fortunate to find work delivering disassembled kitchen cabinets to private homes and some small stores. As an extra tax-free income, he would sometimes return after work to help some of the customers assemble the cabinets and even install them. He had purchased some basic tools secondhand that he left in the boot of his car. This wasn't going to be the vocation that he expected for the rest of his days but for now, until something better came along it would be adequate.

The extra input of cash had thankfully come before his savings had run out. He had been able to have his car serviced and purchase some new clothes. His room at the pub wasn't much, but for now it sufficed. John had become a good friend and the free board for working the bar was also a benefit.

The pub he found had other fringe benefits; women of all ages would often flirt with him and surreptitiously follow him to his room for sex. One of them called him a 'lone wolf' which she said was a big turn on. John didn't seem to mind, if it was done unobtrusively and that the female had left the building before morning.

He had begun to smoke again, probably because of the bar but to make up for it he had also started jogging. His favorite route took him around the beautiful reservoirs over the Grane, it helped him to stay fit and the memories it brought back seemed to ground him. His drinking had also become quite heavy at times. Living and working in the pub had a lot to do with it. In the navy at sea there were rules as to how much booze one was allowed... legitimately. After the centuries old free tot of rum at lunchtime had stopped in nineteen seventy, men were allowed three cans of beer per day. On some strict ships they would even have you pull the tabs on all three to stop men hoarding beer. It was difficult for anyone to become addicted under those circumstances. Being in a shore base was a whole different story though. He had witnessed a lot of his shipmates going through cold turkey after the ship left Harbour. He had always thought of himself as being a binge drinker, one nasty hangover would usually put him off for a while, negating becoming a typical addict. But it was now becoming the norm to sneak a quick scotch behind the bar or a half pint when the urge hit him, and he couldn't remember a single day when he hadn't had a drink.

As the many months passed, he was also slowly beginning to realize that he just didn't fit in. He wanted so much, in a lot of ways, to blend in with the fun crowd. But the conversations were shallow and uninteresting; the main topic between men at the bar was how the local football or cricket match had progressed, of which he had absolutely no interest. In the rare occurrence of a different conversation that was more to his interest about the world outside Haslingden, he gave his opinion based on his experience. The bar occupants would immediately fall silent, and he would hear whispers, *who the fuck does he a think he is... fuckin' know it all.*

I'll tell you who I am, you ignorant pig. I was there in the Suez helping the CDs clear the god damn mines. And that my friend is no fairy story like the one you just made up! ... Wanker!

In the last year he had dated more than just a one-night stand, but few had lasted no more than a couple of weeks. That was until he met Shauna, she had lasted for over four months. At twenty-one she was two years younger than him. Recently divorced and she also had a baby girl. It was kind of uncanny even though she had auburn hair and comparable dark eyes to Annie, those were the only similarities.

Playing the field, as it were, since he had arrived, had been fun and more to the point easy because of not having to make any commitments. Dave had met Shauna and she was becoming quite serious and had even confessed her love for him. Sex with her was wonderful and although he had played with the idea of taking their relationship further there was still something holding him back. In a lot of ways, she was the perfect woman. But the thoughts he once had of settling down and starting his own family just didn't seem as rosy anymore. The more the relationship evolved the more nervous he became. How could he now release himself from this without hurting her.

He half expected that everything in his hometown, to seem smaller from his youth but it was also looking run down. The once majestic old buildings in the center of town from a different and more prosperous past were now looking dilapidated and shabby. The heyday of the many cotton factories and other industry bringing in laborers from as far away as Ireland and Scotland had ended, acerbated by the current recession. Many old streets like the one he had lived in, with their blackened stone caused by the soot from the many smokestacks, were now boarded up waiting for demolition. It would inevitably rebound as it always did, mainly because northern people were resolute and used to hardship.

In truth, he was becoming bored and somewhat missed looking forward to some new port or excitement on the horizon. All those original ideas of settling down with a wife and kids were slowly becoming a nightmare. Although the Navy at the end felt like a prison sentence, there was always something to look forward to. When he now looked at some of the regulars at the bar drinking the same beer and reciting the same stories, then staggering off to their same home, it made him shake with fear.

What seemed to him to be the sad turning point that tipped the scales had come when reading the local newspaper one morning; Bobby had been found in a house on Rudd Street just around the corner from the pub. He had hung himself.

There you go, open disaster... wherever you tread... yes siree... a friggin walking Jonah.

Dave felt guilty for not being there for his old school chum. He had bumped into him here and there, usually with a pint in his hand. **Bobby's** party trick was to conveniently disappear when it was his round to buy the beer. During his more sober moments he mentioned that he was now working again, and his girlfriend had taken him back. He hadn't slept in the grungy caravan in months. Dave hated to think what condition it might be in. His minimal fond memories of his childhood always included the 'happy go lucky' Bobby and the three other pals in the gang, Keith, Mac and Birdie. They all shared the bond of coming from broken homes and the poverty that inevitably came with it.

What is wrong with me? I have everything I dreamed of having. My drinks and lodgings are pretty much free, I have a beautiful doting and sexy girlfriend waiting in the sidelines to marry and bear the kids I always wanted. You are one stupid fucker! Yes siree... you're gonna fuck it up... I'm in this little brain of yours and its growing cobwebs, shit or get off the pot... OK then, just get the fuck out! Before it's too late.

Chapter 21

Escape.

He had driven to Manchester to visit the merchant navy recruitment office. The few uninspiring papers that he had from his eight years in the Royal Navy still seemed to impress the well-dressed businessman.

"Well sir, this is just what we're looking for, I think you'll fit in very well, many of our men are ex-Royal Navy like yourself. When can you start, I'm sure you would need to get your existing responsibilities in order?"

"Nope, I can start tomorrow, how's that?" Dave quipped smiling.

The man smiled thinking it was a joke.

"No, I'm serious give me your next ship, I'm outa here. It's all sorted with my landlord," he lied.

"Well, we will have to do a quick police check and we do have a container ship leaving Liverpool with an opening in three days on the understating that you get the 'all clear.' It has a regular run to Amsterdam if you're interested?"

He gave Dave all the relevant information and who to report to at the Liverpool docks.

John was disappointed, especially since it was at such short notice. Dave explained the situation. He couldn't possibly stay in the same town after leaving Shauna. There were only two choices, he explained: stay and be married and always have some regrets or leave and start with a new slate.

"So, when are you leaving Dave. I need to sort something out for the weekend."

"John, I'm going to see Shauna now and explain, then I'll be leaving right away. I'll find accommodation in Liverpool until I board the ship. I'll be back within the hour," Dave explained sorrowfully.

John seemed to understand his decision and had admitted that he should have done something similar many years ago.

Shauna was a different story, that he was dreading. She met him at the door.

"Oh, I thought we were going out for dinner on Thursday. Come on in, there's a good program on the telly in a minute, Becky is in bed already. Can I make you a cup of tea?" she asked with an expression on her face knowing there was something wrong based on Dave's solemn frown.

"Shauna, you need to sit down, I have something to explain."

"What is it Dave, are you OK? you look like you have something dreadful to tell me."

"Yes, I'm afraid so," he could feel his body trembling. How was she going to take this?

"Shauna... I'm all messed up. I've told you some of the stories from my past. I thought I could be the person you want me to be but eventually I know that I will let you down, and *you* don't deserve that. You are a beautiful and caring lady; you'll undoubtably meet someone that will be more worthy of your love. Unfortunately, I'm not that man," Dave explained feeling like a low-down dog as she began to cry.

In between her deep sobs she said, "Dave, I love you, whatever this big problem is, surely, we can work it out. I'm willing to wait; you can't just leave me like this."

He had to be strong and could not allow her sadness and tears to sway his decision. He had once been in her position remembering how Annie had once made him feel. He could never lower his guard again to feel that pain, which was plain to see he was now inflicting. He had to remove himself as the sadness welled up, tears were simply not an option as he stood to leave.

She was crouched over in her chair openly sobbing into her hands when he leaned over to kiss the top of her head like his mother had once done.

"Goodbye Shauna," he said as he opened the door to leave.

Driving back to the pub he knew he had to do this quick and not give himself a chance to be weak.

John was behind the bar serving drinks when he entered the pub. "John give me a large scotch please," he asked, then downed it in one.

"You OK Dave? you look like you've seen a ghost," John said with concern.

"John, my holdall is packed and ready to go in the back of my car. I'm leaving now," as he reached across the bar to shake John's hand.

"Do you have to leave right away, we could have a wine evening later, what do you say? Best to leave fresh in the morning," John said now looking very concerned.

"John you've been my rock this last year, I couldn't have hoped for a better friend. You welcomed me into your home and even gave me a job. More importantly you gave me hope that there are still good people in this world. I will forever be in your debt my friend." He let go of Johns hand and walked toward the back door where his car was parked. John left the bar unattended and followed him.

"Dave, I'm going to miss you, you had better stay in touch, eh?" He shouted as Dave closed the door to his car.

As he drove away, he could see that John was openly weeping. He would never see Haslingden or John again and he never stayed in touch.

Was a place called home

Sometimes I hear, a whisper... in my ears

Though it's been so many years

And through a sea of many tears

Was a place called home

Photo's yellowing with age

Faces rising from the page

Was a place called home

Water... passing under bridges of time

Those memories – all mine

Through rose colored glasses... sublime

Those memories, was it such a crime

Through blackened walls and secrets in the mold

Holds stories never told

Of a lifetime to unfold

It was a place called home

Belonging and ready to forgive

Family never to deceive

there was a place called home

Water - passing under bridges of time

Those memories – all mine

Through rose colored glasses – sublime

was it such a crime

Those memories– was it such a crime

Kevin Firth 27 April 2019

Chapter 22

Merchant navy.

This was very different from what he had been used to in the Royal; he had his own small but comfortable cabin, the showers and bathroom he shared with the few other men. The Skipper didn't have the la di da accent of the Officers he had known in the Royal. But he made it abundantly clear that he was in charge and the men respected him for it.

The ship was a medium sized container ship. It had been fully loaded when he first arrived onboard, and it would be sailing the following day. The junior Officer had shown him around and seemed pleased that Dave was quite familiar with his deck duties as an Ordinary seaman. He helped with the mooring lines when the ship left the wall and was given instruction via a walkie talkie as the tugboats helped to steer the ship out of the busy harbor. Once at sea, he took a turn on the steering controls on the bridge and made it obvious that he knew his way around. The entry into the harbor in Amsterdam and subsequent unloading and loading of the many containers was also straight forward. He felt very confident in what his duties were and had impressed the First

Officer and the Skipper to the point that he was promoted on the next voyage to Amsterdam to an Able Seaman.

For the remainder of his first year, it had been suggested that he take some courses where he could be promoted up the ladder. The back and forth to the same cities had become repetitive and the money was marginally better. Inasmuch as he felt that he had landed on his feet with the work, it wasn't enough, and he didn't feel that the investment in time and money to attend these courses was what he really wanted. Again, he found himself treading water, as it where, until something better came along.

In his second year he had asked for a change and was given an oil tanker that would be transporting oil from the offshore platforms via an SBM* to the onshore refinery in Scotland. This seemed to keep his interest.

SBM* Single Buoy Mooring. Oil is sent to these structures from the offshore platform so that tankers can connect to fill then transport to shore.

Aberdeen had very quickly become a gold rush town with all the commerce from the oil and gas bonanza being found offshore. He had rented a small flat which would be his temporary home in between the many excursions at sea.

He had made a few friends and would take in many fun evenings in the busy bars and nightclubs. Women from all over Scotland and even England would flock to Aberdeen looking for the men with their overstuffed wallets. This was the complete opposite from what he had found in the navy, where most women stayed clear of the men from the sea.

He had dated a few women but when the relationship started to become serious, he would make it clear his lack of interest in that department. Some, who were of the same mind, had become friends and would share a meal or a quiet sociable evening. It had become abundantly clear, the more he thought about it, that he would probably end his days alone. He just could not imagine being out of control and going through that amount of pain again. He was reasonably happy with his life; it hadn't turned out that bad. Most men would be happy with the life he now led.

The ship had just completed several runs in the Norwegian sector to a refinery in Stavanger and had returned to Scotland for some minor repairs. The crew had been allowed some time off. He visited one of his favorite bars which was popular for the oil patch men. He had a few friends that he would sometimes bump into, some were ex-Navy like himself. He had arrived late in the afternoon for a couple of Scotch Whiskeys before meeting up with one of his female friends that he would be taking out for dinner. He saw a familiar face further up from where he was sitting at the bar, it was one of the CDs he had worked with in the Suez.

"Wanger fuckin' Woon how the hell are ya?" He called up the bar.

"Well, I'll be fucked, Swiffy, what are you doing here?"

"I work on one of the oil tankers, how 'bout you?" Dave asked, shaking his hand.

"Oh, I got myself a job workin' on one of those oil rigs as a diver. It's a fuckin' good number mate and pays well."

"Jeez isn't that a dangerous job, it's always on TV that some poor fucker has 'bit the bullet'. It was only last week they lost a diving bell. By the time they got a rescue ship with a diving bell they were both dead, hyperthermia I heard. It got major publicity, and they said parliament was going to be setting some new rules." Dave exclaimed.

"Yea that was a sad one mate, I didn't know any of the lads, but the buzz is that it was a fucked-up bell wire: bad splice in the bell lift coupling. They then tried to pick it up with the umbilical, stupid idiots because that broke and lost them comms, hot water, and gas, the fuckin' lot. They should be fuckin' hung for allowing that to happen. Now there's one dive supervisor that ain't gonna be finding work anytime soon."

Dave remembered Wanger as one of the many colorful characters he had met in the diving team. His nickname came from the fact that he had a rather large dick or 'wanger' in his case. He would boast of his many sexual encounters with the opposite sex and would also like to walk around the mess after a shower or before going to bed naked flaunting his big rubbery dick around.

For fuck's sake put that thing away before you do someone a mischief.

"Hey, some of the lads on the team are here too that you'll know. 'Tug' Wilson, 'Creature' Foote and 'Biscuit' McVittie. Biscuit has done well; he's been here for over two years and is now a dive supervisor. A whole bunch of other ex-Navy lads too, but you might not know them."

"The team was working in Gus (Plymouth); a trawler had snagged a wartime bomb. Anyways after the job we all went to the pub and were drinkin' that Scrumpy cider shit. A yank came into the pub that we were in. He told us how much money we could be making offshore and guaranteed us jobs. Most of us immediately put in to buy out the navy and were accepted. You should come onboard mate."

"Well, I was only a Ships Diver, you were the ones using the rebreather mixed gas sets. I was just on air," Dave answered.

"No-no-no, mate that doesn't matter. Lots of ex-navy ships divers work for the company, one of them is even a top manager. You would have no problem, they're always looking for people, especially ex-Navy divers. It's an American dive company but most of the people in the office are Brits. Friggin good money; we gets eleven hundred dollars a month and that's only working for two weeks because then we gets two weeks off. And just to add the icing on the fuckin' cake, 'if' we do have to commit to a bottom dive then we get paid an additional eleven dollars an hour for the total time we are under pressure. Which for a bounce dive of say an hour or so on bottom at three hundred feet for example using the US Navy sat tables would generally get you, up to thirty-six hours in the decompression chamber. Often the dive would be longer, say over four hours then you're into saturation which would take three days of decompression. So, when you're asleep dreaming of all those lovely dollars... guess what? you're still making eleven bucks an hour, cool huh?"

"Well how much is that in English," Dave interrupted.

"The exchange rate right now will net you about six hundred pounds." Wanger said grinning.

That's three hundred pounds a week, that sure beats my measly twenty-six a week... yes siree... better check this out.

"Yea, but what about the danger? They can pay you all they want but it ain't worth tuppence if you end up being fish food." Dave said.

"That's a joke mate; I've been on the rig for six months and we've dived only once to the bottom at three hundred feet. And that was the two lads that had been on the rig the longest. It's basically first come first serve. I've done two exercise bell diver rescue dives at seventy feet on air."

"On the rig the food is top class, you can have sirloin steak for breakfast if you want. Unless we're working on the dive system, we're usually playing cards and sleeping. I tell you, its fuckin' money for old rope. As far as safety goes, the company has a clean record, barring a few minor bends and that was because of a bad supervisor, they haven't lost a diver yet. They are always looking for experienced divers because of their clean record, they are picking up many offshore contracts from the major oil companies."

"Wanger, it sounds too good to be true mate, but it's certainly food for thought."

"OK no prob mate, listen I'm waiting for a chopper to take me out to the rig tomorrow. The weather doesn't look too rosy, I doubt it'll be flying. If you want, I can meet you here tomorrow and take you out to the office and give you the intro. To be honest, I'd rather have you on the team than some of the plebs they send out. I'll even get Biscuit to vouch for you, as he's a big wheel now."

He went back to his flat as soon as dinner was over, disappointing his lady friend. His mind was full of mixed thoughts. Was this what he had been waiting for, he had done danger before so why should he stop now? Like everything else he had done, it was at least worth a try. If the whole thing proved to be insane, well he still had a job to return to.

Chapter 23

Deep sea diver.

The interview had progressed very well, not only had Wanger vouched for him, but Biscuit had also been contacted, who was out on a different oil rig job that also spoke highly of him. The manager handed the phone to Dave as Biscuit had asked.

"Hey Swiffy, how are you? It's been while, eh?" Biscuit asked cheerfully.

"Oh' ya know, I'm still at sea, she's a hard mistress. I hope they're not going to expect me to dive right away, I'm a bit rusty and from what Wanger has told me, this deep mixed gas diving stuff sounds quite complicated."

"Don't worry about that mate, I'll speak to Jock the supervisor out there. He's a good man and will put you through the paces. Ask Martin in the office to give you a US Navy dive manual. You'll have lots of time to read through it. Don't be afraid to ask questions and learn the inside of the bell to the point you know where everything is with your eyes closed. In this business, the more you know the longer you live. OK ol' mate hope to meet up with you soon. Now pass the phone back to Martin," Biscuit asked sounding very professional.

He had joked with the older British offshore manager who had also been a navy Ships diver many years ago. He was immediately hired and introduced to the American in charge of operations. When asked if he was ready to go out to the same rig as the one Wanger manned, he readily accepted. He later telephoned the ship office and asked for extended leave because of an emergency. It didn't make sense to burn his bridges in case this, hard to believe scenario, fell apart.

The following morning, he had donned a survival suit and was in a helicopter with Wanger and eight other men heading out to the oil rig. In the two-hour flight he read through the first few pages of the manual. This was all heady stuff and very exciting, especially when the chopper landed on the huge floating oil rig far offshore in the familiar North Sea.

He felt a bit awe struck when Wanger took him out to the substantial and complicated dive system to meet Jock in the dive control room (dive shack). He had already learned that Jock had been one of the original Mk 5 brass hard hat divers (6) who worked in many of the dockyards in Scotland.

"Och now laddie is there any chance you know anything 'bout 'lectricks. Ave got a wee problem wi arr hot water machine oer therrr." As he pointed to a stainless-steel covered machine across the deck.

"Sorry, no sir but if you have some manuals I can learn," Dave nervously answered.

"Firrst off ye dinne need to call me sir. They call me Jock... that'll do, call me Jockey an ye'll get me boot up yer arse," he said smiling.

Wanger and two of the other divers were laughing, standing behind Jock in the very complicated dive shack. "An' whatever you do Swiffy don't call him short arse as well cos he fuckin' hates that."

Jock was a feisty looking fit, ginger haired man and even though he lacked a little in the height department, he didn't look like someone you would want to get on the bad side of.

"Oh, verry funny Wanger, well I've got a nice wee job for you today, cleaning the toilet in the transfer chamber. You can take Dave here and show him the inside of the chambers and while you're at it disinfect the whole inside wi that special chamber cleaner."

At that moment they heard a loud wolf howl at the doorway as a tall man with curly hair and long dangling arms entered. He came up behind Jock and commenced licking the top of his head.

"Git tae fuck Creature I told yu to stop doing that. Next time yu'll git a fuckin' knee in the bollocks." Jock yelled.

Dave remembered the very colorful and extremely funny 'Creature Foote' that he had met in the Suez. If you didn't know any better at first meeting, you would have thought he was ready for the loony bin. He had told Dave once in confidence that he wasn't just any old dog, no, he was a pure bred Austrian Ribber Hound. It was common to pee over the side of a ship or in this case an oil rig. Creature would cock his leg up like a dog to pee over the side causing many strange glances from other ship mates. To gain your attention on deck he would bark at you. It was common to find a meat bone on the pillow of his bed.

When he first saw Dave, he scampered over to the side of the dive shack toward him pushing Jock and the others away and pinned him to the wall. He was licking his forehead and saying, "us dogs missed Swiffy, can you take us for walkies," as he sniffed his shoulders.

"Yes, Dave has missed his dog too," Dave replied laughing.

Biscuit had once told him that Creature had indeed come from a very well to do upper class family. It was much to their dismay that he had joined the RN as a Clearance Diver and later became a bomb disposal expert. His real name was Neville Bartholomew Foote. The surname had links to royalty. He was a very intelligent man and usually the first one to volunteer for any dangerous task. He would later become the deepest diver for the company with a record deep working dive of over eight hundred feet done off the oil fields in Brazil.

Ian, an ex-Army diver was the assistant supervisor and the other diver, 'Don,' was another ex-dockyard hard hat diver making up a total crew of six.

Right from the very beginning he felt that this was what he was meant to be doing. He just had to get over the first hurdle of learning how all this worked. The thought of being committed to a dive before he was ready gave him the creeps. Don, the other diver he learned had even less experience than he did, this was his second trip offshore.

The routine on the rig for the diving crew was very lax and he felt some resentment particularly from the rig management. The big chief of operations seemed to be the tool pusher in charge of drilling. The driller on the drill floor had the responsibility of the roughnecks, a crazy job much more dangerous than any diving job. Then there were the roustabouts, who were basically deck crew loading and unloading containers from the various supply vessels. They also had a support vessel that continually circled the rig in case of an emergency or a rig evacuation. Under him was the 'company man' who was the link to the oil company in this case British Petroleum who had hired the rig to do the exploratory drilling. Then there was the captain of the vessel in charge of the ballast control personnel, anchorage and moving the floating oil rig to future drilling sites. Most of the personnel were on continual twelve-hour shifts. In comparison, the divers struggled to get out of bed by ten in the morning. Complete a few hours on the system... if needed, then sample the five-star meals every six hours of the day and night and watch movies. It was tough going!

A typical oil rig in the seventies cost the oil companies over one hundred thousand dollars a day. Much of the complicated BOP or Blow Out Preventer equipment lay on the seabed, in this case at just over three hundred feet. Four compensated guide wires attached to the BOP which guided tools and hydraulic lines to operate the system. In case of a blowback of oil or gas it was imperative that this could be closed in an emergency. If this failed, not only would there be a massive spill but the gas bubbles rising to the surface would aerate the water and the massive floating oil rig would sink like a stone. This had happened in various places in the world. Also, the telescoping riser pipe connecting the rig drill floor to the BOP that the drilling collars ran through would also need to be disconnected. All this equipment was controlled hydraulically. BUT if one of those simple one-hundred-dollar hoses were to be damaged what ya gonna do?

Call ghost busters?

To obtain insurance to drill offshore from a floating semi-submersible rig, they had to have a team of divers onboard for those issues that needed hands on or even to simply hold a handheld video camera on the bottom.

Dave was determined to learn everything he could, not only about deep-sea diving but about the complicated diving system. He remembered the advice that Biscuit had given him.

He could already see why some of the disastrous diving accidents had happened. How would he fare if he was asked to do a dive today? He didn't even know how to wear one of the strange looking masks and hot water suits. He had a general idea of how the mixed gas system worked. The typical SABA set in the Navy was very similar to the civilian SCUBA amateur set. It comprised of two air bottles; only one of the bottles was used, when it was seen to go below a certain pressure by a gauge the diver would pull a lever which allowed the full bottle to cascade into the partially empty one. On the second equalization it was time to surface. If there were any in water decompression stops to be made the diver had to ensure there would be enough air to complete the dive. Generally, an experienced diver controlling his breathing could last approximately an hour at thirty feet.

The navy had also given him some very basic instruction on the SDDE* system. The SDDE diver had a smaller bail out bottle used only for emergency; his main supply of air would be from the surface via an umbilical hose. In this manner, the diver could stay in the water much longer so depths and bottom time could be extended.

SDDE* Surface Demand Diving Equipment.

In the navy he had completed a few dives at one hundred and twenty feet and had experienced a slight narcotic effect and compression or suit squeeze as he had not utilized his suit inflation bottle. Atmospheric air pressure is roughly fifteen pounds per square inch. Every thirty feet depth of water the pressure doubles. Therefore, to counteract four times the pressure than on the surface at one hundred and twenty feet the diver had to be breathing four times the volume of air than on the surface. As air is twenty percent oxygen(O_2) and Nitrogen(N_0) the remainder minus a few trace gases the diver would now be breathing the equivalent volume of eighty percent O_2.

Nitrogen is an inert gas but breathing the equivalent volume would be roughly three hundred and twenty percent. At these volumes and more, the average diver begins to feel the narcotic effect of that nitrogen. The slang name for this that was probably first introduced by the famous Jacques Cousteau, 'the raptures of the deep' or 'the narcs.' The official term was Nitrogen Narcosis.

To counter the exposure to the narcs, the diver could breathe a higher percentage of oxygen in the supplied mix thereby lowering the percentage of nitrogen. Which also helped with decompression. The bends that most people have heard about are bringing the diver too quickly to the surface and not allowing enough time for the nitrogen to gas out. A good example of this is opening a pop bottle quickly, not allowing enough time for it to remain in its liquid form. However, now you have another situation at greater depths as the diver could be breathing the equivalent oxygen level of two hundred percent or higher. At those partial pressures oxygen then becomes poisonous with horrible convulsive side effects.

What are we gonna do now?

The answer was of course to change the mix removing those nasty euphoric effects of nitrogen (damn it). Helium is also an inert gas which seemed a good choice except for the Donald duck voice side effect and lowering the oxygen percentage in the mix to give the diver the equivalent percentage on the surface of one hundred percent.

As an example, to send our diver to three hundred feet and have him sane enough to complete meaningful work, How about we get sneaky and give him a mix of ten percent oxygen and the rest good ol' helium?

Works for me! Yes siree... You too damn shmart!

Only ten percent oxygen on the surface would be quite dangerous; therefore, when pressurizing the diver to three hundred feet on the ten percent mix it is done relatively quickly. As an example, in the diving bell on bottom the supervisor would give a countdown much like in the space program. At zero he sets the clock to register the beginning of total bottom time to use the correct decompression schedule needed to safely return the diver to the surface.

Move over Buzz Aldrin.

The bellman would control the speed by opening the blow down valve in the bell usually at fifty to a hundred feet per minute. Once the pressure inside the bell is equalized to the outside pressure, the bottom door would open by its own weight. It would generally be quite warm with the added pressure but would cool off very quickly to the surrounding sea water temperature. Another side effect of helium, probably because it is such a light gas, is that the human temperature control system ceases to be as effective. A slight drop in temperature can feel very uncomfortable. An outside source of heat is imperative to counter the onset of hypothermia.

Dave would rise before the rest of the crew and have a quick breakfast then don his overalls, work boots and safety helmet and head out to the system with his manual. He remembered seeing the tube-shaped emergency decompression chambers in the Navy. He was very fortunate to have never used one. He had witnessed one of the CDs having received a hit (bend) as he hadn't adhered to the correct time at his last in water stop. He was slid into the narrow tube on his back via a stretcher. There was a six-inch port to see his face as he laid in position. When he was surfaced hours later looking quite relieved, he had explained that it had felt like a hot knife in his elbow. Looking at this massive structure there was little in comparison. There were two vertical chambers probably ten feet in diameter and ten feet high. Looking through the small circular ports there were two small bunk beds in each. The two chambers connected to the bell transfer chamber in the center, this was a sphere-shaped chamber of around eight feet. Above the transfer chamber was the ominous and complicated looking sphere-shaped diving bell. On each of the living chambers there were heavy circular hinged door entrance hatchways. Wanger had given him a tour of the system. Climbing up a metal ladderway from inside the transfer chamber up into the bell had given him a bit of a jitter which he was trying not to show. They had both sat facing each other on the small fold down seats. The bell had looked a lot bigger from the outside. Wanger's face was just over a foot away from his face. Behind each of them were the two, one hundred-and twenty-foot umbilical hoses. Wanger had given him a quick rundown on the many valve's, gauges, and strange looking devices. There was a clear plastic covering over the bell check list with a colored pencil attached with a piece of string.

He now sat inside the bell alone wondering if he would have the balls to be in this small cramped, bubble at the bottom at three hundred feet in the fierce North Sea. He had read through some of the diving manual decompression tables. A short dive of say a couple of hours on bottom would still warrant a three-day decompression. He tried to visualize a dive that the crew had mentioned the previous evening when he had asked. The bell would be detached from the system and winched over to be above the moon pool door where the bell stage was kept. The bell would be moved via an above rail system, lowered, and attached onto the stage. Two fully dressed-in divers would climb into the bell and close the bottom door. The bell and lower stage would be lifted to allow the moon pool door to slide open on a similar rail system. The bell would then be lowered through the floor of the deck to the sea eighty or so feet below. Once the bell entered the interface (sea) the bottom door would seal as the pressure increased. The bell would then be lowered to three hundred feet where the sea water pressure would be one hundred and fifty pounds per square inch (ten atmospheres). There would be literally tons of pressure keeping the door closed. One of the divers would set himself up to dive by attaching the hot water hose from his umbilical to his hot water suit. He would don his Kirby Morgan full face breathing mask that was attached to a neoprene hood. The bell man would then blow down the bell (pressurize) with the helium, oxygen mix, supplied from dive shack via the bell main umbilical. Once the inside pressure reached the same as the outside, the bell bottom door would swing open, (having previously undogged the two clips). The diver would after doing a final comms check turn the hot water on to his suit and exit the bell. Depending on what the task was at hand he would be committed up to three days of decompression. He had even heard stories of being in for a month if the job required additional dives. Either way there would still be the same three-day decompression to be accomplished prior to surfacing the chambers. At the end of the dive with both divers now inside the bell, the bottom and inside door of the bell would be closed and the inside top door sealed by adding more pressure via the blow down valve. Once sealed the bell could now be raised and attached to the dive system on deck that had been previously pressurized to the same as the inside of the bell. The bell would then be returned to the system for decompression or would even remain under pressure for numerous future bell dives. The bell would be attached to the system transfer chamber with a large clamp or in this case stainless steel bolts. The top door of the transfer chamber would be closed from the pressure inside the chamber. So, the only remaining drill would be to now equalize the pressures in the transfer trunk allowing the divers to open their top door in the bell and climb down the trunk undoing the dogs on the transfer hatchway. With the whole system now pressure equalized, they could now climb down to enter the transfer chamber where there was a shower and toilet facility. Once cleaned they could climb through the hatchway into one of the vertical living chambers. Once there they could dress in regular clothing and pass out all the wet suits and clothing through a medical lock system to the outside. Food and dry clothing could also be passed back into the system ready for future dives or to slowly decompress adhering to the correct dive table for that depth and time at depth.

In the first few days, the thought that he had bitten off more than he could chew, was front and center. How could he conveniently ask to be returned to shore? Fortunately, the thought of doing that and cowardly walking away was just too foreign to the way he had lived his life so far. No, he would at least hold out for the two weeks and see how he felt then. It was the comradery and being included in this crew of characters that had given him confidence. There was so much to learn, in fact as the week wore on, he realized that diving was secondary to the tasks he had to learn on deck. He had picked up a little bit of electrical experience strangely when he had been installing cabinets. Re-routing electrical switches in kitchens and wiring under cabinet lighting. This was of course the English two-twenty-volt system. He was now being asked to work on the US one-ten-volt system. No one else on the crew seemed remotely interested in fixing the hot water machine. Jock had given him a manual and he had spent a couple of days studying and taking apart some electrical boxes. He had found a loose wire and re-attached it fixing the machine impressing Jock.

"You know Swiffy they can teach a trained monkey how to dive. It's what you do when yerrr down tharr that matters. In my experience, I find if a guy is practical on deck, he won't let you down when the going gets tough. When I've got a diver on bottom and a dive shack full o' big wheels breathing down me neck, it makes all the difference to know the laddie can figure something out. Yer on yer own dune tharr. The whole fuckin' rig is on standby waiting for the laddie to fix wots wrong or at least cum up wi an intelligent suggestion," Jock had intimated to him one day.

He had learned that this dive system had been one of the first in the North Sea so there was always something to fix. In his second week he was helping Ian to weld. Ian had shown him how to get around the rig welder to borrow a long welding wire from his shack to the diving system.

There was so much to learn that had absolutely nothing to do with diving. The two weeks had gone by extremely fast. It was all incredibly interesting, and he was feeling like a beneficial part of the crew.

Flying back to shore with Wanger was such a relief and most of his initial fear was a thing of the past. He was warmed by the feeling of achievement. Receiving his first payment he hit the town to celebrate.

Is this what he had been waiting for? He always felt that eventually something would come along. This seemed tailor-made; it had just the right amount of fear to overcome, and he was being paid accordingly. The money was just the icing on top of the cake.

He was a little nervous having his first diving medical, it had been extensive, but he had come through with no issues. This, he was told, would be an annual examination.

The call to the shipping company had gone well and he felt that he had not burnt his bridges. He would be welcomed back if he so desired.

Chapter 24

First dives.

On his third trip out to the rig he would be tested. The rig had been moved to a new site and one of the many anchor chains had fouled, fortunately it had not stopped drilling operations. The Captain had asked the diving crew for help in freeing the chain. It was suspected that the chain had fallen inside the 'cow catcher' frame. This was a frame of heavy piping protecting the front of one of the two pontoons that the rig floated on. For safety's sake, the Captain wanted to resolve the issue in case of bad weather, when the chains could be tightened to hold the rig in position. Jock and Creature had given Dave instructions on wearing the mask and hot water suit. There would be a cage where the two divers would be lifted by the rig crane and lowered over the side above the fouled chain location. Dave suspected that this would be his first trial dive to prove to the rest of the crew that he was ready. A hot water hose had been extended from the machine to the corner of the rig. A quad of air bottles was crane lifted into position and Jock would supervise the dive through a remote dive panel and one of the dive shack radio helium unscrambler sets.

Once in the metal basket cage both himself and Wanger wore their band masks and were in voice contact with Jock. The hot water from their respective umbilical's were dumping via the control valve on the hip of their suits. The suit was a heavy neoprene material with small, holed rubber tubes running through the complete suit. One tube also led to the back of the neoprene hood and there were tubes also running into the separate booties.

After a final comms check the cage was lifted and carefully lowered over the side. Jock held a two-way radio transceiver to give instructions to the crane driver and wore a headset that was in contact with both divers. Dave was going to be the diver and Wanger would stay in the cage as standby. From the rigs main deck, the sea looked calm but as they were being lowered the swell seemed quite large. Should the swell hit the cage it could be smashed into the side of the rig's leg. Dave had them stop lowering at the approximate height than the largest swell. He threw out enough of his umbilical into the sea and timed the highest swell before jumping into the sea. He had previously put enough lead weights into each of the suits thigh pockets to be heavy not wanting to be wallowing around on the surface and risk being pushed into the leg. He had pushed the nose clearing device in the mask hard into his top lip knowing that he would be clearing his ears quickly as he dropped into safety. As he was sinking, he turned on the valve for the hot water to his suit and was immediately enveloped in warm water. He tried to hold his breath when talking or listening to Jock as the bubbles were quite loud from his heavy breathing. It had been a few years since his last dive, and he knew that Jock would be listening to his rapid breaths as he tried to control his breathing rate. This he knew were all the signs of a professional diver. He was more concerned of not fucking up than his own wellbeing.

Eventually at around thirty feet he saw the massive pontoon and the cowcatcher pipe. He swam closer to the leg and found the anchor chain.

"OK, Jock, I've found the chain and yes it has gone through the inside of the cowcatcher. Send me down the tugger (winch) wire which had been set up prior to the dive. He held onto the chain until he saw the tugger wire which had a six-foot eyed strop and a large shackle attached to the end. The heavy current and swell could be felt even at thirty feet which had pushed the wire away from the rig. He swam out and pulled the wire back to the chain. Within minutes he had found the snag where the chain had been caught and attached the shackle to the chain.

"OK, Jock, have them come up with the tugger," he asked.

It took them ten to fifteen minutes of pulling and loosening before the chain noisily let go crashing over the cowcatcher. He had stayed clear while all this was going on as he held on to a fitting on the pontoon. The whole operation had been relatively simple, but it was easy to see how it could have become dangerous seeing and hearing the heavy chain as it noisily sped over the cowcatcher. He was then able to have them loosen off the tugger wire so that he could now disconnect the shackle.

"OK Swiffy, stay clear we're goin tae drop the cage into the sea. Once yea see it let me know an we'll all stop. Dinne go close until I tell yea... over."

"Roger roger Jock... standing clear, you can drop it now," Dave answered sounding very professional.

It was easy to see the cage in the clear blue water as it was lowered to his depth. He waved at Wanger as he pulled up on his umbilical and coiled it into the bottom of the cage. Dave swam out and entered the cage then closed the metal door.

"OK Jock, all secure, you can come up with the cage... over."

"Roger roger Swiffy, coming up on the cage... hold tight it might be a bit bumpy coming up through the interface... over."

"Roger roger Jock... holding tight... over," Dave answered.

As the cage was lowered onto the deck, he could see Jock's smiling face which made him feel contented that his first commercial dive had gone well.

They both stepped out of the cage and removed their masks.

"Well done lads, the Captain is really pleased. I'm guessing one o' these roustabouts are gonna get a kick up the butt for allowing the chain to get caught in the first place. Go an git yersel changed lads a'll get the others tae clean up this lot."

Creature was busy coiling up the umbilicals with Don, but he looked up and gave Dave a wink and a thumbs up. Dave had confessed to Creature earlier that he was a bit nervous about using all this new equipment and didn't want to let down the diving crew in front of just about everyone on the rig. It was a relatively rare event to see the diving crew in action. Creature had said the definition of a rig diver is long months of absolute boredom punctuated with moments of sheer terror.

When he left the rig after that trip, he felt a little more confident and pleased with his decision because of the simple dive but still had reservations about an actual deep bell dive.

He had been with the company for over four months before he experienced the diving team in full action. One of the hydraulic hoses on the BOP had a suspected leak and rather than bringing everything to the surface that would cost them days they had asked for a dive.

Dave had felt very nervous thinking that this might be his time to show his true mettle. He had purposely spent many hours in the diving bell and had replaced both masks from their respective umbilical's more than once. Each valve, gauge, and instrument inside the bell he knew like the back of his hand. He had even chased back each hose and power line from the bell's main umbilical back to the dive shack. And had made himself a pain in the butt with Jock continually asking him every question until he knew how it all worked. The US Diving manual had been read through many times becoming his bible. But the thought of being at three hundred feet having been committed after blowing down to depth, would he have the balls to lock out of the bell to do meaningful work. Then there would be the lengthy decompression that could take days.

He felt much guilty relief when Jock had chosen Creature and Wanger to do the dive. Creature had done a deep dive with the company, but it would be Wangers first ever deep bell dive. Wanger was going to be the diver and Creature would be the standby diver and bellman.

Dave could feel Wanger's nervousness as he climbed up into the bell that was now attached to the bell stage. Dave helped the divers inside to close and dog the bottom door of the bell. It was two o' clock in the morning before the rig gave the go ahead to commence the dive. It had been a long day of getting everything prepared, which had been a small blessing considering everything they had to do.

One of the chambers and the transfer lock had been blown down with the heliox gas to match the bottom depth. The mix inside the chambers had been checked with the special sensor gauges in the dive shack for the corresponding percentage to match the bell mix. The hot water machine would now be heating the chambers as well as the two divers below. The carbon dioxide (CO_2) levels were closely observed with sensor probes in the bell and the chambers. Both the chamber and the bell had CO_2 scrubbers which were basically twelve-volt fans that removed the poisonous CO_2 using a granular chemical called sodasorb. This chemical powder would have to be replaced, based on the levels shown on the sensor gauges. The diving bell had two spare cannisters.

As soon as they got the order, the bell and attached stage were lifted with the bell winch. The deck moonpool door was slid open.

Dave had to lower a forty-five-gallon drum of set concrete as an anchor via a deck winch to the seabed. The bell had a short pennant wire that had previously been shackled to slide on the anchor wire, this would stop the bell from dangerously swinging back and forth like a pendulum between the rig deck and the sea eighty or so feet below. Once the wire slacked, Dave waved at Ian who was on the bell winch controls. Ian relayed the message via his headset to Jock in the busy dive shack that was now full of rig management. The bell commenced to be lowered pulling with it the bell umbilical through a large pulley wheel. The moonpool door was then closed enough to allow Dave and Don to attach the umbilical to the bell lift wire every fifty feet. Dave then waved at Ian that the bell was entering the sea so that he could increase the speed thus not allowing the sea swell to swing the bell. Inside the bell the bellman would be instructing Jock that they had a seal on the bottom door before the lowering could be continued.

Inside the bell the bellman would be instructing Jock every fifty feet from their outside gauge viewed through one of the ports. Jock would have a similar gauge inside the shack to confirm depth. Eventually the lowering stopped. The bellman had seen the BOP from one of the ports in the bell and had stopped the lowering roughly twenty feet off the seabed. Ian gave Dave and Don the thumbs up denoting the bell was in position. Dave headed over to the busy dive shack and could barely see Jock over the heads of the tool pusher and the rig manager. They were going over the final bell checks before blowing down. Jock had his hand on the bell gas quarter turn supply valve. The bellman could control the speed of blowdown but if it was seen to be going too fast Jock could close the supply valve. They did the countdown and blowdown commenced. The noise of the blowdown could be heard on the radio even where he was standing. Dave was going through the procedure in his head that he had been shown and read more than once. He was trying to imagine how Wanger was feeling knowing in a few minutes he would be out and attempting to find and fix the hydraulic leak as quickly as possible so as not go into saturation*.

Saturation* Once the dissolved gases in a diver's tissues reach the saturation point, decompression time does not increase with further exposure, as no more inert gas is accumulated. Up to that point much shorter bounce diving decompression tables can be used.

Not only did the divers have to know this complicated dive system but they also had to be knowledgeable about all the rigs equipment on the seabed. He guessed that having a diver on bottom cost the oil company extra, so time was of the essence.

The noise of the blow down stopped as he heard a Donald duck voice mumble something undecipherable. Jock had the radio on speaker so that the rig bosses could hear. Jock turned the dial on the helium unscrambler as the diver was talking which brought the high pitch lower and slightly more understandable. Nobody seemed to know what the diver was saying except Jock. Eventually he guessed that Wanger had exited the bell as he could hear the familiar hissing and bubbling.

The BOP had color coded valves and lines and each of the guide wires that were connected to the four corner posts were numbered. There was also a remote video camera and light mounted on a frame attached to two of the guide wire posts. There was a small monitor screen that had been placed above the radio in the dive shack showing part of the BOP below. The tool pusher was giving directions via Jock to the diver as to where he thought the problem was. A few times Wanger had swam across the camera's view. Dave couldn't help but admire Wanger for his professionalism and guts. Outside the dive shack it was a pitch black and cold night, and the wind was picking up. On bottom, at just over three hundred feet in the inky black sea, Wanger was completing what he was being paid big bucks to do. Time was ticking on but eventually Wanger had found the leak that he had managed to fix with a crescent wrench from the bell stage toolbox. The pusher needed to know for sure that the expensive fix had been completed. He had instructed by his hand-held radio to have another video camera sent down one of the guide wires. Wanger had returned to the bell stage as he waited over an hour before he was instructed that the camera should be on post number four. Wanger made his way over and unshackled the camera and pulled more wire to allow him to closely video the fitting that he had tightened showing that the leak was fixed. He was then instructed, always via Jock, to video other certain areas of the BOPs fittings. When the pusher was satisfied, he instructed Jock that he was happy with the results and the bell could be returned to surface.

The dive shack emptied, and Ian, Dave and Don took various orders from Jock to ready everything to return the bell to the system. The divers were both now in SAT so thankfully it would be a standard US Navy sat decompression table that would be used. It would take three days so they decided which shift the crew would take during the decompression.

Dave heard Creature's distinct voice even though it was an unscrambled helium voice that the bottom and top doors were closed, and he was going to blow down the bell a few feet to ensure the top door was sealed before leaving bottom.

"OK lads back out on deck with ya, let's get em put tae bed safely." Jock ordered.

Bringing the bell up was exceedingly harder than putting it down, as the hydraulic wheel to aid pulling up the heavy umbilical was not very efficient. Dave and Don had to take turns pulling and coiling the umbilical in its cradle while the other undid the ropes attached to the bell lift wire. Eventually, after a lot of sweat, the top of the bell could be seen. Dave gave Ian the thumbs up to quickly pull the bell through the interface. After the last rope was undone from the umbilical, the moonpool door was slid fully open. Once the bell was up and clear of the door it was slid closed allowing the bell to be lowered back onto the deck. Dave and Don then climbed into the bell stage to open the dogged clips on the bottom door which allowed the heavy door to swing open. They then clipped the door fully open. The fixtures to hold the bell to the stage were then opened allowing the bell to be lifted onto the above trolly system. Another winch would pull the bell along the rail until it was directly above the transfer chamber. This looked like a jury-rigged system because the wheel on the rail kept getting stuck so the bell and its occupants had to be swung back and forth before the wheel would move. Dave had glanced into one of the ports to give them the thumbs up and sorry for the rough ride. Through the dim twelve-volt light he could make out Wanger looking wet and tired, but he still returned a smile and a thumbs up. Eventually, after a lot of messing about, the bell was lowered carefully onto the top flange of the transfer chamber. The many stainless-steel bolts were fastened to hold the bell bottom flange to the chamber. Ian, who was still on the headset, listened to Jock as he opened a valve on the trunk to allow gas to equalize the pressure in the trunk to the same as the bell and transfer chamber. Creature gave Ian the thumbs up when the top door unsealed allowing them to pull up the inside door. Once they had both climbed down into the transfer chamber, Jock gave them the instruction to hold up the top door until it sealed by releasing pressure in the bell and increasing in the chamber.

They were now safely in the decompression chamber, showered and waiting to have their wet clothes taken out of the medical lock system. Ian came out on deck to inform Don and Dave to go up to the galley and see if they could scrounge up some hot food and a drink. The chef was quite willing to give them the food and drink and they passed it into the chamber via the lock. Dave had mistakenly put the drinking glasses stacked on top of each other. Creature came to the port to show him that the two glasses were impossible to part. The cream that was on their dessert lemon meringue was completely flat.

Eventually, they both climbed into the small bunk beds, Jock turned off the lights and they slept. It was now just before six AM and Dave was tired. Jock had given Dave and Ian the first shift until twelve mid-day. USN Sat tables stopped decompression every night from twelve midnight to twelve mid-day then it was a slow linear decompression during the day.

The hot water machine was acting up again so he had a busy morning keeping it running otherwise it could get dangerously cold in the chamber for the boys. His bed felt so good when he crashed at midday.

The day they came out of decompression they both looked pale and tired but happier about the extra cash they had just made. The following day was the end of Dave's two weeks so he would be flying ashore, normally Wanger would be with him. After decompression divers had to stay onboard for a minimum of thirty-six hours as the reduction in pressure in a helicopter could trigger a bend. Wanger wasn't too happy seeing Dave dressing in the survival suit ready for the chopper.

"Hey, no worries, buddy I'll have a couple of cold beers and think of you with all that extra cash. Oh, and the lady you met last time ashore, I'll look after her too, no prob."

"You'll have to grow another couple of inches mate she's got pretty used to having a real man," Wanger replied holding himself between his legs.

All the rigs were dry, any smuggled alcohol or drugs would be reason for immediate dismissal.

On the next trip out to the rig, Jock informed him that on the next calm day both he and Ian would be doing an exercise bell diver rescue. Ian spent much time with Dave in the bell explaining the exercise. Dave then spent many hours on his own going through the bell check list and knowing everything in detail about all the equipment. Jock made it very clear the importance of the exercise and that it had to be completed within three minutes. He would be allowed a couple of attempts but if he didn't complete the exercise in the allotted time there would be a high chance that he may be sent ashore.

The day came as he nervously climbed into the bell with Ian. He was more nervous of fucking up than his own safety as the bell entered the sea. The bell was jostled back and forth as it passed through the interface but eventually Ian called topside through the bell speaker that they had a seal. At seventy feet Ian had topside stop the lowering of the bell.

"OK Swiffy, after we blow down you are going to go out first and I am going to rescue you. All you must do is fin out to the full extent of your umbilical. I will inform topside when it's all out and Jock will relay that info to you. When he is ready to start the exercise all you must do is play dead. I'll come out and rescue you and bring you back to the bell and winch you in. It's all basic really," Ian said confidentially grinning. "No worries, mate you'll crack this."

He knew from the rest of the crew that it was imperative to be completely ready to leave the bell when the bottom door opened. It not only showed professionalism but if the dive on bottom was a bounce dive, then every minute counted that would increase the decompression time. For that reason, he had Ian hold off on the blow down until he got his shit together. He put enough weights in his pockets to keep him heavy then donned his KMB hooded mask. He was breathing through the mask and checking comms. When all was good, he gave Ian the thumbs up. He could hear Jock doing the countdown through the bell speaker then Ian opened the noisy blow down valve. Dave had the nose clearing device pushed under his nose busily clearing his ears. Ian gave him a couple of thumbs up to ensure he was OK. Ian then reached down to un-dog the bottom door. He could hear Ian informing topside that they had reached fifty feet. Dave began to feel warm, so he put his hot water suit on dump. The bottom door swung open, and Dave immediately dropped into the bell stage. He unlatched a pair of fins on the bell stage and put them on then began swimming out toward the massive pontoons. "Diver leaving the bell," he informed topside.

"Roger Roger Swiffy, OK you know the drill, all you gotta do is play dead."

"Roger Roger topside... playing dead," Eventually he felt a tug on the umbilical, Ian was signaling it was at the end. He was guessing that Ian would be informed and be leaving the bell shortly. It seemed like only seconds had gone by before he felt his umbilical being pulled toward the bell and he could see Ian finning toward him. Ian dragged him onto the bell stage and connected the inside bell pulley to the loop on the front of his harness. He then quickly made his way into the bell and hoisted Dave into the bell. As soon as Ian could reach his head and chest, he pulled off his own mask then Dave's.

"Diver in the bell giving mouth to mouth," Ian informed topside.

"Well done lads, that, was very quick. OK let me know when you're ready for the next exercise," Jock informed them.

It took them another fifteen minutes to get everything cleared up in the small bell but a little more spacious now that both umbilicals were mostly outside of the bell.

"OK lads, git a fuckin' move on we ain't got all day," Jock said over the bell speaker.

Ian gave Dave a thumbs up and a questioning expression not wanting Jock to hear.

"Yea no problem, Ian out you go... I got this."

Dave still had his fins on and his hot water on dump. His mask was on his knee. He had a quick check around the bell to ensure all the valves were in the correct position as he rolled off the remainder of Ian's umbilical into the bell trunk. He could feel Ian's breathing as the umbilical pulsated in his hand. Creature had explained to him the importance of being the bellman. It was tempting to nod off or be distracted in the boring hours that the diver is out. Always hold the diver's umbilical and be ready for any change in how it pulses, you can even feel if the diver is exerting himself. Constantly check the CO_2 level in the bell and change the scrubber cannisters when needed. Be aware of any situation that could possibly occur and always be ready. The supervisor is probably very busy with the dive so it is always wise to let topside know that all is well in the bell or anything that may be a concern.

As the rig raised and lowered with the sea's swell so did the level in the bell trunk, sometimes allowing the air to bubble out causing a slight difference in pressure in his ears. He gave Ian a tug once that his umbilical was all out and shortly thereafter Jock informed him to rescue the diver. He expected that Jock would be watching the clock in the dive shack as he exited the bell pulling Ian's umbilical. The whole exercise had gone to plan, and he had made it well within the regulation three minutes. After coiling up the umbilicals and clearing the confusion in the bell Ian pulled on the rope attached to the bottom door. The door was closed and dogged then the top door was closed and sealed with a few feet of pressure from the blow down valve.

"Both doors closed and sealed ready to raise the bell," Ian informed topside.

The bell began to be raised and Ian gave the instruction to Jock when the bell reached fifty feet then coming through the interface. "Bell out of the water... Bell on deck."

He could now feel the bell being decompressed by the popping of his ears and of course the reading on the inside gauge. This had gone very well and most of his fears had been quelled. He felt good as they exited the bell climbing down onto the stage. Jock even met them. "Well done lads, a good exercise and the rig is always happy to see us doing something besides sleeping and eating."

A few months later he did the same exercise with Don. He felt confident and had even looked forward to the dive. Much like before, everything had gone to plan. He didn't ever want to get lackadaisical and always ensured to stay refreshed with all the controls and procedures. Eventually, he would be asked to do a deep dive, although he was still a little nervous, he was hoping it was going to happen sooner so that he could sleep a little better.

His life had changed so much, he now felt like a valued part of the team. There was always something new to learn. He had made it a goal to acquire everything he needed to know about not only the diving but the complicated system on deck. When everyone else was playing dominoes or cards, he had his nose in a manual. Jock and Mike, the other shift supervisor, always seemed to come to him first when something needed fixing, and with this ageing system that happened a lot. The money was great and even his life ashore seemed happier.

Chapter 25

What the heck happened?

He woke feeling awful, his chest felt like he had been hit by a freight train. When he could focus his eyes, he slowly perceived a bright light shone in his eyes. As this weird fog cleared, he could now make out various concerned faces looking down on him. Only one seemed to be mildly familiar.

"Dave Swift, can you hear us." The voice asked.

He tried to reply but because of the tubes in his mouth and nose and the oxygen mask he could only mumble.

"That's good enough Mister Swift, these tubes will be removed shortly. We're glad that you are with us again. Try to relax, we will be administering pain killers to help with the pain."

His eyes closed as he was again returned to the blackness.

He woke again to the same face asking him questions. The pain in his chest seemed to be much alleviated.

"Dave, do you feel any pain?" The voice asked.

"No, it's not as bad." His voice sounded raspy with the dryness he felt in his throat. "Where am I? What happened?"

"You're in Aberdeen Royal Infirmary. You had an accident but you're in good hands. Mister Swift, I need to ask you some questions?" the soothing, quiet voice asked, "What is your date of birth?"

It took him a few seconds as his mind concentrated on the question. "Eighteenth of March nineteen fifty."

"What is the name of the company you are currently working for."

"That would be Sub Sea International," his crackly muffled voice answered.

He could hear various voices in the background cheering. "Jeez, thank god for that," one of the now familiar voices said.

A new familiar face appeared looking down on him. "Swiffy, how ya doing you old wanker." It again took him a few seconds to recollect the Lancashire accent of Biscuit McVitte. Another face then appeared that he recognized as being the company offshore manager.

"What the fuck happened? Why am I here?" he asked.

"It's a long story we'll get into that another time. The most important thing now is that you're back with us. You're on the mend and the doc here tells us the next few days of your recovery is important." Biscuit said before being interrupted by the Doctor.

"Mister Swift, you need to rest, your body needs time to recuperate. Let us know if you feel any pain. You will have to be patient; you are obviously a strong young man, and we have confidence you will recover. We are now going to administer some more pain management."

The next time he woke feeling a little better. His mind seemed clearer as he glanced around the empty hospital room. He was connected to a drip feeding his left arm. It gave him time to recollect how he had gotten here. It sent shivers down his spine as he remembered running out of air and the terrified feeling knowing he was about to die. But then the weird elation he felt letting go and meeting his Dad. As much as he tried to remove those thoughts they kept returning. Eventually a cheery nurse entered the room to check on the drip.

"Ah! Mister Swift you're awake. Can I get you a drink or something? I'm not sure you're ready for solids just yet, we'll see what the doctor says when he does his rounds."

His throat felt cakey and dry. "I'd love a juice, if you have that?"

"Yes of course, how about an orange juice?"

"Oh yes please, that would be great," he answered.

Removing his oxygen mask, the juice felt cool and quenched his thirst immediately. After his second juice, the horrible dry taste in his mouth had gone and seemed to be helping also with his sore throat.

He had forgotten to replace the mask when the nurse returned to take away the glass.

"Mister Swift until the doctor says it's OK, you must wear the mask. Sorry, I know it must feel uncomfortable."

"Oh, sorry I forgot," he answered.

Chapter 26

Decision time.

Chalky White was replaced two days after the accident by another diver from head office. Chalky was questioned by a plain clothed police officer and sent home on indefinite leave. One week later he quit the company and he never dived again. The nightmare of the incident would stay with him for many years.

Dave was eventually released from the hospital where he had stayed for almost a month. He returned on a weekly basis as an outpatient until his breathing and all pain had subsided. The company even paid for psychological counseling for a period after Dave had mentioned many sleepless nights. The company also still paid him as though he was still working his normal two weeks per month schedule offshore. Being classed as self-employed, he was surprised at the way the company had treated him. It gave him precious time to evaluate his life and decide what his future might hold. The hospital had suggested light exercise, so he had joined a gym and was slowly bringing himself back to where he wanted to be.

Boredom began to fill his days so after his three months of absence with nothing to show for any ideas as to a new vocation, he asked to be returned to his old job. Just the idea of being a deep-sea diver and making the big bucks still excited him. He had met many professional divers that had worked offshore successfully without any accidents. And the idiom 'a lightning never strikes twice' kept coming to his mind. He reconciled his life threatening event to simply being in the wrong place at the wrong time, exacerbated by reckless inexperience. With all the big diving construction jobs the company was involved in, accidents were very rare.

Biscuit had explained that as it was an American company, they worked for, most of the high paying jobs went to the American divers. Granted most had many years of experience welding and arc cutting underwater. However, there were a few Brit divers that had broken through and were now part of the company's dream team. He explained that the exploratory floating oil rigs that Dave had worked on were mainly just for the rig's insurance purposes. Deep dives were quite rare. On the massive oil production platforms there was almost a constant diving presence on the seabed where all the pipelines and complicated machinery lay. At any time of the day or night for pretty much twelve months of the year there were divers on bottom welding, cutting, and moving huge pieces of machinery around like a child's Meccano set. On some of those dive systems, whether on a specially designed rig or a D.P ship,* there were three six-man chambers constantly pressured to a bottom depth of anywhere from three hundred to six hundred feet.

*(DP) Dynamic Positioning is a vessel with the capability via computer control systems to automatically maintain a vessel's position with the use of hull thrusters.

Some had two separate diving bells working twenty-four hours a day. It was normal to be in Sat (saturation diving, living in a chamber) for thirty to forty days then work on deck for ten days or so to then return for another thirty or more days. Biscuit was averaging one hundred and twenty days a year in Sat which meant he was living offshore for up to three hundred days a year. In the late nineteen seventies Biscuit was making over a hundred and twenty thousand dollars a year. And that was BIG money in that period. Considering the average income was around eleven thousand dollars a year. A rig diver was making somewhere around fifteen thousand but that was for only two weeks per month, some men also had other jobs or businesses ashore.

He felt privileged that Biscuit had taken his valuable shore time to enlighten him and convince him to return. Usually, the few drinks in the bars would end up in a drunken spree in the many Aberdeen nightclubs.

The specialist doctor at the hospital eventually gave him the all clear and was very surprised that Dave was returning to the same dangerous profession. The Dive company was even more surprised the day he came into the operation managers office to ask for his job back. It was a foregone conclusion that the company would not continue to pay indefinitely. He also thought that they were quietly relieved that he had not sought legal advice for any severance situation. This was also a blackmark on their record that they did not want to advertise and probably the reason for his pay and help over the last three months.

Chapter 27

Back tae work.

"Yea got tae be fuckin' nuts comin back tae wurk Swiffy. We all thought yea wur a fuckin' gonner when they put ya on the chopper that day," Jock said when Dave strolled into the dive shack.

"Yes, I know, I think I got a screw loose upstairs." As Dave grabbed Jock in a neck hold and licked the top of his head. "But ah missed you soo much ma little jockcroach," Dave answered giggling.

"Git tae fuck off, ya fuckin' wanker afore ah kick ya in the fuckin' bollocks," Jock said grinning and holding out his hand to be shook.

As they shook hands Dave remembered what Don had told him ashore weeks ago about the rescue and Jocks quick actions and life preserving decisions.

"Jock, I can't thank you enough for saving my life. I don't think I'd be here today but for your quick decisions. I would have liked to see Chalky and thanked him too. I know it was because of his actions this this happened in the first place, but accidents occur, it's what you do next that makes the difference. Because of you... and Chalky and everyone else involved I'm alive and not brain damaged... well maybe a little ha!"

"Aye we jus need to get on we it an learn from our mistakes eh laddy? Are ya all cleared tu dive 'cos we got a possible dive comin up soon. I expect yae want tae git back on the horse, eh?"

"That would be good Jock, I'm glad I haven't lost my place in the queue. I'm good to go and have the 'all clear' from the diving doctor ashore. You read it right Jock; I need to get in there soon. I'm going to climb in the bell right now and bring myself back up to speed. The sooner I get this over with the better."

It was two weeks later before the dive was called for, he was due for crew change but asked to stay on and complete the dive. Keith, a new diver on the crew would be his bellman. Jock spoke highly of him; this would be his second deep dive.

The rig was now working in the Argyle production field and was involved with replacing some of the aging coflexip pipelines from the various surrounding wellheads to the production platform.

After many unnerving hours, the dive was finally called for. Both he and Keith had been dressed in hot water suits for over three hours. They had been sitting in the deck change room on wooden benches where they had eaten supper from a tray. It was nine PM, they had spent most of the day preparing the bell, and the dive system had been blown down to depth. The seabed at this location was just under three hundred feet. Nine percent Oxygen and ninety one percent Helium would be the mix. They both followed Don to the dive shack that was now crowded with the rigs top brass. Jock made his way through the crowd and with the tool pusher went over again in detail what the dive entailed. The bell sat ominously on its lower stage (cage) on the moonpool door. They both climbed up into the cramped bell and folded down the small metal seats also raising and latching the heavy bottom door. The dim twelve-volt lamp was their only light as they went about the final bell check off list calling out to Jock in the dive shack through the bell mic/speaker. The general deck noise had been immediately silenced and replaced by the steady whirring noise of the CO_2 scrubber fan. A fresh CO_2 sodasorb scrubber canister was placed on its fan mount which would usually keep the CO_2 level down for at least four hours. There were two spare replacements in plastic garbage bags. A small instrument panel showed the CO_2 level in the bell and was also transmitted to the dive shack. They heard the distinct sound of the bell lift electric motor starting and being transmitted down the bell lift cable.

Jock informed them, 'LIFTING THE BELL' as they both readied themselves for the primary shaking lift. Looking through the lower viewing port they could see Don on the winch that slid the moonpool door open on its rails then moving over to another winch to lower the clump weight to the bottom. Eventually he looked up to the viewing port and gave them a thumbs up as he informed the dive shack through his headset that the weight was on bottom.

"OK lads lowering the bell, everything OK in thur?" Jock asked.

"Yes Jock, good to go," Keith informed him over the bell mic/speaker.

There was a jerk as the lowering began. The bell began to swing from the rigs listing movements but spinning back into position as the pennant wire attached to the clump weight wire controlled the swinging motion. Looking through the ports they could now see the rigs' giant legs disappearing into the inky black sea below. As they got closer to the interface, they could see the motion of the sea as the huge swells came toward them. The lowering of the bell momentarily stopped as Keith timed the waves then quickly informed Jock to quickly lower. Jock was in direct contact with the assistant supervisor Ian on the bell lift winch. They both held on tight as the bell crashed through the waves jostling the bell from side to side. A little water came in through the bottom door before it sealed. Keith informed topside, 'WE HAVE A SEAL' (the bottom door was sealed with the pressure of water from the outside). The bell outside lights were then turned on, from the outside gauge seen through one of the ports, Keith informed topside every fifty feet of the depth as they were slowly lowered. Although Dave's stomach churned from his nervousness, he wasn't going to let that show as he busied himself attaching the umbilical with the attached KBM mask to his harness and checking yet again every valve in the bell. He placed a couple of lead weights in his suit pockets and attached the hot water supply to his suit. Primarily, he did not want to fuck up, which took away most of the nervousness. Eventually Keith could see the top of the BOP and asked topside to, 'ALL STOP.'

"OK lads you know the drill let me know when you're ready for blow down." Jock said as Keith looked over at Dave questioningly as Dave donned his hooded mask. Keith leaned down into the bell trunk to undog the latches on the lower door. When they were satisfied everything was in order. Dave gave Keith the thumbs up.

"OK topside, we're ready for blow down," Keith informed Jock.

They did the usual countdown then Keith opened the noisy blow down valve. Dave pressed his nose onto the rubberized clearing slider in his mask and felt his ears popping rapidly, he was eventually able to apply just a yawn to clear his ears. As they came to matching outside depth, the inside of bell became quite hot. He had sensibly left his hot water suit valve closed. In roughly three minutes* they had reached depth and the bottom door swung open under its own weight.

*In later years this would be changed to a maximum of fifty feet per minute to ease the sometimes-dangerous situation with HPNS (high Pressure Nervous Syndrome) causing violent shakes, tremors, and even seizures.

"BOTTOM DOOR OPEN," Keith informed topside with his high-pitched helium, almost undecipherable voice.

"DIVER LEAVING THE BELL," Dave informed topside as professionally as he could muster feeling slightly dizzy from the speedy blow down.

Dave gave Keith the two thumbs up as he dropped down into the depths of the cold Atlantic. Freezing cold water rushed down his spine reminding him of his navy dives. He quickly opened his hot water bypass valve to his suit and was immediately bathed in hot water.

He unlatched a set of fins and put them on then grabbed a flashlight from the bell toolbox in the stage and descended into the darkness.

"OK Swiffy, can you see the Christmas tree below you (well head cage). The tool pusher wants you to first check for any leaks from any of the hoses."

He went about this task diligently following the many hoses from valve to valve finding no leaks. Although he was concentrating on the job at hand he didn't feel completely alone as there were thousands of miniature sea life swimming across his mask attracted to the light. Large Ling Cod he noticed here and there were seemingly staring at his intrusion. There were strange sounds occasionally that he figured were propeller noises from the rig's safety and supply vessels in the area. But there were also other sounds that he couldn't put a name to. He knew that sound travels much faster and further in water, he had learned that from his navy days.

Eventually, Jock from the pusher's directions, guided him to a six-inch flexible hose pipeline. He followed it to where it was attached to the Christmas tree with a large clamp. There were two jaw type clamps holding the two flange plates together. He was instructed to remove the two large nuts and bolts then remove both jaws releasing the pipeline from the BOP. It seemed like a relatively simple task as he returned from the bell stage toolbox with two large wrenches. He tried to unscrew the nuts, but they must have been rusted on as they were completely seized. He waited for further instructions. After many long minutes they decided that the bolts would need to be cut. An arc cutting torch would be sent down the clump weight guide wire beside the bell. He had used arc cutting under water and even a little welding in the navy. He had also been shown on deck how to use Brocco rods. These were three eighth inch thick rods with tiny metal rods inside, one of the tiny rods was made of manganese. Basically, you would strike an arc with a grounded piece of steel then pull the trigger allowing pure oxygen into the arc. In doing so it was possible to cut through three-inch steel like a knife through butter. This was all new stuff, and he was hoping not to show his inexperience. He waited outside the bell for over an hour while they lowered the cable.

Dave attempted to keep his mind occupied with the job at hand, which was OK for a while, then he decided to think about sex especially with Annie. It was not arousing but kept his mind from thinking about where he was; at the bottom of the North Sea in almost complete darkness with just a small flashlight and all these tiny fishy things floating around his mask. When he spoke, he could hardly understand his own voice let alone Keith the bellman on the few occasions that he popped his head into the bell trunk. After what seemed ages, he saw the cutting torch beside the bell.

He swam up to unscrew the shackle releasing the cable and torch, then as topside released more slack he pulled it toward the job. He placed the ground lead on the opposite side of the flange away from him knowing that not doing so would cause a possible electric shock. When he struck an arc and pulled the trigger, it seemed to light up the whole seabed around partially blinding him. A metallic taste appeared in his mouth that he guessed were from the fillings in his teeth. Mild electric shocks zapped the end of his nose from the metal nose clearing fitting in his mask. This he would have to get used to in many future dives. The two large bolts were cut through easily. He half expected that the two jaws would drop allowing the flange to part... but it didn't. He tried to pull it apart with a crowbar, but it wasn't budging. In a last resort, he beat on the jaws with a five-pound sledgehammer and a chisel. Eventually he seemed to be making some headway as a small amount of oil sprayed out clouding the water in a dark red.

"Topside, there is oil spraying out of the flange, this isn't under pressure by any chance," he asked.

Long minutes passed as the area around him became quite cloudy. He imagined the conversation going Back and forth between the rigs tool pusher and the personnel on the production platform nearby that the other end of this flexible pipeline was connected to. Eventually Jock explained that the platform had checked, and it was indeed not under pressure. He could hear the voice of the pusher in the background telling Jock to have the diver beat the shit out of it and get the job done as this was taking too long.

"OK I guess you heard that Swiffy just beat it off but be ready to move quickly."

"Are you sure about his he asked," wishing that they could see what was going on down here in front of his eyes.

"Swiffy, just get it done we're wasting valuable time." Jock asked more forcefully. Obviously, the loud American tool pusher was pressing the issue.

He didn't use the chisel and just beat once with the hammer on the bottom jaw which immediately dropped. The six-inch hose literally flew off the BOP flange and was whipping from side to side like an angry snake. He swam back along his umbilical in the cloud of oil praying that the hose with the heavy metal flange at the end wouldn't hit him. His mask was so covered in oil he could hardly see as he climbed into the bell.

"The fuckin' hose is under pressure and almost took my frickin' head off," he screamed at Jock, not caring how that would be received in the busy dive shack.

As he climbed into the bell, he could hear Jock asking Keith if what Swiffy was reporting was fact.

"It sure as hell is. Swiffy is covered in oil, and I can see through the port a huge cloud of oil coming toward the bell," Keith replied.

"OK close the bottom and top doors and blow a seal quickly, we're bringing you up." Jock replied.

Once the top inside door was closed Keith opened the blow down valve and sealed the door.

"BOTTOM AND TOP DOOR CLOSED AND SEALED BRING US UP," Keith called as clearly as he could with his Donald duck voice.

Dave felt relief when the bell and stage were finally set on the moonpool deck. Coming through the interface they had been jostled around a bit. The bell lift wire winch had stalled halfway to the deck and for long minutes they had been uncomfortably swung and spun beneath the rig. The fun wasn't over as now with the bell disconnected from the stage it was raised onto the above rail system. They were truly at the mercy of the deck crew. He remembered from the outside the difficulties of moving the bell along the rail to the decompression chambers. Every swing and ding as the bell hit the bulkheads was exaggerated inside and made them cringe. They were eventually lowered onto the transfer chamber flange and the many stainless-steel bolts were screwed into place firmly attaching the bell to the system. Dave felt relieved when Jock asked them to slowly open the equalization valve in the top door to pressure up the transfer chamber trunk. Keith had opened the bell blow down valve fully so that Jock could control the pressure in the bell from the dive shack. The top door seal slowly popped, and they were both able to lift it to the open position. Keith climbed down the metal ladders and undogged the chamber upper door of the transfer chamber which then swung open allowing them both to climb into the comfort of the small transfer chamber. It was only slightly larger than the bell but without all the hoses and assorted equipment. There was a small toilet and a shower hose. They both lifted the heavy door back into position as Jock released some pressure in the diving bell, sealing the hatch. They had both noticed their ears popping in the last half hour in the bell as Jock had already reduced the pressure to match the holding depth of the chambers. They both stripped off and Keith with his dry 'wooly bear' under suit climbed through the hatchway into the decompression chamber. Dave showered attempting to remove as much of the oil from his hair, face, and hands. Keith had pressured up the medical lock and one at a time they passed through their wet and oily suits and wooly bears to the outside.

He had spent over four hours in the water and was quite tired but relieved as he later lay in his small bunk bed. Although he was hungry, he just needed to sleep when Ian asked them from the dive shack if they needed food. Ian had obviously relieved Jock in the shack with Wanger as his runner. They were now essentially in SAT (saturation) so from twelve midnight to twelve midday they would be held at depth. During the day they would be slowly decompressed unless there were other dives to be completed. If so, they would remain at holding depth until all diving was complete.

Thankfully, the following day brought bad weather, as they were informed that more dives had to be completed. The small deck crew were split into twelve-hour shifts. Several more dives were completed mostly without hitch as he and Keith took turns for diver and bellman. One of the busy dives lasted over twelve hours on bottom as they each swapped out diver and bellman. Nine days later after a three-day decompression they opened the chamber door to breathe the sweet fresh air. Jock and the others had crew changed out, so Mike and a couple of new divers had relieved them. Mike had them sit in the dive shack for a little while until the slight dizziness at breathing air again, ceased.

One of the divers was an American. Now that the rig was involved in partial construction and possible many sat dives, the company's dream team were now hustling for some SAT time. Dave had calculated that he had been in SAT for two hundred and nineteen hours, at eleven dollars an hour he had made two thousand four hundred extra dollars to his monthly salary. Which made all the hassle seem worthwhile. Two days later, after the customary time on deck before boarding a helicopter to not risk decompression sickness from the reduction in pressure, he flew ashore. He felt good about himself; he had taken a lot of risks and had learned so much. The chopper back just made him feel important and kinda proud. He was hooked!

The old rig with the very old diving system had proved itself formidable in getting the job done... cheaply! Once the work in the Argyle field was completed the rig moved on to the Tartan field. Dave was averaging sixty days a year in SAT and was now a leading hand making a day rate of one hundred and twenty dollars a day for every day he spent offshore. The company still paid eleven bucks an hour in SAT and not the normal fifteen, as the rest of the company's construction jobs. However, he was making more money than he had ever dreamed of but felt like he was becoming a risk junkie. His reputation of having died and returned to diving proceeded him. There were many situations where the risk was close, but he now had the experience to be able to tell topside, 'NO, let's do it this way instead' and get away with it.

He had purchased a brand new red TVR Taimar sportscar, which he had already damaged twice to very expensive repairs. His new flat was the envy of many of his wealthy visitors. Granted he was now spending two thirds of his time offshore, which was beneficial as his many days of alcohol and drug abuse ashore were starting to take their toll. The time offshore where booze was illegal at least gave him time to recover and return to a semblance of health and sanity.

He had worked from a DP dive ship in the Norwegian sector for a few months which crew changed out of Stavanger. On the few days onshore, he had picked up the habit of rollup cigarettes from the locals (mostly women). These seemed stronger and with his chewing tobacco habit offshore, that he had picked up from the many American divers, it was also having an adverse effect on his health. He was only just making it through the annual stringent diver medicals. A dark patch had appeared from the X rays of his lungs. The doctor had warned him that unless he changed his lifestyle his days of diving would be limited.

Chapter 28

Bren.

The DP dive ship had gone into Aberdeen to pick up a huge reel of coflexip pipeline. It was being welded to the aft deck much to the glee of the diving crew who were now comfortably making their offshore rate sitting in the bars on Union Street. Two men were even making hourly SAT rate in the chambers. A fishing ship had snagged the main pipeline coming in from the offshore rigs. The problem had been all over the national news and Whitehall had even got involved with the disaster. Previously, high profile oil men and, 'brave' politicians had been flown out by helicopter and winched down to the wildly moving deck. The dive crew had been taking bets as to who would make it alive landing on the rolling deck. The ROV* crew had been busy videoing the damage to the valuable pipeline and precious commodity having been halted on its way to the onshore oil terminal.

*Remotely Operated Vehicle; ROVs are unoccupied, highly maneuverable underwater machines that can be used to video seabed equipment and diver support at depth, being operated by a tech in the ROV shack on deck.

Dave had checked that everything was in order with his flat and decided to wander down to his favorite quiet bar for an afternoon scotch before returning onboard. The ship would be sailing in the morning. He had been attempting to manage his smoking and alcohol intake knowing the risk he would take if he let it get out of hand again.

"A grouse whiskey please," He asked the friendly bartender.

"It's a fuckin' low flyer yea sassenach bastard," came a retort from a large burly man further up the vacant bar. He seemed to have a faint smile as he looked his way, so Dave took it as nothing to be alarmed about.

"Well, I'm sorry to insult such a pleasant whiskey from beautiful Scotland. But why may I ask, fair gentleman from the North."

"Grouse... It's a fuckin' low flying bird yea dinne ken? Yea fuckin' sassenach."

"Oh, sorry kind Sir for my ignorance in these matters. Kind barman could I have a wee low flyer, och tha noo!"

"That's better, now dinne forget it," said the large man now grinning.

Fast forward approximately six hours and Dave found himself being driven up Union Street at an unimaginable speed skidding around roundabouts. Callum was an off-duty traffic police officer who was now showing off his driving skills but was just as inebriated as himself. Even noticing the few police, they passed on the sidewalks, he would wave, and they would nonchalantly wave back seeing nothing wrong with the sound of the squealing tires. The quiet bar they had been drinking in had now closed at the legal time of ten PM. Cal knew a few illegal late-night bars which was where they were now heading. Although an unbelievable situation, it just seemed like a requirement in the life he was living. He would just go along with the flow, with no idea what adventure... or mishap would come his way. Cal would give a secret knock on the basement bars and a tiny slit would open in the door welcoming constable Callum Campbell into the busy labyrinth to many free drinks. At around four in the morning after another death-defying drive down Union Street, Cal dropped him off at the ship which was tied up alongside in the busy port.

Four weeks later the ship again returned to port. The offshore leak had been fixed but there were other parts having been manufactured ashore to be installed on the seabed.

The ship had just been tied up alongside the busy dock and the gangway installed when the dive superintendent rushed over to speak to Dave who was on the stern of the ship. Dave had got on famously with the ex SBS diver, they both had many interesting stories of their naval experiences to tell in the long boring evenings offshore.

"Swiffy we'll keep the cop talking on the gangway, you can scurry up the dock ladder, we can let you know when he's gone. The cop is asking to see you. What the fuck ya been up to Swiffy?" the dive superintendent said concernedly.

Dave cast his mind back, had he done anything illegal beside smoke a little pot. He *was* on his last set of points before losing his driving license. The women he had been seeing were definitely above the age of eighteen.

"Brian, I haven't done anything illegal... I don't think." As he strained to lean over the ship's guard rail from the aft deck to look up toward the gangway seeing his new pal Callum waving to him. He was in his full police uniform with an intimidating and flashing shiny police car parked close by strangely making all the divers run for cover.

"See yea in the barr this aft," he shouted down, miming drinking a glass.

Dave looked up giving him a thumbs up with many very concerned and mystifying expressions coming from his crew mates. Cal roared off in his police car leaving everyone on deck staring at Dave in complete disbelief.

"You got to be fuckin' kidding me," Brian said as a few of the other lads came out of hiding.

"Ah he's OK, he is just a traffic cop... no biggy," Dave answered walking away chuckling to himself at the absurdity of the moment.

Callum, he later found, was a scotch connoisseur, as they both took turns in ordering top shelf scotches for each other. Dave had in the past enjoyed a good scotch and had a few choice bottles in his liquor cabinet at the flat. Instead of drinking their faces off at the bar, he took Dave on an enjoyable country drive to some of the rare distilleries, where they tasted top notch scotch whiskies.

On their return, he invited Dave to his house to have dinner with him and his wife and kids. When they arrived, Cal was surprised that his wife's sister with daughter was also visiting. The small room became busy and a little noisy, so the kids were sent to a bedroom to play. The adults could now talk and sample Cals special whiskeys. They seemed intrigued by his diving job and asked many questions to the point Cal had to intervene and return the conversion back to malt whiskies.

After dinner, he found himself alone with Brenda, the sister who was visiting from Yorkshire. She had asked him to call her Bren as everyone else did. Both sisters were originally from Leeds and were nurses. They had both worked in the busy Aberdeen Infirmary where her older sister had met Cal. Bren had met her husband through Cal, he was also in the police. After a short rocky marriage, they had divorced, and she had returned with her daughter to Leeds. This was one of the many visits she would take to spend time with her sister and her daughter would also spend time with her Dad. She seemed a little shy but the more they talked the more she opened, and she had a cute giggle that seemed to draw him to her. With her dark slightly auburn hair she reminded him faintly of Annie. With her child, the coincidence seemed a little uncanny and that she was also in Yorkshire, held him back somewhat.

The evening came to a close, he thanked Cal and his wife for a wonderful meal and evening. They exchanged phone numbers; he told Cal that the boat would be alongside for the next couple of days, and he would contact him when he was next in town. They shook hands, Bren was a little hesitant but came to the door to also shake his hand. For a split second, as he felt her soft hand in his and their eyes met, there seemed to be a chemistry.

Laying in his bed that night he tried to examine his thoughts. He had been offshore for over a month, so it felt time to have female company and of course sex. He could pick up his phone and call various lady friends to share his bed, with no holds involved. But there was something new that seemed to be missing. He needed to connect. It had been too many years. There was a part of him he had buried deep inside that he feared would awaken and would inevitably let him down. Could he risk going down that road again? He was in his thirtieth year and still felt that awful pain. Would that rejection stay with him for the rest of his life? Could he ever trust another female with his heart? But he knew deep down, and given the chance, he would give himself completely and with no reservations.

The following morning, he awoke feeling fresh, it was a beautiful sunny day. He had called the ship and he was not needed until it sailed the following day. He felt light and ready to take on the world. He didn't need those depressing thoughts that he had fallen asleep with.

Don't even think about it ya wanker. Just grow a set, and fuckin' call her, yes siree... what a wanker.

He felt slightly nervous as he dialed Cals number.

"Hey Cal, how's it going? That was a nice evening last night. I'd like to thank you again. It was great to be with your family."

"Hey no problem, Dave. What ya up to today and when is your ship sailing? You know I can call my friend, the harbor master office and know exactly when any ships arrive and leave."

"Ha! yes, I guessed that the other day when you scared the living shit out of everyone onboard." Dave quipped. "Listen, I hope you don't mind but I was wondering if Bren is doing anything today. I'd like to ask her out for lunch."

"Well, I'm certainly not her keeper, why don't you ask her yourself?" Callum replied.

The phone lay dead for a little longer than expected. As he began to think this was a bad idea.

"Hello Dave, are you back on your ship," she asked. He wondered if she was just trying to come up with something to say.

"No, we don't sail until tomorrow. I was wondering... if you're not busy that is... if you would like to come out for lunch? I know a nice place where we could sit outside in this lovely sun, it's a little cool but we can go inside if you like."

"Yes, I would like that. Joanie's going to her Dad's today. He'll be picking her up shortly. I don't have a car, so you'll have to pick me up."

He felt a slight jolt in his heart and reprimanded himself.

Hey loser... don't count your chickens, no siree!

She seemed suitably impressed sitting in his fancy sports car. "Jeez, I bet this thing is a lady puller, Mister deep sea diver. Just so you know I don't like being driven fast; it scares me."

"Yes, I'm afraid it has gotten me into a lot of trouble in the past. No worries I'll try and keep it below one hundred miles an hour," he grinned. He guessed she was in her late twenties by the fact she had an eight-year-old daughter. She still seemed a little shy and hesitant to look at him directly.

The conversation seemed disjointed with too many long silences as they both ate. When he did see her eyes, they were a beautiful brown tinged with green. She wore a sensible yet fashionable dress with a loose top. They had moved to be inside the restaurant as it was cold outside, even in the sun. When she stood to remove her short jacket, he noticed she was well proportioned in the breast department, and he was forcing himself not to stare. She seemed mysterious, yet when she spoke, her obvious Yorkshire accent drew him in like a magnet. He needed to break the ice, so he decided to tell her how he and her brother-in-law had met those weeks ago, exaggerating the Scottish accent somewhat. This seemed to hit the spot as she laughed uncontrollably.

"Oh yes that's him for sure, he can be a right laugh when he wants to. My sister is very lucky to have him, and they are still madly in love after all these years. Kinda makes me a little jealous sometimes. My X and I just didn't see eye to eye... on anything really but I'm happy that he has found his partner. She's a nice lass a bit younger than me and pregnant now... wouldn't you believe!" she said a little sadly then stopped short to look away, slightly embarrassed at opening up, like that.

"Hey Bren, I know what it feels like losing a partner, nothing to be ashamed of."

He realized that he had probably crossed the line. She now looked at him directly in his eyes and her demure smile had disappeared as she laid down her utensils.

"I'm not ashamed, at all, what would make you think that?"

"I'm sorry Bren that was inappropriate of me, please forgive my rudeness. If the truth is known, and I don't know why I'm telling you this; it's me that is embarrassed and probably a little ashamed. I've been bouncing around from one relationship to another because of things that happened to me many years ago. I'm a pretty screwed up individual; I now seem to be a risk junky or even have a death wish in the job that I do. If I'm not careful, you'll be reading about me on some obituary page. I don't know what it is but just speaking to you last night and today has made me rethink my life and... 'what could be.'" He immediately felt tears appearing in his eyes. "Excuse me, I need to go to the washroom." He only just made it into a cubicle as the tears flowed uncontrollably. The last time he cried like this was when his Dad had died so many years ago.

What the fuck is going on, am I having a friggin' breakdown, yes siree get it together ya fuckin' idiot.

"Are you OK?" Bren asked, looking a little concerned as he sat down at the table again.

"Bren I am so sorry; I don't know what came over me. This has never happened before," he said embarrassingly knowing his face to be flushing red. "I should drop you off back home," he said not wanting to look into her gaze.

She reached out with her hand and laid it on his with a concerned expression.

"Dave, really, no need to apologize. Although I'm a little confused, there is absolutely no reason to explain. However, I am touched that you can show your feelings. My last relationships have been disappointing to say the least. I hate lies. Over the last year I have pretty much given up on finding Mister right. Joanie and I do all right on our own. She still loves her Dad, but I like to think we are very special together. She will always be my number one concern."

They were both now looking directly into each other's eyes as he now held her soft hand in his.

"Bren, are you ready to take on a crazy motherfucker like me because I would certainly like to get to know you better."

"You know what Dave, yes, I would, but you will have to be patient with me and I'm nobody's fool. I would appreciate it if you would take me home now as Joanie will return soon. I'll give you my home telephone number in Leeds. I travel to Aberdeen often, when I'm not on duty at the Leeds general hospital. Call me when your next onshore and hopefully we can figure something out."

He drove her back to Cal and Linda's house; she had the door open to the car and had almost stepped out then, seemingly as an afterthought, she returned to her seat to reach over and kiss him. It was a deep sensuous kiss as he held her tight. There was a definite stirring as she left the car and waved from their front door smiling.

Now what was all that about? Am I up to a real relationship? Is this what I'm ready for after all these years? Or is this going to come crashing down and be another huge disappointment? Could I cope with that if it happened? He wondered as he drove back to the ship.

He needed company and a few stiff ones to calm his nerves. This was a 'wet' boat in that you could drink alcohol offshore unlike most other dive jobs, especially on the rigs. Most of the lads were ashore probably drinking their faces off. The duty supervisor and his assistant were taking care of the two lads in SAT. Wanger, his old buddy was one of the divers in SAT, so he had gone over to one of the ports to tease him holding a beer. "God this beer tastes so good Wanger," he said later over the radio in the dive shack.

"Fuck off Swiffy... Oh hang on a minute let me consult my trusty calculator. Hmm sixteen days with only seven actual dives at fifteen bucks an hour. Oh, would you look, that... a cool five thousand seven hundred and sixty dollars. That's gonna buy me a whole lotta beer when I get out." Wanger said with his unscrambled Donald duck voice.

Dave replied, "Oh, before I forget Wanger, that chick you were seeing ashore. Well just so you know I looked after her last night. She told me something about, 'it's not the length of the chain that counts its what's in the chain locker that's important.' What did she mean Wanger? I'm confused."

"Hey Mister Swift... go away in short jerking movements i.e., fuck off." Wanger said laughing.

"OK my old friend, over and out... I am now fucking off!" Dave added.

He made his way up to the dining room rest area and sat in one of the comfortable chairs to read a little to take his mind off his deep thoughts. There were a few noisy poker games going on as they all drank their duty-free alcohol purchased offshore outside the legal duty zone. It would of course be illegal to drink it onshore but who was going to know?

One of the seamen came rushing into the room. "The cop... he... he's back," He stuttered breathlessly. Making one of the lads immediately put out his marijuana joint.

"Hey no problem, he's cool. Don't have a frickin' bird." Dave attempted to calm everyone as he made his way up to the gangway.

Cal was in civilian clothes and looked like he had been partaking in a few malts.

"How ya doin Dave, permission to come aboard? No worries I'm off duty," he added.

"Yeah, sure but your gonna have to keep yer blinkers on,"

"Oh sure, and I didn't when we hit those afterhours facilities?" He replied.

Dave gave him a tour of the dive system where he seemed very impressed. They then made it up to the rest area room to witness much shuffling of booze, dope, and money.

"Hey lads, relax I'm off duty, throw me one of those cans and I'm blind tae everything. I'm a fricking traffic cop. If yea miss a stop sign driving up Union Street, well I'll be the one on yer tail," Cal said as the money and booze was gingerly replaced on the tables.

Chapter 29

Pulling a sicky.

He had been offshore for six weeks, during which the last three he had been in SAT at four hundred and eighty feet with five other divers. Two divers had recently been replaced; they had been in for their normal max of thirty days. Two fresh divers had been pressurized up in one of the decompression chambers and once equalized opened the hatchway into the six-man living chamber where the exchange had been made. Five days later all six divers had come down with a nasty and painful ear infection, which had obviously come in via one of the new divers. With the humidity and close contact with wearing the same diving helmets, this wasn't rare. The whole system had to be surfaced, disinfected, and scrubbed clean. It would take almost five days to decompress with little medication allowed to take away the pain. This was also a costly procedure in wasted helium and time.

Dave had decided to take some time off to recuperate and asked to go ashore. As normal he and a few others were crew changed, by lifting them off the boat holding onto a rope cage from an oil platform crane. Later in the day he was on a chopper somewhat excitedly, flying toward Aberdeen. He had contacted

Bren a couple of times via the ship's radio phone during the six weeks away. She had been suitably impressed by this and seemed keen to meet up again.

He and a few others had shared a cab from the heliport to Aberdeen. He had checked on his flat and picked up his car then drove out to meet Bren at Cal and Linda's as they had prearranged via the last radio... telephone call.

Cal met him at his door with a big welcoming smile. "Well, neow look what the fuckin' cat dragged in. Are yea ready for a wee snifter, sassenach?" Cal Said holding out his hand to be shook.

"Aye, I could do wi a wee one, me ol' mucker," Dave replied smiling. It was hard not to return a smile; although Cal was a large burly guy, he had an engaging way about him with a red almost purply tinge to most of his face, in particular his nose and forehead.

"The doc said I should stay off the booze while I'm on antibiotics but... what the fuck eh?" Dave added.

They walked down a short hallway into the living room where Linda and Brenda sat on a sofa together. He felt like he had interrupted their conversation as they both looked up inquisitively, he wondered if he had been the subject. Brenda looked beautiful and everything he had dreamed about these many weeks. She wasn't overly dressed in a knee length black skirt and colorful top showing her shoulders. He did notice fresh lipstick and her medium length hair had been permed into curls at the back, as was the latest eighties fashion. She seemed shy and slightly blushed at his gaze. He dearly wanted to hold her but was trying as best he could in the situation to be calm as he sat on one of the armchairs across the room.

"Hi... everyone... how's everyone been... long time no see huh?

Oh god what a dick head you are, that was so lame, yes siree anymore of that and they'll be running for the fuckin' hills.

"Hi Dave," they both seemed to reply at the same time seemingly waiting for a witty reply that sadly wasn't forthcoming.

Linda stood and asked if he would like tea or coffee.

"No thank you, I think Cal is bringing me a drink."

"Oh, I better go and see where he's at, I hid the key to the booze cabinet, he'll be climbing the walls." She said laughing and breaking the embarrassing silence.

As the door to the living room closed Brenda patted the seat next to her on the sofa. "Why don't you come and sit here Dave," she said reservedly.

He didn't need to be asked twice as he sat next to her putting his arms around her shoulders and pulling her close to kiss. She didn't resist and it was a long passionate kiss. Her perfume filled his senses. He had waited so long for this moment.

"Brenda, I have thought of you so much over the last weeks. I would sure like to get to know you better."

"Me too, Dave. After you left, I felt disappointed and hoped you would call. Six weeks is a long time, but I was so encouraged when you called from your ship, thanks for that. It's obvious that we have both been hurt badly in the past, so we need to take this slow."

They heard footsteps down the hall a little too heavy that made it obvious they were about to enter the room. Brenda smiled as Dave quickly removed his arm from her shoulders and placed his beside hers on the sofa. Linda entered holding a small plate of smoked salmon on sliced bread rolls and a pot of tea with cups. Cal followed with two large whisky cut glass tumblers.

"Take a wee snifter o' that Davey boy, its verry special. It's only available every five years or so. I have a special rapport wi the owner o' the distillery. Caught him speedin' once too many times ha!"

After a couple of whiskies and a comfortable relaxing conversation Dave suggested that Brenda and he could go for a drive somewhere. The weather wasn't that great, but it would get them some private time together.

"OK, I'd like that, let me get changed into something a little warmer," as Brenda left the room.

"OK, I'll clean up these dishes love," Cal said leaving the room with the tray of dishes. Leaving only Linda and Dave together, sat across the room from each other. It was a little obvious that Linda wanted words privately.

"Dave, you seem a nice chap. Bren and I have always been very close, especially since we lost our parents. She's had a particularly hard time, since her marriage break up. Her last couple of relationships have also been complete disasters. Awful men seem to gravitate toward her. Cal and I dearly love her and Joanie, we've spent a lot of time together. If you're one of those awful men then my door is open for you to leave, 'right now.' She would be very angry if she knew I was talking to you like this. Cal is a pretty good judge of character and speaks highly of you. I know he comes across as a bit of a bruiser and you sure wouldn't want to cross him, but he has a heart of gold."

They heard footsteps coming down the stairs as Linda quickly crossed the room to shake his hand with a stern expression on her face.

"No worries, Linda. I can't vouch that our relationship will flourish but I'm not here to outwardly hurt anyone either. You have my word."

At that moment Brenda entered the room seeing them eye to eye with a look of concern on her face.

"Am I intruding on something here," as she glanced at her sister disapprovingly.

"No not at all love, you two have a great day. Joanie is with her Dad today, we can pick her up later, no need to rush back." Linda said smiling, defusing what could have been an embarrassing moment.

Brenda wore tight jeans, slightly belled at the bottom with comfortable black pumps, an open necked silky shirt, and a loose buttoned sweater as he helped her into the car.

"OK, so what was all that about, I hope she wasn't reading you the riot act." Brenda said as they drove away.

Dave smiled, "No not at all, they both obviously care for you very much. A bomb could drop on me and no one would give a flying shit ha!"

"Aww come on that's not true Dave. You must have lots of friends. Isn't your Mum and Dad still alive?"

As they drove over the beautiful Scottish Highlands, he gave her a brief synopsis of his life so far. Not wanting to ruin the day he tried to make fun of the sad moments of his despair. In turn she also gave him installments of her unhappy episodes. As a nurse she had also witnessed death many times which had affected her deeply. He changed the subject as he felt it was becoming depressing. He talked about the many funny and somewhat unreal characters that he worked with. She found it almost unbelievable that one of his enviable characters thought of himself as an Austrian Ribber hound dog and liked to go for walkies on the rig. He also told her the story of one of his diver pals, 'Scouse' who was pulled over by a cop in Liverpool in the early hours of the morning. As the police officer leaned into the car to check for booze or drugs, Scouse unclipped the officer's chest radio; 'for fucks sake Spock, beam me up' he had said grinning. Fortunately for Scouse, the cop had found this mildly amusing. Later after learning that Scouse was a deep-sea diver from his license information, he immediately called his friends in the force who were police frogmen*.

*Frogmen – policemen trained in underwater rescue.

Within a half hour there were four patrol cars of cops asking him many questions about his dangerous profession. They all eventually escorted him home. He felt like a film star or someone important.

He mentioned many of the unbelievable situations that had occurred leaving out the time that he had physically died. They had stopped a couple of times on their drive. They found an ancient country pub with huge original oak beams where they had an enjoyable lunch. Nothing was planned as they seemingly drove without a care, enjoying each other's company, leaving all the woes of work and life behind. They lost track of time in their reverie but were reminded as the sun began to sink leaving a beautiful sunset as they drove West.

"Where are we going?" she asked between various conversations.

"I haven't a clue, I thought you might know. We can turn around and drive back if you like?" Dave suggested as they slowed down to a halt in a roadside layby. The day had seemed so perfect, neither of them wanted it to end.

"Well, we could drive on and find a hotel and return in the morning if you don't have to be back." he suggested gingerly. In the last couple of hours, he was feeling so relaxed that he had to admit sex was on his mind. She had held his hand on a few occasions and had even stroked the top of his hand which had brought on a severe erection that he hoped she hadn't noticed.

After a moment of silence as she looked out of the window, obviously in thought. He was beginning to feel like he had overstepped.

"Cal and Linda could look after Joanie I suppose. I would need to get to a telephone though, but yes Dave, I think it would be OK."

Before the sun had completely set, they found a small bed and breakfast linked to a country farm. After booking in they asked the owner where the nearest restaurant could be found. Being in the country it would be a twenty-minute drive to a pub that served evening meals.

The restaurant inside the pub was ready to close as they entered but Dave had convinced them to stay open long enough to finish their meal. After their enjoyable and conversation-filled meal, they sat at the bar for a few drinks before heading back to the B and B. There was a moment of slightly embarrassing silence as the door was closed to the room leaving them alone. Brenda sat on the bed looking away from him.

"Bren, I can sleep on these two chairs if you like, we don't have to sleep together, if it doesn't feel right."

She held out her hand and pulled him toward her sitting on the bed. He kissed her and it felt wonderful as they both fell back onto the bed.

The many weeks of emotional promise was prevalent in their lovemaking. He felt mildly surprised and somewhat gratified that her need was the same as his. She might have come across as a shy, quiet lady in her mannerisms but when the lights went out, she made it perfectly clear what she wanted. It was also wonderful to later have this beautiful woman fall asleep in his arms. Everything felt so natural, the world would spin around to bring another day, but this moment was precious, it needed to be treasured, caressed, and nurtured. Although sleep called him, he didn't want to waste a single second and forced himself to stay awake to hold this gem, just a little longer, lest she be taken from him. In another moment he reminded himself that they had only known each other for such a brief time. How could he allow himself to be lulled into thinking that something so wonderful could happen in *his* life? Again, for the second time since they had met tears began to form in his eyes.

No, I can't allow this to not work. This time I must try a little harder. What will it take to wake beside her every day? To have her near, to love someone and... feel loved!

Sleep eventually came with many strange and disjointed dreams; in one he was with her as they danced in a summer meadow; in another she was leaving on a train, and he felt the pain of his life being drained from him. He was choking... he couldn't breathe!

He felt a hand stroking his chest. He opened his eyes, and his cheeks were wet with tears.

"Dave are you OK?" she asked quietly.

He had fallen asleep on his back with his arm around her. She was cuddled in his arm lightly kissing his chest. Fortunately, the room was in darkness so she could not see his tears. However, a dim light showed through the heavy curtains, it was early morning.

"Yes, I'm fine, silly dreams that's all," He answered.

The kissing developed into a mild biting of his nipples and her hand had reached down to feel his fast-developing erection. She rolled over on top of him and reached down to place him between her legs. He noticed that she was quite wet as she slowly pushed him into her. She moaned and began to move, pulling and squeezing him inside. She then sat up to ride him. As she rocked back and forth her breathing became fast. He squeezed her ample breasts and felt her hard nipples which excited him even more. He wanted to let go to feel his orgasm but held on as he felt she was near. She let out a moan and literally fell onto his chest. He tried to keep on moving as she trembled in his arms until he also came.

"Oh my, what must you think? I needed that so bad. A girl must take advantage when sex is so very rare. Last night was wonderful, I just wanted more, sorry," she said breathlessly.

"Sorry? You must be kidding. I've never had it so good. If that's the case you'll just have to be sorry more often, eh?" Dave quipped.

They laid in each other's arms not saying very much but invisible questions were seemingly transmitting back and forth through the ether. Eventually Brenda spoke.

"So, what was the dream about?"

Kevin Firth

"Oh, silly stuff really, I guess I have a few hang-ups if the truth was known."

A few moments passed before she asked again. "OK, so you got me in a conundrum... give me a clue?"

"I don't know if this answers your question and I hope I'm not going to blow it by telling you all this. I never thought I'd make it to thirty years old. No one is more surprised than me. For a while I thought I had a death wish and I know that sounds crazy. Time drags on when I'm offshore. Sure, it is a dangerous job but most of the time it is extremely boring. I've spent more of my life at sea than I ever have on land. The sea, sure is a cruel mistress, but it does give you a lot of time to contemplate. I probably have some serious relationship issues, from everything that I have read. I know we have only known each other for such a short time. But my time ashore... living! Especially with you is very precious. I want to let every moment count. So here it is... Brenda I think that I'm already in love with you! There I've said it... please don't run a mile!

There was another quiet moment that went on a little too long as Dave was beginning to regret what he had just confessed.

"Dave, I'm a bit gob smacked, and I don't exactly know what to say. I certainly like you a lot and would be happy to see where this goes but Love? No, I've also been hurt once too many times to allow myself to go down that road."

She got out of bed to go to the washroom with her clothes in her arm, not saying another word. He also stepped out of bed, dressed, and opened the curtains to a gray day as it began to rain. This was not how he expected this to transpire. He questioned himself repeatedly, why had he even said those things?

She returned clothed and ready to leave.

"Brenda, I'm so sorry for messing this up saying those things. Can you forgive me?"

She then came up close and put her arms around him laying her head on his chest.

"Of course... There is nothing to forgive Dave. I am flattered... but a little wary if I were to be brutally honest. Can we just take it as it comes? I do, however, feel closer to you but you're going to have to give me time."

"Brenda, take all the time you need. At this point I just do not want to lose you. By the way I'm starved, you ready for breakfast?"

They ate a hearty full farmer's breakfast as they were introduced to the friendly owner's wife of the small B and B. After the huge meal they were invited on a tour of the farm. The rain had stopped, and the morning sun peeped through the clearing clouds. There were corralled horses, goats, and pigs. In the meadows there were many grazing sheep and in a small enclosure even a pair of beautiful peacocks, the male showing off his colorful spreading tail feathers.

Returning to Aberdeen the drive was pleasant with lots of conversation as they both learned more about each other's lives. Brenda informed him that she would have to leave later in the day to catch her train back to Leeds. Joanie would go to school in the morning of the following day, and she would start her evening shift at the hospital. Dave offered to drive them back, but Brenda seemed reluctant to accept.

"Dave, I know you mean well, and I do want to spend more time with you... really! But this is all happening too fast. When do you have to return to your ship?"

"Well, I'll be lucky if they allow me more than a week. The job we are completing is probably going to take a couple of months and who knows what's next. This probably sounds a little crazy but there is usually a lineup of divers wanting to get into the chamber to make the big bucks. It's basically on a turn basis and totally dependent on how you fare on deck. The dive superintendent is like a god out there. I'm on pretty good terms with one superintendent. They generally spend a couple of months before they change out. The other super is an American and generally has most of his buddies in the front of the cue. It's a crazy business. Although we work year around there is generally a summer season when most of the big jobs are done. I mostly end up on one of the slow rig jobs for Winter when most of the Americans have returned home. It has taken me a few years to be where I am now, but I have no reservations that should I not make myself readily available, I would be replaced in a heartbeat. And unbelievably, at my age, I'm beginning to be old when the average diver in SAT is in their mid-twenties. I've met a few oldies but usually they are super qualified welders. We tend to do all the heavy work setting up their jobs.

However, I have a few years left in me before they put me out to graze.

I know that it's a lot to ask Bren, but would you be willing to wait for me? I've painted a sad picture here, but I know what I want when I see it and I would like you to be part of my life. Something has happened with you and me and I don't want to chance losing it."

Chapter 30

Alexander Kielland disaster.

Four days passed, and the office hadn't called him yet, which he felt was a little strange. He had called Bren a few times, she would have a change of shift in a couple of days and asked if he would like to come and stay with her for a couple of days. He didn't need any prodding as he accepted. He couldn't seem to get her off his mind as he sped down the highways. He arrived at her door in just over six hours. She was apologizing for her small rental council house accommodation as he entered.

"Bren, please, I'm here to see you not your house. This looks quite comfortable for you and Joanie."

"Oh, thanks Dave, I was a bit nervous. It's not much but it's ours. I wasn't sure when I'd see you again. I still have a couple of days shifts then I'm off again on the weekend. Are you sure you don't mind hanging around while I'm at work?"

"No, not at all, I might have a drive around and check out the scenery while you're at work. Like I said on the phone, I'm expecting a call at any time. They don't usually give much time to get your life in order before you're expected at the heliport dressed in a survival suit ready to fly at a moment's notice."

She came over to him and hugged him tightly. "Dave, thank you for coming down to Leeds. After that drive we had and getting to know you, it just feels so right. I feel like I've known you forever. Now it's me coming on strong huh?"

"Bren, life is short, I never seem to know what's coming next. I've learned to just take it as it comes. But when something comes along which is sweet and soft..." He kissed her neck lovingly and held her tight. "You just have to make the absolute best of it," he said smiling.

She reached up to kiss him tenderly. "Dave, I will have to pick Joanie up from school shortly," as she smiled sexily leading him to the bedroom.

In the following two days he tried to get to know Joanie, especially when they sat down for their meals together. He fully expected this to be a package deal; to win over Joanie would be paramount to also winning Brenda's heart. Before Joanie went to bed at night, he tried to make it obvious that he was sleeping on the sofa. And was always on the sofa when she woke up for her breakfast. In between would be highly satisfying but quiet sexual romps in Brenda's bedroom.

During the day when Brenda was working, Dave drove around the area checking on real estate.

This wouldn't be a bad place to live if our relationship flourished. But it probably wouldn't be a good idea to mention this to Brenda, remembering her thoughts on taking things slow.

On the third day came his call. He had been connecting with his answering machine at his flat in Aberdeen regularly to ensure he didn't miss the call back to work. Upon calling the office, he was surprised and a little confused that he was being sent to another job. Biscuit had asked for him to finalize the installation of a dive system on a small DP dive vessel. He felt mildly disappointed that he would miss out on going into SAT again on his previous job. But it was good to know that the company thought enough about him from his experience with all the machinery on deck.

It was sad to leave Brenda again as he set off on his drive back to Aberdeen, but it seemed their budding relationship would sustain him until their next meeting.

The ship was in the Norwegian sector so he would be flying fixed wing to Stavanger, Norway then later in the day would be flown out by helicopter to the oil rig, Alexander L. Kielland. The floating drill rig was not used for drilling purposes anymore but served as a semi-submersible 'flotel' providing living quarters for offshore workers. Accommodation blocks had been added to the rig so that up to three hundred and eighty-six men could be accommodated. In nineteen eighty, the rig was providing offshore accommodation mainly for the production platform *Edda* 2/7C. He would later be crane lifted by cage and lowered on to the deck of the DP vessel when the weather permitted. The chopper landing on the swaying rig was a little hairy with the wind blowing up. He had quickly removed his survival suit and handed it to the personnel returning to shore, a little relieved to at least be off the scary chopper.

The following day the wind had picked up even more and was blowing a gale at forty knots. Looking over the side of the rig after his breakfast, it was a miserable rainy and misty day; he estimated the waves at almost forty feet. They sure weren't going to be crew changing him to the ship today.

The rig was a little unusual in that it had five legs in a pentagon shape. Each leg had its own separate floating ballast tank. This was unlike the semi-submersible rigs he had been on before; in that they had several legs attached to two separate large pontoons that could be flooded to lower or raise the rig depending on weather.

Later, in the early evening, just after his evening meal, he made his way over to the rig's makeshift cinema. He'd seen the movie many times, but he needed to take his mind off the negative thoughts of what 'could' happen in his new relationship. Little did he know what was ahead.

Because of the increasing bad weather, the floating rig had released its bridged gangway over to the fixed 'Edda' (Jacket) platform and was using its anchors to pull away to a safe distance.

The movie had just started when there was a loud ripping sound and a severe jerking movement. The whole room suddenly tilted to one side as chairs and tables flew across the room. They were all plunged into complete darkness and there was panic and confusion everywhere. Dave managed to climb up to the entrance door where he could see daylight at the end of a corridor. Making his way in the darkness almost walking on the walls of the corridors there were many men attempting to climb the obtuse angle of the stairs leading to the outside. Relieved that he had at least made it to the outside, he then had to climb down an escape ladder from the temporary accommodation container. He was dressed only in a tee shirt, jeans and trainers as the cold wind blew against his bare skin.

Chaos was all around as men attempted to scramble to safety to the highest part of the rig still out of water. It was obvious that the rig was slowly overturning as the rigs crane fell crashing over, killing many men. The anchor wires that so far were holding the rig from overturning were now one by one snapping and whipping across the decks decapitating many men still holding on for dear life. A massive stanchion came crashing down toward him hitting him on his shoulder and pushing him into the cold sea. He knew that he had to make his way clear of the overturning rig as he swam desperately away. The huge waves lifted him and with each ensuing trough he struggled to stay afloat. Fortunately, the weather was at least pushing him away from the disaster. His training had always taught him never to panic under any circumstance. Eventually he saw a rope, he swam anxiously toward it then pulled along the rope. At the end was a floating bag that he then climbed on to. As he shivered, he was reminded that unless he removed himself from the sea, he would only have minutes before hypothermia would cloud his actions and death would undoubtable follow. He was much relieved that when the bag overturned with his weight, it was a life raft. He quickly went about removing as much of the seawater from the raft as possible. It was only then that he looked back to see the carnage of the overturned rig. All that was left of the massive rig was the ballast tanks that now bobbed on the surface. One of the legs had been ripped off and was floating to one side. There were broken lifeboats and much of the rig's flotsam close by, many men were still swimming for their lives. He made every attempt to rescue as many as he could and drag them into the raft with him. There were now seven others beside him, some were injured and would need medical attention soon.

A supply vessel came close by in a bid to rescue them, but it was obvious from the way it was being beaten by the weather that it would be far too dangerous. Its massive propellers rose out of the water many times squealing and crashing into the waves.

In the five hours before they were finally rescued his thoughts were of how he had reacted to the danger. He had kept a level head concentrating only on survival. He wasn't sure if he was shivering with the cold or the horrible thoughts of drowning again. Many of the large waves constantly threatened to overturn the raft. The only positives were that they had at least been washed away from the rig. A bright light suddenly appeared above them in the darkness. It was a helicopter. They lowered a rescue swimmer but after a few attempts at attaching a separate harness onto the hurt survivors, he let loose of his own harness and swam into the raft. One by one each of the men were then winched from the raft into the chopper. They were then flown back to the platform to safety as the chopper left again in search of any other survivors.

He had a nasty gash on the back of his shoulder that needed stitches that he only recognized as he was being winched up to the chopper.

A day later the weather calmed enough to allow the personnel choppers to fly again, he and many others were transported to shore, some directly to hospital. Of the two hundred and twelve men aboard the Alexander Kielland only eighty-nine survived. The capsize was later publicized as the worst disaster in Norwegian waters since the second world war. (9)

Much later, after extensive investigation, the fault was laid on defective work during the rig's construction. Lamellar tearing in a flange plate and cold cracks in a weld together with the cyclical stresses commonly found in the North Sea caused a complete leg to be detached. The design of the pentagon shaped rig was also flawed owing to the absence of structural redundancy. Losing one of its legs would surely cause the complete structure to overturn.

After being checked over by a doctor and with his arm in a sling, he was released from hospital. Again, for the second time in his diving career, the diving company gave him some time off with full offshore pay to recover.

"Swift, we just can't seem to get rid of you," the offshore dive manager joked.

"Yeah, I know, I'm becoming a bit of a Jonah I suppose. You just can't keep a good man down, eh?" he replied.

Chapter 31

The Rue.

He called Brenda from his flat and gave her an abbreviated version of what had occurred. The story had been all over the international news, but she had no idea that he had been on that particular rig. She seemed shocked and very concerned about his health. He dearly wanted to see her and suggested that he would pay for a rail ticket for them both to come to Aberdeen. She readily accepted and as it was the weekend Joanie would be off school.

Joanie was dropped off at her Dad's and Bren returned to Dave's flat. She seemed very concerned as she removed the sling to check on the wound. With her obvious nursing skills, she replaced the bandaging and suggested some pain medications that he refused. For three days she constantly fussed around him making him feel cherished and loved. She had even confessed her love and wanted to take their relationship further. They later collected Joanie and returned to Leeds as she had to go back to work.

He was surprised that it was beginning to feel like the home that he had never had. While she was at work, he drove around again, now in earnest looking for a possible permanent home.

On the fourth day of his covert research, he found the perfect home. It was a little further from her work but had much more to offer than her current residence. It needed a bit of work; the past owner had begun to upgrade but had run out of funds, so the real estate person had mentioned. He needed to do this and quickly before he was called back to work. He hastily gave the very surprised salesperson a cheque as a deposit.

He couldn't wait for Bren to return from work. He surprised her by meeting her at the hospital as he had previously arranged over an excited phone call.

"What is it, Dave? Why can't it wait? I can catch the bus, like I always do."

"No, no this is special... and I can't wait," he had replied. Refusing to let on, as much as she insisted.

They later pulled up outside the detached house. She looked confused as he said, "so what do you think?"

She looked around completely bewildered as to what he was referring to.

He glanced over toward the house as she met his expression.

"I bought me a house, wadduya think?"

Her confused smile turned into mild concern.

"You bought this," as she pointed hesitantly toward the house.

"Yup, just a few minor details and it's in the bag," As he opened the car door beckoning her to follow. She followed somewhat trancelike as he opened the gate to a small parking area and pathway leading through the front garden to the front door. Once in the vestibule he then unlocked the front door to allow her in. There was a slight musty odor as the house had been vacant for a few months. She stood on the carpeted entrance hallway looking toward a spacious kitchen. Her confused expression turned to a slight grimace as the realization began to set in.

"Dave, please take me home," she said looking at him very concerned.

"Don't you like it? I know it needs some work, but I can do all of that, no problem," he said as his stomach began to churn. This wasn't what he expected.

"Dave, we have only known each other a matter of months and you expect me to be ready for this?"

"Bren, *I* need a place to call home, I don't expect you to up sticks and move in right away. Sure... I might have jumped the gun a little."

She interrupted him, "A little... you think so?"

"Bren, I love you and I'm willing to wait for however long it takes. I feel like I've been treading water for so long but now I have found my home... in you. This is just bricks and mortar; allow me to build on what we have got so far. I'm not asking you to move in tomorrow. Even though, I know, *I'm* ready."

She seemed to ease up at what he was saying as she allowed him to show her the rest of the house.

He explained how he was going to completely replace the entire kitchen and expand one of the three bedrooms. She seemed slightly impressed when he showed her the back garden which was spacious and had obviously once been well kept. It had many privacy bushes, a sitting area and even a small fishpond.

She seemed to have had enough when she asked a little more relaxed this time to leave as it was almost time to pick up Joanie from school.

Dave felt disappointed but tried not to show it as they drove back and spent a quiet evening together.

He spent some time the following morning after she had left for work pondering if he had made a huge mistake. Had he read things differently than Bren? But he kept going back to his original thoughts that eventually they would become a couple. He would finalize the house and make it comfortable. Like a bird building its nest, she would soon warm to his plans. Eventually she would learn to trust him, and they would become a happy married couple and his life would be fulfilled.

He put his flat in Aberdeen on the market, which quickly sold. The cash input from the sale would put a sizeable dent in the mortgage and pay for some of the renovations that he had planned.

Everything was put in motion and his arm fully recovered by the time he was called back to work.

The dreaded annual diving medical time was due when he returned to Aberdeen. The dark spot on his lung had grown and the doctor explained that he really should not be diving under this condition. He pleaded with the doctor to give him just one more year and he would be out of diving anyway. He wasn't sure whether the doctor had granted his request when he eventually returned to the ship. He didn't seem to be getting 'in the pot' (Saturation diving) as often as he wished. When he did, he noticed that he was becoming more tired than he ever was before. He hoped that it wasn't as obvious to the other divers, especially his shared dives in the bell. There wasn't much that one *didn't know* about your bell partner hundreds of feet below the surface.

During that year he was also spending more time offshore trying to build up the extra funds he needed for the expensive renovations. Not only had he sold his flat, but his fancy sports car also had to go. He now owned a sensible Ford people carrier that he used for transporting building supplies. Bren seemed to become a little more distant every time he returned home. They had a few intense arguments over what he thought were minor issues. Even though most of the renovations were complete she still seemed hesitant to stay in his house. Her excuse was that the bus route meant a change of buses and extra time back and forth. When he was home, he offered to take her to work and pick her up at the end of her shift. During his time offshore she would sometimes drive his truck. He had promised to purchase another small car for her use when things became more permanent.

The glut of oil worldwide caused by the Saudis in the early eighties had a direct impact on offshore oil. Diving jobs, especially in the North Sea, became thin on the ground. At the end of his first year in Leeds he had been home sparsely, attempting to save for the renovations. But because of the lack of offshore work at the end of that year he had been home for just over a month and was somewhat relieved when he received his usual call back to work. His medical was almost due, and he needed to squeeze in the last trip offshore before the contract was completed. He was only gone for six weeks with not a single dive to be had. He fully expected to be grounded anyway.

Things hadn't been going very well at home. Bren had been expressing her loneliness because of his long periods offshore in her letters.

When he arrived home, she told him that she was pregnant, he felt ecstatic. She was crying when she told him. She repeated that it was a huge mistake as she had mistakenly stopped taking the pill when he was away almost three months ago. On that trip he had surprised her by coming home earlier than expected.

"Bren this is amazing news why are you so unhappy? I'm probably not going to be going offshore again soon anyway. Diving work is thin on the ground and I'm about ready to quit anyway. I'll find a local job, no worries. The house is pretty much finished. Isn't it time that you left your rental to live here? This is all I have ever dreamed about."

"Yes, it is all *YOU* have ever dreamed about Dave. I have tried to follow your dream this year. But it is not what *I* want, and this is a huge mistake that I am just not ready for," as she stormed out of the house.

He was shaken, what was going on? Surely this was a good thing. He had a couple of scotches to steady his nerves and the queasiness he felt inside that there was more to this than he realized. He drove to her flat and there was an expensive-looking Jaguar car outside her house. This shook him to the core. She saw him from her window and came out to sit in his car.

"Dave what are you doing here?"

"What do you mean, what am I doing here? Who owns that car?" he pointed at.

"It belongs to Doctor Hynes, one of the doctors that I work with at the hospital. I have known him for a long time. He is a good friend and seems to know what I am going through right now. Dave I am so very sorry to tell you this... but we are through. I tried to make this work but those long months that you were away brought me to my senses. Although I care for you, it just isn't enough. To be fair I did ask you many months ago to take it slow, but you seem to have bulldozed yourself into my life. I have made so many mistakes particularly with the men in my life. For a change, I want to be the one to follow my instincts to find happiness. And now with this huge mistake," as she pointed to her stomach, "I just feel trapped in the worst possible way." she began to sob.

"I don't understand Bren. We seemed fine the last time I was home. This didn't come from Scotch mist," as he also pointed to her stomach.

"*This* was the sad wakeup call Dave, and it should have never happened. You really need to leave now."

"Are you having an affair with this... Doctor Hynes?"

"Dave, it is none of your business AND it is time for you to leave. Please do not make this any more difficult than it already is," as she left the car.

He went home feeling delirious from thought and finished the whole bottle of scotch whiskey.

He called and left messages on her home phone and drove past her house a few times over the next days to see that there was no one home. To say he was distraught would be an understatement. His life yet again was in complete disarray.

He had gone to a pub to drown his sorrows and had met a drug dealer that in the past he occasionally purchased marijuana from. He needed to sleep and take the harmful thoughts away even for a few hours. The dealer gave him some downers.

"Ye'll sleep like a baby wi those mate, just don't take too many. Three will usually do the trick." He had warned.

When he awoke the following morning, it was as if someone had just turned the lights off.

Four days had passed, and he had hardly eaten. Empty scotch bottles and strong roll up cigarettes littered the floor. It was eleven o' clock at night and he was ready to take his three pills to 'turn off his lights' when he heard a loud knocking at the door. In a haze he staggered to the door. It was Bren. The sleek looking Jaguar car was parked by the roadside beyond his front gate.

"Dave, can I come in, we need to talk," she was ashen looking with dark rings under her eyes.

He opened the door, and she went into the front room to sit. He quietly sat across from her. Just by her expression he knew that whatever she was about to say, it was *all* going to be bad.

"Dave, you are a nice man and deserve to find someone to be in your life... However, that someone is not me... You need to move on. I hope in time that you will forgive me," tears appeared in her eyes.

"Bren, I don't know where I went wrong but surely you can give me another chance," He was mildly surprised at his quiet and crackly, dry voice as he had spoken to no one in days.

"Sorry Dave but that is never going to happen," as she began to openly cry.

"What are we going to do with the baby? Can I at least be in its life. I think that I could be a good Dad," he said weakly.

There was a long silence as she took out a tissue to wipe away her tears.

"Dave, there isn't going to be a baby."

"What do you mean, no baby, your still pregnant... aren't you?" he whispered almost under his breath, half expecting what the dreaded reply would be.

"No Dave, I have had an abortion. I couldn't risk leaving it any longer. I hope in time Dave that you can forgive me." As she stood to leave.

He just felt a numbness as she left closing the door behind her. A severe anguish seemed to spread and surround his very being. Eventually tears began to drop onto the floor between his feet leaving a damp spot on the wooden floor. It was completely uncontrollable and reminded him of the tears he had shed for his father all those years ago. However much he tried he could not think of any outcome where he could be anything... but lost. Sure, he had made a few friends in his life but there was no one that could make any difference at this moment in time. As always, he was alone.

In the many months and years, he had spent at sea, whether spending his time in a cabin or in a diving chamber, he had dreamed of a different life. It was a simple life by definition; a loving and caring wife, a few kids and to be connected to a labyrinth of aunts, uncles, and grandparents. Was that too much to ask?

It was time to say sayonara. Maybe in the next life it will be different.

He reached into his pocket and pulled out the bottle of pills and washed them all down drinking from the bottle of scotch.

At one point, just before oblivion, he staggered to the front door. He attempted to reach for the handle. Panic overcame him, he couldn't even scream when he opened his mouth. He desperately tried again to reach for the handle. His legs gave way as he stumbled onto the floor. He was now sitting with the door to his back as he tried to force his eyes open.

"I need to say goodbye," He heard himself whisper. "Please let me say goodbye." However much he strained to open his eyes they would close, and the darkness would return. The very last vision he had was looking down on himself from above. His mother was stroking and kissing his head. "It's OK son, Mum's here for you. I've always been here and always will. Come... it's time to go now."

"Mum, you came back! I always knew you would. Where's Dad?

"Oh, he's here too son... we've been waiting for you."

What did I do wrong? I still need to say goodbye... no siree, it can't be my time to leave yet.

It was four days later when a concerned neighbor knocked and tried the front door. She looked through the front window to see the empty whisky bottles and pill container. The police were called, and they later forced the front door open, sliding Dave's lifeless body to one side to allow entry. They had looked through all his meagre possessions to find not another living person's address except Bren.

Two police officers came to Bren's door, the somber looking female officer gave her the sad news. Bren was distraught and had to return to her kitchen to sit and weep. They asked if he had any other family or friends that they could contact. She knew of no one. The diving company was contacted, and they circulated the news to all the divers that knew him of the sad event. Biscuit, Keith, and Wanger were especially shocked to hear of their friend and wished that they could have been there to help him through whatever had caused the woeful event.

RIP Dave (**Squiffy**) **Asquith.**

The end

Please see the following afterword:

AFTERWORD

Although this is mostly a fictional story, there are many unfortunate events that aren't. In order of where the events happened in the book I will attempt to elucidate. With respect to any living family of the deceased I will only give first names.

They say when writing, you should always write about what you know. 'Swiffy' or Dave Swift in the book is in fact a combination of a few characters that I have been quite fortunate to have known in my life.

Kenneth K. was my close friend at the senior school in Haslingden, Lancashire. At fourteen he very sadly found his only surviving family member 'his Dad' deceased. I visited his dilapidated house in Station Steps, Haslingden a few times in my youth. I think my memory of him, and his home is quite intact. And later his stepfather Arthur Clarkson is again as true as I remember right up to him, and his ten-year-old son being lost climbing the Matterhorn (See note (1) in the following bibliography section).

I lost contact with Ken a few years later and the last I heard he may have emigrated to Australia.

'Birdie' my other childhood friend (in our gang). We joined the Royal Navy at slightly different times. He went on to the HMS Ganges boys training facility at fifteen when we both left school. From the stories he told me of the ancient facility, they are also correct. Like myself he bought himself out after the agreed two thirds of his man's time (beginning at 18) which would mean he would serve eight years of the twelve we had to sign up for. He would spend the rest of his unhappy life a bordering alcoholic. He died a lonely life a few years back, no doubt from alcohol abuse. RIP Alan.

(Pricky) Price was a very colorful individual navy friend I made on my first ship HMS Zulu (tribal class frigate). He was older than me by a few years and wanted out badly to the point he went AWOL twice. He spent a customary thirty days at the Royal Navies Detention quarters (DQs) and told of the many disgustingly shameful events that they put him through. He went on the trot (AWOL) again and when he was caught, he returned to the ship for trial. He had a tattoo across his forehead that read 'I HATE THE FUCKIN NAVY.' He served three months in DQs and returned a different person. Normally a fun-loving guy, he had become a much-changed person that couldn't be spoken too before he would threaten violence. They forced him to have the tattoo removed so for the rest of his life he would have a nasty scar across his forehead. Please see the short video exposé that was bravely made by the British Granada TV film crew of the Navy detention Quarters. (See note (2) in the following bibliography section).

I will also put it on my web site https://kevinfirth.ca/ as I'm sure it will eventually be taken down. It is shameful that not only the government but the admiralty right up to the royal family knew what cruelty was occurring inside the walls of this establishment.

I saw with my own eyes young men attempting suicide by cutting their wrists in a bid to get out of the navy. One of my messmates even staged himself sleeping with another to be caught by the officer of the day to hopefully be dismissed. A couple of messmates I served with also ended up in mental institutions. Most of these facts can be read in my autobiography 'Below the Surface.'

Bobby S was another school chum (in our gang, we all hung out together). We were easily noticed because our parents couldn't afford the obligatory school uniform. None of us had an intact parentage. The once fun-loving boy became an alcoholic drain on society after his overprotective mother died. The caravan story and the Trades drinking club story are all facts including his sad demise of hanging himself. RIP Bobby.

Bernard (Biscuit) McVitte One of my lifetime friends from a very early age. He was the one who got me the job deep sea diving offshore. His experience, input, and the courage he gave, helped me to stay alive in a very dangerous job. I don't think I would still be here telling these stories but for him.

Although he now lives alone, he seems quite comfortable living in Devon, England, mostly playing golf.

(Wanger) Woon. I believe, later lived an idyllic life, be it short. He owned a boat in his birth county of Devon. A lifetime womanizer (with his wanger). His wife caught him, 'in the act' with a lady friend on his boat and divorced him. Shortly thereafter he died of a heart attack. RIP Wanger.

Neville (Creature) Foote (the dog). One of the bright lights in my memory of the many long months offshore in the U.K. I think with his craziness it kept *us* all sane. The last I heard he had become an important oil company rep. He would report directly to the oil companies of the various diving companies working on their operating rigs offshore. The proud, 'Austrian Ribberhound' is now a dog to be reckoned with.

John Merchant. The past landlord of the Commercial pub in Haslingden, whom I was proud to call a friend. Special regards go out to his remaining family here in Canada. RIP John.

Dave (Squiffy) Asquith. Lastly but not least; my trusted diving bell partner on a few jobs in the North Sea off Scotland. As mentioned in the book, when there are only two people in a small metal sphere hundreds of feet underwater relying on so many mechanical and human decisions above it is imperative to have ultimate trust in your partner. Many divers were killed in the mid to late seventies right up into the early eighties. In one year alone twenty-seven divers were killed.

Squiff, was a typical Yorkshire man in the fact that there was absolutely no bullshit in anything he said or did. He never seemed to have any fear no matter what scary events happened to us on the seabed. He just went about the job matter of factly in a practical manner. There were only a few other divers that I knew, with whom I felt the same.

He was ex-Royal Navy like me with many similarities excepting he was a seaman. He had also worked as a seaman in the merchant navy before getting the job as a diver. He experienced a couple of bouts of the awful Royal Navy detention quarters and told me of the many harrowing events where they had tried to crack him. He was about five foot ten and a bit on the skinny side. He had a large protruding nose (sorry Squiff) that had obviously been broken a couple of times and muddy blonde thinning hair. If you met him on the street, you would not believe he was an actual deep-sea diver. But he was as hard as old nails and not someone you would want to tangle with. He smoked roll up cigarettes and just went about his work like he was packing books in a library. If there were any jobs that were particularly dangerous, difficult, or dirty, Dave was our man. Sadly, most of the supervisors knew this. The details of him physically dying during a practice bell diver recovery in the story are all fact, which I remember at the time shook me to the point of nightmares.

In the years that I knew him, he was a lifetime bachelor and made fun of us married men. I never really got into it, with him as to why, simply because men usually don't pry knowing touchy issues. I had the distinct feeling that he had been jilted and hurt badly and had decided to be safe and single than to repeat that kind of hurt. We had many conversations in the many hours and days we spent in the bell and decompression chambers, sometimes for weeks at a time. So, with some of the small things he hinted at, it gave me clues.

I had emigrated to Canada and returned a few years later to Aberdeen in the early eighties. I was looking for diving work when I was given the details at the diving company where I used to work of Dave's demise. He had fallen in love with a lady close to where he lived in Yorkshire. She had got pregnant with him and later had an abortion. His sad ending, as I wrote, was somewhat factual from what I was told. RIP Squiff.

Keith. in the story is of course me. The exploding pipe flange was my dive with Dave in the bell. Some of the other parts of the story are also me but I'm going to leave that to your imagination.

BIBLIOGRAPHY

1. Arthur Clarkson and son

   https://www.lancashiretelegraph.co.uk/bygones/10259449.f
   und-set-missing-rossendale-dad-
   son/?fbclid=IwAR2VLCxje_B9x-
   RkxyD6jEuArJ9RYDDEuShaN1r0LUnnTQ7KRBqxot6xjCk

   https://www.lancashiretelegraph.co.uk/bygones/10065400.c
   limber-7-head-
   heights/?fbclid=IwAR186wbNEY0ibat1F__OfnFTbZBZFadttxQ
   uA0GHwDD5thD6-a1JJijY8hgo

2. British Granada TVs exposé of the Royal Navy
   Detention Quarters in the 1970s
   https://www.youtube.com/watch?v=Eezm9WBYayY

3. Beira Patrol

   https://en.wikipedia.org/wiki/Beira_Patrol

4. Splice the mainbrace

   https://en.wikipedia.org/wiki/Splice_the_mainbrace

5. Jenny side Party https://www.navyhistory.org.au/obituary-jenny-of-jennys-side-party-hong-kong/

6. Hard hat diving

   https://en.wikipedia.org/wiki/Standard_diving_dress

7. HMS Ganges mast climbing.

   https://www.youtube.com/watch?v=mkmADkG13XU

8. Aggie Westons

   https://www.google.co.uk/search?q=https%3A%2F%2Fwednesdayswomen.com%2Fagnes-aggie-weston-mother-of-britains-royal-navy%2F&source=hp&ei=h9WEY935LfvmkPIP-J2OoAQ&iflsig=AJiK0e8AAAAAY4TjlyLXRQE8G1zqOk2JHn8H55PnbJIK&ved=0ahUKEwid2dqZmtH7AhV7M0QIHfiOA0QQ4dUDCAo&uact=5&oq=https%3A%2F%2Fwednesdayswomen.com%2Fagnes-aggie-weston-mother-of-britains-royal-navy%2F&gs_lcp=Cgdnd3Mtd2l6EAM6DggAEI8BEOoCEIwDEOUCOg4ILhCPARDqAhCMAxDlAlDuC1juC2CyHWgBcAB4AIABaogBapIBAzAuMZgBAKABAqABAbABCg&sclient=gws-wiz

9. Alexander Kieland Disaster

   https://en.wikipedia.org/wiki/Alexander_L._Kielland_(platform)

ABOUT THE BOOK

Dave Swift (Swiffy) begins his life in the industrial north of England under traumatic conditions. Little did he know that matters could get much worse. Through a series of sad events at fifteen he is given a choice to join the Royal Navy or go to a boy's prison which was the norm in Britain in the nineteen sixties. He is taught to be a ships diver where his toughness and resilience seems to shine. His life seems to take a turn for the good when he seemingly meets the love of his life.

Unfortunately for Swiffy though, through a series of events he finds himself in the Royal Navies infamous detention quarters which history has proven was little more than a torture camp for young men.

This tough individual with his many scars later becomes a deep-sea diver working on the oil rigs off Scotland. He soon realizes that he is tailor made for this type of extremely dangerous work. But for Swiffy even though he has faced his many fears it would not be enough.

Although a fictional story it is based on true events.

ABOUT THE AUTHOR

Kevin Firth joined the British Royal Navy at fifteen years old and became a diver. He served several tours of duty on ships mainly in the Persian Gulf. He later became a deep-sea saturation mixed gas bell diver working on various oil rigs and diving support vessels around the world. His noteworthy book, Below the Surface, is mostly about his diving exploits, in particular with the salvage of the famed Ocean Ranger oil rig off Newfoundland, Canada. Later after a successful business career he and his wife travelled extensively throughout the world finalizing in Costa Rica, where they lived for over twelve years. In this period, he was able to fulfill his passions for writing and music. An avid naturalist and humanitarian, this is his fourth novel.

Author's Amazon site:
https://www.amazon.com/Kevin-Firth/e/B07BGH4JPF
Author's personal web site : http://kevinfirth.ca/
Email: kevin@kevinfirth.ca

Go to my web site at https://kevinfirth.ca/ for additional information and photographs on this book and others. From a future CD there will be clips from the songs that appear in this book. There are samples from the author's previous CDs, REUNION and IT'S WHO I AM.
See also the amazon site.
https://www.amazon.com/s?k=kevin+firth&i=digital-music

OTHER BOOKS BY KEVIN FIRTH

Below the Surface ISBN:978-1-98060-169-2
Rengat Ericksen–Chronicles of Humanity ISBN: 978-1-98054-4173
Thor Lindstrom–Chronicles of Humanity ISBN: 979-8-671691-993
The Miner - ISBN: 979-8- 420936-863